WHERE THE DEAD LAY

www.rbooks.co.uk

WHERE THE DEAD LAY

·

DAVID LEVIEN

BANTAM PRESS

LONDON · TORONTO · SYDNEY · AUCKLAND · JOHANNESBURG

TRANSWORLD PUBLISHERS
61–63 Uxbridge Road, London W5 5SA
A Random House Group Company
www.rbooks.co.uk

First published in Great Britain
in 2009 by Bantam Press
an imprint of Transworld Publishers

A CIP catalogue record for this book
is available from the British Library.

ISBNs 9780593059340 (cased)
9780593059357 (tpb)

Addresses for Random House Group Ltd companies outside the UK
can be found at: www.randomhouse.co.uk
The Random House Group Ltd Reg. No. 954009

The Random House Group Limited supports The Forest Stewardship
Council (FSC), the leading international forest-certification organization.
All our titles that are printed on Greenpeace-approved FSC-certified paper
carry the FSC logo. Our paper procurement policy can be found
at www.rbooks.co.uk/environment

Typeset in 11/16pt Sabon by
Kestrel Data, Exeter, Devon.
Printed and bound in Great Britain by
Clays Ltd, Bungay, Suffolk.

2 4 6 8 10 9 7 5 3 1

To Brian Koppelman,
a great friend

ONE

THE MORNING WAS grey, with a cool that wouldn't last. Frank Behr steered his Toronado across East Prospect, and appreciated the empty streets at 5.45 a.m. His neck still throbbed from a guillotine choke he had barely escaped a day ago, and he was having trouble turning his head to the left, but at this hour the city was his. He had a jump on the world, and that felt good. As he drove, he tried to leave his mind distant and unfocused. Better not to dwell on the soft bed he'd just left, or on the physical challenge that loomed ahead of him. In twenty minutes' time he'd be soaked in sweat, his heart hammering, arms and legs turned to molten lead, as he attempted to gain limb-breaking position against a virtually impossible opponent.

Pummelling, clinches, fire feet and sprawl drills, takedowns, guard escapes and technique work. Topped off by lunge walks with a 100lb ground and pound bag on his shoulder. It was enough to cause a replay of last night's dinner, and that was just for openers, before they began to 'roll', which was what they called sparring at Aurelio Santos's Brazilian Jiu-Jitsu Academy.

Behr cut right on Sherman. There wasn't much traffic, but whatever cars were out at this hour would be along 74, so he avoided it. Behr trained alone with Aurelio himself, and because of that made damn sure he was on time for their 6 a.m. starts. It was a matter of respect. Behr had tried the normal group classes in the evenings at the Academy, but leaving the hardest thing of the day until the end was exactly the opposite of how it worked for him now. The spectre of it tended to hang over his entire day. It was a concession to his age, he figured, which was a little chunk on the wrong side of forty, but nowadays he needed to clear the physical effort first.

Aurelio charged him the regular fee of a hundred and fifty bucks a month despite the private lessons that should have cost that much per hour. For that, Behr figured, he owed Aurelio plenty. He had to consider, though, that it might not be a straight-up favour. Behr had a habit of accidentally breaking people. Six foot plenty and two-fortyish was a handful for the recreational martial arts practitioner and Behr had caused some unintentional injuries to various training partners during the decade and a half he'd studied karate, boxing and kickboxing before taking up Jiu-Jitsu. Regular-sized, civilized, often white-collar folk, plying techniques on someone of his mass and dimension, tended to lose faith in a system when the moves suddenly didn't work. Even those of a much higher belt rank weren't immune. It wasn't unheard of for someone to quit outright and not come back after practising with him. Plain and simple, Frank Behr could be bad for business. Maybe Aurelio had gamed that out.

Behr hit a string of green lights along Campbell, letting the big car drift around some potholes, and then steered towards the Academy on Cumberland. He felt it before he saw it, as he rounded the corner and clicked his right-turn blinker: there was too much activity in the parking lot, which should've been quiet. His eyes zeroed on a pair of patrol cars, done up in graphite and black, the colour scheme for Indianapolis Metro PD since the consolidation with the Sheriff's Department, which still wasn't the norm in his mind after all those years of taupe and brown. There was also an ambulance in the lot. The ambulance had its flashers on, no siren. The patrol cars were split and parked in a wedge, one directly in front of the Academy, the other at the door of the neighbouring cheque-cashing establishment.

That doesn't make much sense, Behr thought, as he pulled in and parked and saw that the metal grate over the door to the cheque-cashing place was securely closed and the lights turned off. Then his eyes found the door to the studio, which was swung wide open.

Who the hell robs a martial arts school? he wondered. That is no kind of score. Anyone who's ever been inside one could guess the office would contain only disorganized paperwork, out-of-date liability waivers, mouldy addresses, and instead of a safe to break there'd be a petty cash envelope holding fifty dollars maximum. Not even worth the trouble.

Maybe somebody hit the studio hoping to go through the wall into the cheque-cashing place, Behr considered, shutting off his car.

If that was the case, and Aurelio had arrived to discover a thief with the bad fortune to not be finished . . . Well, Behr supposed, that would explain the ambulance. He opened the car door. He wore sweats over shorts and a rash-guard top, and automatically grabbed for his gear bag, which contained mouthpiece, towel and dry clothes for after, and walked towards the studio. *No workout today*, it occurred to him, knowing too well how long the bullshit paperwork with the cops would drag on, until the morning class started to arrive. Then his experience reminded him that burglaries didn't happen at 6 a.m. very often. He quickened his pace.

*   *   *

The air inside the Academy was thick with it. It was unmistakable. Behr stepped through the door and saw it in tableau. Two paramedics sat back on their haunches, idle and staring at the walls. A pair of cops stood, arms crossed, heads down. Silence. Between them, on the ground, was Aurelio, his face and skull blown away from his neck like a snapped-off match head. Dark blood spattered the blue mat. The once supremely powerful and intelligent body lay there, simply turned off, now just a pile of bone, sinew and other dumb tissue.

Behr edged closer. What stared up at him from the ground made him go cold: death, still and final. He felt his stomach knot and threaten to turn over. He bit back on it hard and held his mud. It was the least he, the living, could do.

Then, even as he stood there, stunned, not saying a word, his eyes began to work, undirected. Aurelio's fists were clenched, the knuckles raised and purpled, as to be expected after his fourteen-year mixed martial arts career. There were damp patches on the mat. Water or sweat? The few pieces of furniture in the studio – chairs and a table – were upturned. A chunk of drywall was caved in. On another wall were a few small, round holes, buckshot pellets lodged in them. The blood streak on the mat grew chunky with solid matter as it neared and stopped at the body.

It came together in an instinctive rush in his mind: Aurelio had been shotgunned under the palate. It had been an interrogation finished by an execution, but not before a struggle. No *two* men he'd ever met could've held Aurelio down. A gun changed any equation, to be sure, but Behr's gut reaction was that there had to have been three, at least. The body had been dragged a distance, but then abandoned.

'Ah, goddamn it,' he breathed. It just slipped out. Behr cursed himself for the words. He could have used an extra few seconds to take in the details.

But now one of the cops turned to him, 'Regan' printed on his nameplate. 'This is a crime scene. You can't be here. Who are you?' The kid in uniform was blond, maybe twenty-five, but his blue eyes were already going flat and probably lit only when his son or daughter was around. It was what happened.

'Frank Behr. I train here.'

'Behr. You used to be over on the Near Northside?' the other cop, a dark-haired, dark-eyed thirty-year-old, said. His tag read 'Dominic'. 'My uncle Mike's said your name.'

'That's right. A while back,' Behr said, and tried to think. 'How'd the call come in?' They gave him the courtesy.

'Bread truck delivery driver went by on Cumberland. He saw a flash in the window. Didn't think much of it at first, but it stayed with him enough to call 911 further on along his route,' Regan said.

'Don't suppose he saw anybody or any cars in front?' Behr wondered.

'Nah. Course not. Detectives are on the way to question him anyway.'

'You know *this*?' the second cop asked, gesturing to the body.

Behr bristled, but nodded. 'Aurelio Santos.'

'Like the name on the sign.'

'Yeah. It's his place.' Behr heard the defeat in his own voice. He'd seen enough of them to know that this was one cold crime scene. It looked icy. How many dozens of prints and partials would be all over the place thanks to the student traffic? And no witnesses either. A grim, hopeless feeling looked for a place to grab hold in his belly at the waste of it, at the empty hull that was now all that remained of a man.

Then anger settled on Behr, hot and familiar. He felt his breath come in short stabs, a bellows of fury working deep within him. He tried to control it, to not be a 'belly breather', the way Aurelio had taught him when an opponent had knee on chest and was going for full mount and every cubic centimetre of oxygen left in the lungs meant the difference between light and blackness. His jaw set and he knew in that instant that whatever the police did or did not do, no matter how much or how little they threw at the case, no matter how quickly they might try to clear it, *he* would invest the minutes, the hours, the days, the months it would take to hunt down the scum, the animals, the maggot-motherfuckers who had done this.

A random killing? Behr tried it out in his head. Not the norm for Indianapolis. There'd been too many murders in the city lately, but they all had a crime-on-crime connection and Aurelio was the furthest thing from a criminal. It wasn't right. He felt it again: *someone had wanted something.*

Behr's eye fell on the office in the far corner of the main room. *Information.* It wasn't a mere idea but an imperative that pulsed deep in his cortex, like a reptile's desire for food. He figured Aurelio's Rolodex would be on the desk, and his best hope of a lead would be found inside. But it would be only a matter of moments before the officers threw him out, regardless of whether he'd once been on the job, and went ahead and locked down the crime scene. Like the cop saying went: *when you're in you're a guest, when you're out you're a pest.*

Taking a chance, Behr started for the office, going wide around the body and blood trail, staying on the edge of the mat. His movement seemed to stir the others into action. As he passed the high shelves holding tall, elaborate trophies from Aurelio's wins in the Mundial and Abu Dhabi and Tokyo, the paramedics started closing their unused medical kits and the cops looked to each other.

'Ho, buddy. Where you headed?' asked the dark-haired officer, Dominic. Behr felt them starting after him.

'You guys are gonna need to notify next of kin, I'm gonna get the number,' Behr tossed back over his shoulder.

He reached the office, nudged the door open with a toe, and in the half-light saw an address book with a worn cloth cover on the corner of the desk. Leaving the lights off, Behr dropped his gym bag on top of the book, covering it. Then he took a paperclip off a file cabinet and used it to gently click on the light switch without disturbing any possible prints.

'He's from Brazil. Unmarried. No family in state. Are Homicide Branch and Crime Scene on the way? No one's touched anything, right? You guys seem like you know the dance steps. Goddamn, he was a great guy . . .' Behr used the patter to distract while his eyes darted around the office looking for something he could use before they clocked his bag on the desk. The cops filled the door-way.

'Look at that, huh?' Behr said, of a calendar sponsored by a Brazilian beer called Brahma featuring beautiful copper-skinned girls in dental floss bikinis playing volleyball on Ipanema beach. The young cops glanced at it for a long moment and then Behr saw a sheet of notepaper tacked to the wall over the phone. It was covered with scrawled Portuguese first names and digits with the +55 prefix needed to call Brazil. Aurelio was from a large, close-knit family, and the list was his frequently dialled numbers back home.

'There you go,' Behr said, stepping back, letting the officers move in. 'If there isn't a family member on that list I'd be real surprised, and there'll at least be a close friend.'

'Thanks,' Regan said. Dominic just grunted. Then the pair raised their notebooks and started copying down the names and numbers. Their backs to him, Behr took the opportunity to pick up his bag, and the address book under it, which he made disappear into the waistband of his sweatpants, pulling his shirt down over it. It didn't look as if the office had been disturbed by whoever had killed Aurelio, and the worn fabric of the book cover wouldn't hold a print very well. The risk had already been taken anyway. There was no going back now.

Behr stepped into the main room again. The blond cop, Regan, followed him out, on point now.

'OK, Behr, Frank,' he said, writing.

'B-e-h-r.' Behr spelled it for him.

'Phone numbers, home, office, cell.'

Behr supplied them, and his address.

'We train four days a week here, for an hour, hour and a half. Then the other instructors, some private students, start to arrive. There's a morning blue-belt class at eight most weekdays,' Behr went on. He began to feel his emotions beating at the door of the cold recitation. He didn't know how long the barrier would hold.

'Blue belt, what level's that?'

'Fairly beginner, but guys who know their way around.'

'What belt are you?'

'We weren't doing it that way.'

'So, no wife.' Regan shrugged. 'He got an ex-wife?'

'No. Had a girlfriend but they broke up maybe ten months ago. No one steady since then.'

'Uh-huh. I'll need that name.'

'If I can think of it. Maria something.'

'This guy have any beefs?'

'None that I know of. Everybody loved him.'

'Teachers he'd fired? Pissed-off student? Creditor?'

'I'm telling you, everybody loved the guy.'

'Someone didn't fucking love him. Or had a strange way of showing it,' the dark-haired cop, Dominic, said as he joined them.

'Why don't you shut your mouth?' Behr bored holes in him with his eyes. The one paramedic who remained, writing notes on a clipboard, froze.

'Oh.' Dominic turned. 'What're you, gonna cry now?'

'Be a professional, asshole,' Behr said.

'*You* be one.' They stood nose to nose, or thereabouts, since Behr had a good couple of inches on him. The truth was, the guy didn't mean anything by it and Behr knew it. It was just the way cops talked to each other to get through their shift. That didn't make Behr let off any, though.

'Look, you've been helpful, but you're gonna need to fall back for us,' Regan said. 'Watch commander's coming to set.'

Behr broke off with Dominic, nodded, and took one last look at the scene, drinking it in with his eyes. Aurelio wore a green satiny warm-up suit that could've just as easily been his outfit from the night before as it was for that morning. He was wearing Puma track shoes, which he wouldn't have stepped on to the mat with ordinarily, but under the circumstances that didn't seem to mean much. The body still appeared supple. Rigidity hadn't yet set in. The blood was wet. He couldn't have been dead for very long. Behr was turning away when something struck him as wrong. He turned back and tried not to be blinded by the obvious, and then he saw just below where the wound started, Aurelio's neck.

'You didn't remove anything from him, did you?' Behr wondered. The paramedic looked up at him.

'Yeah, a mole from his left butt cheek – ' Dominic started in.

'Like what?' Regan said, his voice sounding tired.

'You gonna give us a lesson – ' Dominic tried again.

'Jewellery,' Behr said. The paramedic shook his head.

'Nah. There was none,' Regan said. 'Why, you thinking robbery?'

Behr shrugged. He wasn't in the mood to volunteer it but Aurelio wore a thick gold rope chain around his neck that held a figurine of Christ the Redeemer, like the one up on the Corcovado in Rio. He took it off only when he went out on the mat, but like the cop said, it wasn't there. The paramedic finished and exited. The detectives would be showing up within minutes and it would be better if he wasn't around when they did, especially with a piece of evidence tucked into his waistband.

Behr kneeled, almost in communion, near Aurelio's feet, and the room got quiet. Even Dominic gave him the respect. Behr made a final, silent promise, then stood and headed for the door.

TWO

THE SPARE WAS out and leaning against the rear quarter-panel even though none of the tyres was flat. Bobby Brodax stood by the Gran Fury parked on the side of South White River Parkway and smoked. He had a .45 ACP in his hand and tucked under his crossed arms inside his sports jacket. If a passing motorist even slowed, it was coming out.

He looked down the slope towards the railroad tracks and the curve of the White River and beyond. Tino and Petey were taking their sweet fucking time. It seemed that way at least. Brodax checked his watch. It had been only ten minutes, he saw, and they did have a hell of a heavy load.

Brodax's thoughts drifted to his employers. These Indy boys were not pros; they'd made a pretty decent mess a few weeks back, and that had led to him getting the call this time, but they were sitting on a real good thing and they could afford to hire pros. *Which was better?* Brodax had to ask himself. *Being one or being able to hire one?*

Brodax could still taste last night's bourbon. It had taken a lot to finally catch those fancy black-shoed suckers speccing out their lie. But he'd done it, and that was that.

Tino and Petey humped and dragged along the riverside. They could feel their quads burning, and sweat was running down the sides of their faces, matting their hair.

'This fucking mud's trying to pull my shoes off,' Tino said.

'Don't lose a shoe. You lose one, stop and find it,' Pete answered.

'I just said it was trying. I didn't lose my fucking shoe.' The bags were heavy, the plastic stretching and cutting against their fingers, which were already raw from the shovel handles. They tried switching hands, but the bags were fairly equal in weight. There was no respite. And the heat, even though it was the crack of dawn, was beating down thick and meaty. Sometimes the summer sucked.

'Those guys said the reeds past where it gets marshy, right?' Tino asked.

'They said the marsh. Where it's reedy.' Pete sounded sure. The fact was, the tall grass they were slogging through stretched for a few hundred yards, and then there was some even taller grass ahead. Tino let the bags drop, straightened, and pulled up for a blow.

Pete heard the wheezing and also stopped for a breather, looking back.

'You thinking what I'm thinking?' Tino asked. Pete shrugged, looked around and started for some thick growth in the shadow of the berm under the train tracks.

'Over here,' Pete said.

'I goddamn love working with you, Petey,' Tino said and hoisted his load for the last time.

*　　*　　*

If we leave about now, we'll be on I-70 over to 65 north and back in Chicago by the morning rush, Brodax thought. *But at least we'll be back, and rid of the car by noon.* He flicked away a second cigarette when he saw them coming. Sweating like barnyard hogs, the two of them. Especially Tino. Their shoes, and their pants up to their calves, were smeared in red-yellow clay like they'd waded through sick baby shit.

'Done, Bob B.!' Tino wheezed, climbing up on to the road surface, pushing a hand down on Pete's shoulder to get a leg over the guardrail. Pete's lips pressing together in effort was his only protest. They reached the car. Brodax looked to Pete, who slapped his hands together like he was dusting off crumbs.

'Good,' Brodax said. He pulled a garbage-can liner out of his pocket, snapped it open, and in went their muddy shoes.

THREE

'OOH-AH, OOH-AH,' the little blonde moaned as Kenny Schlegel rode her. The 'ooh' was the downstroke, which she was enjoying plenty, the 'ah' caused by the impact of his new necklace banging into her chin on each thrust. He wasn't so much nailing her as trying to bounce that thing off her face like it was some kind of carnival game. Kenny would've won the smaller prizes and traded all the way up to the jumbo for how good he was getting at it. It had him totally distracted from how tight the little blonde's body was, and that had made him last at least thirty or forty minutes now.

'Ooh-ah, ooh-ah, ooh-oh.' Though they were just taps, the repetition of it was going to leave a bruise on her face, he realized with satisfaction. But she wasn't complaining none, the dirty little thing. What was she gonna say anyhow? Little sophomore bitch. Nice of her to wait around all night for him too. She was pretty cranked up from the day before, so what else did she have to do? Her breath smelled like beer, and her pits reeked a little from the zoot. But in a good way. He put his face into one and took a deep sniff.

'Oh yeah, Kelly, you ready for some skeet?' He looked to her eyes, which opened and flashed because he knew her name was Kathy. That was why he'd called her Kelly. But she didn't hit him as he'd hoped. She just upped the tempo. Maybe it was for the best, considering the big-ass bruise he had spreading all over his own cheek. He took another deep whiff, then reared back, ripped off the jimmy hat and gave her an eight-roper across the belly. She moaned and groaned like some porn she must have seen, and as it subsided, all he could think about was last night, and breakfast.

FOUR

*A*URELIO SANTOS *KEYS his way into his studio in the pre-dawn gloom. He wears a warm-up suit and track shoes. He's thinking about riding his motorcycle along Copacabana beach and how glad he is that the Indiana winter is over, when they come at him. Three masked assailants appear from around the building and do a push-in. The first one shoves him from behind, but Aurelio quickly recovers his balance, gets hold of the shover's arm and shoulder-throws him into the wall, caving in a chunk of it. Aurelio squares, swings and lands a punch to the jaw of the second attacker, who goes down to the floor, toppling table and chair on his way. Aurelio moves to foot-stomp his face, when the third man racks a shotgun. Merda! Aurelio freezes, then raises his hands. He slowly backs across the mat . . .*

Is that what you did, Aurelio? Behr wondered. Is that the way it went down? Behr drove around, barely paying attention to where, or to the *zoing* and *boing* of morning radio playing low in the car. After a half-hour or so the streets began filling up with the morning rush around him. There wasn't much of it. Three cars in a row seemed like traffic in Indianapolis most of the time. But it was enough to slow him down and piss him off.

First thing Behr had done after he had exited the Academy was to go around the back of the building to look for anything with meaning. The rear door was closed and locked, which, as it was a fire door, it did automatically. There were old cigarette butts and a few broken bottles among the weeds growing up through cracks in the pavement, but the pieces looked too small to hold prints and besides they seemed like they'd been there for a long time. The windows were undisturbed and there was no way to get on the roof short of bringing your own ladder. Just like inside the Academy: he had a big pile of nothing.

The sun was already climbing, a thick heat spreading itself over the city, as Behr went back around front and wrote out a note: 'All Classes Cancelled'. Once the cops were done, they'd lock the door, affix a crime scene sticker and leave, and people who hadn't come that morning, or hadn't heard the news, might keep showing up. Behr stuck the note to the front window and got out of there. He'd wanted to miss the morning students and assistant instructors. He'd talk to them all soon enough – when he interviewed them – but he wasn't in the mood for handholding and hugs at the moment. Then, since he couldn't canvass the neighbourhood for witnesses, as the cops would be doing that and wouldn't appreciate him stepping on their toes, he had started driving.

Behr pulled up in front of Aurelio's house. It was a one-storey brick bungalow with a Toyota parked in front. He needed to get in there and take a long look, but now wasn't the time for that. Police would arrive within minutes, Behr anticipated. He weighed the risk for a split second before hurrying to get a pair of latex gloves out of the kit in his trunk. He tried Aurelio's car, which was locked.

So was the house, both the front and back doors. Behr peered in through the windows but couldn't see much past the horizontal blinds. What he did see looked undisturbed. Behr stripped off his gloves and hurried back to his car. When the detectives went knocking on doors he didn't need any neighbours ID'ing *him*.

Aurelio's place was a mile and a half from the Jiu-Jitsu school, and it wasn't unusual for him to jog that distance to get warmed up before training. That might have been the case today, which would explain why the car was still at home. Or he might have been taken against his will, Behr considered, getting back in his own car and turning over the engine. He was making the left back on to Baker as the first detective's unmarked unit rolled towards Aurelio's house . . .

Cruising around envisioning how the thing could've gone was a pointless exercise, but Behr couldn't help himself. At least for those moments, in his mind, Aurelio was still alive. And when he was done, because he'd run out of things to do for the present, the finality of it was able to surge up into his chest. It was the old vault door asking to be opened, to be filled, to be slammed shut again. All the shit he'd seen on the street as a cop, and then as a private investigator afterwards, needed some place to go. So he'd learned pretty quickly to make a spot for it. An empty box inside him where he could throw the pain, and drop the lid on it before it became intolerable. The tendency was to stop thinking of the victims as human beings altogether. Instead they became a set of facts, an equation to solve, a clue, a piece of meat to be handled. This gave the investigator objectivity. It gave him the ability to reason. It made him powerful and knowing so he was ready when he had to interdict a perpetrator. Problem was, before long, the ability to discern was lost and a lot of other things ended up getting thrown in the vault as well. Good things, like wives and kids and friends. Just about everything really, and if you weren't careful, or even if you were, you could end up zombied out, going through the motions in your life *and* the work, praying that mere competence would get you by.

The evolved cop, the one who distinguished himself, the one who made it all the way, managed to push the pain down some place but not cut it off completely. He carried it and retained his connection to it, and what it meant. The victims remained human beings to the good cop, and despite the pain – or because of it – that became the cop's salvation. Behr wasn't sure in which group he'd spent most of his time on the job. He had his suspicions, especially at the end. But on this one, he swore, he would do it right. So he let the pain come. He let it come.

A loud, angry honk sounded behind him. Behr looked up and saw he was sitting at a green light. He glanced into his rearview mirror at the pick-up truck behind him and raised a hand. 'I'm going. I'm going,' he said, and turned for home.

FIVE

SUSAN DURANT WAS in the bathroom peeing on the little plastic tab when she heard a car pull up and Frank's heavy step sounded on the stairs. It was supposed to take only a minute for the results, but she didn't have time. Besides, she had her suspicions about the answer and didn't know how to handle her reaction. She finished up, flushed the toilet, dumped the contents of the small trashcan, which contained the box and directions, into the drug-store bag and dropped the plastic tab in on top of it. She was in the living room smoothing her skirt over her hips when he entered. She turned from the mirror and smiled as the door closed behind him.

'Hey,' she said.

Frank didn't answer.

'Is this skirt riding up? I put on three pounds the past month. You're gonna have me fat and happy, Behr,' she said, hoping she sounded breezy.

He didn't respond, and instead entered the kitchen. She heard his hand clattering among glass bottles as he fished around the makeshift bar on the counter. She reached the doorway in time to see him find a small bottle covered by a white paper wrapper. He emptied brown liquid into a glass, tried to add club soda from a bottle that was empty, then splashed tonic in the glass and drank. Susan stepped further into the kitchen, still holding the plastic bag.

'You're drinking, what's wrong?' she asked.

Behr grimaced, finished, held up the bottle for her to see. Angostura. 'Just bitters.' He launched the bottle into the sink, where it broke.

'Why are you back so early?'

'Aurelio's dead,' he said. She absorbed the news, a dozen questions raised and checked in her mind.

'How?' she finally asked.

'Murdered. Shot. At the school,' Behr said, watching her try to understand. Then he looked at her more closely. 'What's up with you?'

'Nothing.'

'No?'

'No. God, Frank, that's horrible. I'm so sorry. How could this happen?'

Behr shook his head.

'Are you OK?'

He just stared at her. She went to him, put her arms around him. He didn't return the gesture. He was a log. She stepped back and looked at him. His face was taut, heavy dark brows knit. His black eyes were distant, but focused, as if fixed on something departing far away on the horizon. He wasn't even there in the kitchen with her, not really. She hadn't seen him like this since the beginning between them, when he'd been fifty feet deep on a case.

'Was it a robbery?' she asked.

'No.'

'Was it a random thing? Could it have been an accident?'

Behr shook his head again.

'I mean . . . could he have been . . . what was he into?' she wondered aloud.

Behr stopped shaking his head and looked at her. 'What the hell's that supposed to mean?'

'Nothing. Just that if it's not a fluke thing, then . . .'

'Then what? He was into some shit and had it coming?'

'Frank, no, that's not what I . . . Not how it was supposed to sound.'

'Just lay off the theories then, all right? They're not gonna help here.'

She looked at him. The tension was immediate, thick and unfamiliar between them. They'd been getting along well this past year and change. Too well, maybe, like a couple of frigging songbirds. But now, with all the thorny Scots, German, Irish, Midwestern and Pacific Northwestern blood in the room, an apology was a long way off. She stepped back. 'I'm here for you if you want, but it's pretty clear you don't,' she finally said. 'I'm going to work.'

'Fine,' he said, and nothing more.

After another moment she picked up her purse, kept the plastic drugstore bag she was carrying and headed for the door.

'See you,' she said.

'Yeah—' he answered, as the closing door clipped off the word.

SIX

VICKY SCHLEGEL PUT a plate of egg whites and wholegrain toast down on the kitchen table, and turned back to a pan sizzling on the stove behind her. The *Smiley Morning Show* played on the counter-top radio. Outside, the dogs, smelling the food, were stirring in their run.

'Hold on, I've got your bacon about ready, hon.' She drew on her cigarette and appraised her youngest boy Kenny's shirtless back as he salted his eggs. He was getting big from all the lifting, just like his brothers. He was already bigger than his father, Terry, but not bigger than Terry had been at that age. They'd met when he was a few years older, but she'd seen pictures.

'You know I can't eat that fatty shit, Ma.'

'I know, I know. It's turkey bacon,' Vicky said, shovelling the strips out of the pan with a spatula and moving away from the stove.

'Awesome.'

'You asked me once, that's all it takes, dear,' she said, and put the strips on his plate. He looked up and she saw the bruise purpling on his cheek.

'Kenny-bear, what happened to your face?'

'Training, Ma.' He shrugged. 'It's nothing. Gimme some character, right?'

She smiled, and then her eye fell on the nasty black tattoo on the left side of Kenny's chest. 'RTD', in Gothic lettering. It was some rapper's slogan – 'Ready to Die'. The thought of it made her shudder. All three of her boys wore ink. It was the style now. *Damn disgrace*, she thought. 'Spray paint on a Rembrandt' was what she'd said when Kenny had come home with the lettering on his seventeenth birthday last year.

'You think I could get some OJ, Mrs Schlegel?' the little blonde asked. Vicky turned towards the girl – Karen, was it? – and picked up her cigarettes. Three handsome boys like hers, all with the ladies' man gene courtesy of their father, and it was a constant stream of chippies in the house for Vicky to deal with. She should've held the line when Charlie, her oldest, started asking if it'd 'be cool if his girlfriend crashed on Friday nights'. She should've told him it certainly was *not* cool. And she would've if she had foreseen that the Fridays would turn into weekend-long 'hangs'. By the time her middle boy, Dean, started dating, they had 'guests' on weeknights too. Then, when Kenny made it to high school three years ago, it became a regular flow of horny little things parading through the house. She couldn't keep the names straight and didn't even try any more.

At one point a few years back Vicky had gone to her husband to put an end to it. 'What should they do, go fuck in a car like the tar babies?' Terry had said. 'Besides, you're the one who says you're too young to be a grandma.'

'C'mon, Terry,' she pleaded.

'Rubbers and a room, it's the least we can do for 'em. Boys'll be boys,' he said, and laughed. She had a suspicion he liked having the string of ripe little bouncies around. Now it seemed the house was perpetually running out of toilet paper and frozen pizzas, and the little wenches would've drummed her out of shampoo and make-up altogether if she didn't put her foot down on that.

Now Vicky turned to the latest *skank du jour* at her kitchen table and gave her standard reply: 'Oh, honey, listen, I'll serve my boys till I die, but not their little twists. It's just a rule I have. So get it yourself.' Vicky jutted her thumb towards the refrigerator and lit her cigarette. A short snort of laughter was the only evidence that Kenny had heard it.

The blonde's nose wrinkled in hurt. 'Jeez. Kenny, can we just do the picture now?'

'In a minute,' he said, taking a bite of his food. Then he piled the egg whites and turkey bacon on the wholegrain toast.

The girl made a huffing noise and crossed her arms. Mrs Schlegel just leaned against the counter and drank her coffee.

'All right,' Kenny said, folding the toast into a sandwich, 'let's go, ya little hoodrat.'

He got up and led her out of the kitchen. 'C'mon, *Kenny-bear,*' she said and snapped the waistband of his boxer shorts as they went.

'Get off,' he said, swatting at her, causing her to giggle.

Vicky Schlegel reached for the coffee pot and seethed.

SEVEN

AURELIO SANTOS JOGS *up Cumberland and slows to walk the last block. He crosses the parking area and be-bops towards his studio, quietly singing 'Chuva, Suor e Cerveja'. His keys click and rattle as he spins the keyring around his finger, ready to let himself in. When he reaches the door and inserts the key, the bolt doesn't turn, it is already open. Estranho, he thinks, sure he'd locked it the night before. He walks inside and is hit across the back of his head, a solid blow. The pain comes in a hot rush that makes him see white. He tries to keep his balance, reaching for the chair, but falls through it, crashing into the table next to it and knocking it over as he hits the ground. Knees to armpits. In a rush of instinct, he rolls to his back and curls into a tight ball, finding the position that's second nature to him. He spins on his back to face his attacker. In the dim morning light he makes out a few others coming from behind the first one. One holds a large black shotgun. That's what I was hit with, Aurelio registers, and then launches out a low sideways kick that lands on his attacker's patella. The man goes down. Aurelio seizes the opportunity to kip*

32

up to his feet. But the blow to the back of his head has done damage and he doesn't land solidly. He totters to the side, getting hold of the second man, but not for a clean throw. Instead he lurches forward, knocking the man into the wall, caving it in. Then more white flashes through his eyes, as he is gun-butted in the back of the head for a second time. He feels himself falling, falling through darkness . . .

Behr's feet pounded the pavement, rage shooting up through the soles of his shoes as he hoofed it up Saddle Hill. He wore a weighted vest that added thirty pounds to the effort. The vest was a gift from Susan, who noticed the abrasions on his shoulders from the loaded backpack he used to wear when doing roadwork. *It does sit better*, Behr had to admit of the vest, though it wasn't heavy enough for him to really get into the red zone. Nothing, he'd found, was as tough as extended Jiu-Jitsu sparring. The sets could go on for ten, twenty, thirty minutes without a break and demanded strength, cardio and lactic acid recovery, especially when he rolled with Aurelio. Though Aurelio weighed south of two hundred pounds, the man had had a special relationship with gravity. He knew how to make himself heavy. When Aurelio established side control, Behr felt as if a car was parked on top of him.

He thought back to the beginning of his training almost a year and a half ago. Back then he'd felt as weak as a newborn kitten when on the mat with Aurelio. The strength disparity between them seemed like ten to one. It was disturbing. Especially since he knew he could easily out-lift his teacher when it came to weights. It was leverage that made the difference. As he learned the techniques, though, Behr felt the disparity in strength start to level out.

You try to stay up on your feet, but fights end up on the ground. It was a truth, and one he'd known for a long time, but it took him a long time to finally accept it. Between his hand-to-hand training at police academy, his work on patrol and his time going hard at boxing, Muay Thai and the like, Behr was aware that despite trying for precision with punches, kicks and restraining holds, almost all real-world physical confrontations ended up on the floor. They weren't tidy and organized like in the movies, but messy and savage and full of awkward moves, strange noises and even odours.

In the scuffles he'd had while on the force, and since, Behr had relied on his size, strength and rusty high-school wrestling chops to sort things out when they went to the deck. He tried not to give it too much thought, just like he tried not to think about how much harder he had to work in the gym just to maintain as the years ticked by. He didn't want to dwell on a future where he kept getting older and smaller and weaker, while the guys he came up against kept getting younger and bigger and stronger. Then, one night, he'd found himself in a bar watching an Ultimate Fighting Championship match on pay-per-view and saw a formidable striker square off against an experienced grappler. The striker danced around the ring snapping dangerous punches into the air for a moment before the grappler ducked one, shot the striker's legs, took him down, got the man's back and choked him out in under a minute. The striker had been completely defenceless. Countless hours of intense punch and kick training had been neutralized in one second, and Behr couldn't deny it any longer. As the bar crowd grumbled over how lame the main event had turned out, the winning fighter did his post-fight interview and thanked his training partners and teachers in Brazilian Jiu-Jitsu. The next day Behr found the Academy in the phone book and dropped by to watch a class.

He'd walked in to see a medium-sized but fit teacher with a wide smile, thick, curly black hair, and an almost unreal energy on the mat taking a small group of students through break-falls that day. The man noticed Behr near the door and beckoned him out on to the mat.

'You want to join, huh?' he asked, a lilting Brazilian slur under his English.

Behr shrugged. 'Maybe.'

'You look like you in shape. You take me down, eh?' he offered Behr. 'Off my feet and we done, maybe you don't need the Jiu-Jitsu.' The man stood there barefoot, in surfing shorts and a tight nylon T-shirt. He smiled, bright white teeth shining.

Behr had earned his way through college pushing like-sized and bigger men than himself – men as strong as draught horses – around football fields, so he didn't hesitate for long before nodding and removing his watch, jacket, shoes and socks. But this average-sized man proved immobile on first grasp. They locked up in a collar and elbow clinch and struggled around in a circle. Behr was immediately impressed with the man's balance, which was better than his own, and the smile that didn't leave his face as he yelled merry encouragement to Behr all the while.

Finally, deciding extended duration wasn't to his advantage, Behr managed to wrap his arms around the instructor in a body lock, lifted him in the air, and slammed him to the mat. Behr expected a wheezing bag of cracked ribs to be writhing at his feet as the result, but instead found that the man wasn't hurt or even stunned. He hadn't really hit the ground at all, but instead had held on to Behr's arm. He had also gotten his legs around Behr's arm and shoulder, locked his feet against Behr's neck, and bridged his hips in a way that hyper-extended the elbow and caused Behr to drop to his knees and submit with repeated taps to the man's leg before his joint could be snapped clean through.

'Welcome, huh,' Aurelio said, letting off the pressure and patting Behr on the back. As the awestruck students went back to their practice, he climbed to his feet. 'You strong. You be good, eh,' he said, still smiling. Behr joined up on the spot.

At least that's what Behr had thought he'd said. For the first three months he had trained there, Behr couldn't understand a word Aurelio was saying. It wasn't just the heavy accent but also what the man was teaching. Using an opponent's own weight, strength, momentum and intention against him was not natural to Behr, who typically met force with force. In his life if he ended up facing a brick wall it was a head-on affair until either he or the wall crumbled.

Case in point, Behr thought, grinding his way up Saddle Hill.

But bit by bit, four mornings a week, Aurelio's teachings had begun to sink in. By the end of each hour at the Academy he'd be physically shot, bottomed out and shaky, the proud owner of fresh mat burns, bruises, various painful joint and tendon surprises, and often a wrenched neck thanks to Aurelio's vice-like chokes. The knowledge he'd been gaining sure didn't come cheap. Before the sessions were over he'd know helplessness, futility, outright failure, and invariably feel tiny bits of information seep down into the deep reaches of muscle memory, the only place they'd do any good if needed.

He never did get a submission against Aurelio in open sparring. That moment was at least a good five or six years away with steady training, if ever. After all, Aurelio was world class while he was just a mule. But recently he'd started to take steps – at least the domination wasn't total any more. Behr had also seen the pounds peel off his frame as he trained. Everything that wasn't muscle stripped away until he was as raw-boned as he'd been as a seventeen-year-old farm boy. And a certain kinship grew between them too, like some kind of hardy mountain plant that didn't need tending. When it came to teachers and trainers and the like, it was either hate or this kinship that motivated him. Behr had experienced both, and reflecting on past coaches and police captains, the latter worked a whole lot better for him. He and Aurelio had only gone out for beers and to watch MMA events a few times. Other than that it was just the four mornings a week on the mat. But that was all it took. The bond grew out of the effort and the pain, the stoic lack of complaint in the face of it, in the sharing of knowledge and, as vague as it sounded, in the spirit, Behr concluded, reaching the top of the hill for his eighth rep. After about six months of training he realized he'd made his first friend, save for a client a while back, in fifteen years.

Upon arriving at the top of the hill for the tenth time, Behr bent at the waist and grabbed his shorts. Sweat rolled off him on to the road like a concentrated rain. He felt his right lower leg barking from a knee bar Aurelio had put him in two days earlier.

The hospitals, he thought suddenly. He'd check the hospitals for certain likely injuries that came along with facing someone like Aurelio: a dislocated elbow, snapped wrist, a broken jaw. Behr straightened and began busting it down the hill towards home.

EIGHT

'HOLSTER UP IF you're whacking it, bro,' Kenny said, entering his brother Charlie's room. Charlie rolled over, the bedsheet at his waist. He'd been sleeping.

The Schlegels are hotties, Kathy thought, *not their faces, which were pocky, but their bodies.* Then she saw his right wrist and forearm. It was all swollen and purple. Charlie moved a plastic bag of water, ice that had mostly melted, off the edge of the bed, where it left a wet spot.

'Why so fucking early?' Charlie said. He had a voice that was already getting roughed up by cigarettes.

Hot, thought Kathy, catching a glimpse of his package as he got out of bed and slipped on a pair of camo shorts, *even though he is like at least twenty-two.*

'Mom's runnin' her already,' Kenny said of Kathy, while polishing off his breakfast sandwich.

'What happened to your arm?' Kathy wondered. They both looked at her, as if surprised she knew how to speak.

'Fucking hood of my truck fell down on it.'

'Ouch,' she said.

'Yeah,' Charlie agreed. 'So, give me your licence, I'll scan it in and change it,' he said, pointing at his computer.

Kathy didn't move. 'I don't have one,' she said.

Charlie looked to her, then to Kenny. 'She's only fifteen,' Kenny said.

'OK,' Charlie smiled, 'nice.' He crossed the room and pulled a large piece of tag board out from behind a dresser. 'We'll go old school.' On the board was a blown-up version of a state of Illinois driver's licence. The name on it was Mr Pat McCorkle with an address in some town called Orland Park. The space for the photo on the right, which was roughly the size of a head, remained blank. Kenny went to the bottom drawer of the dresser and pulled out an elaborate Polaroid-type camera attached to a folded-up tripod. Outside, the dogs were starting to bark.

'Photo comes out the size of the licence and we have a laminating machine,' Kenny said, as he telescoped out the tripod legs.

'This is such coolness,' she said.

Charlie found a stencilled letter 'S' among the rubble of newspaper, pens, pencils and coffee cups on his desk. He affixed the 'S' over the 'R' in 'Mr'. Charlie hung the board up on a hook that was already in the wall. She'd soon be Ms Pat McCorkle, twenty-one and a half years old from Orland Park, Illinois, she realized.

'OK, stand over here,' Charlie directed. Kathy crossed over and placed the back of her head against the empty photo space on the oversized licence. Kenny finished with the camera preparations and zeroed it on her. He brought his face away from the eyepiece.

'All set,' Kenny said.

'Should I put on make-up?' she wondered.

'Where's the fifty?' Charlie asked. Truth was, the Schlegels were into a lot better shit than selling fake IDs, but with Kenny still in high school the IDs remained a steady source of $50 bills and fresh pussy.

The girl turned to Kenny. 'But I thought . . . ?' she said.

'That it'd be fifty? You're right,' Kenny said. The girl stood there for a minute in a snit.

'Look, it's either that or a morning blowdjie,' Charlie said, pointing to his groin. The girl looked to Kenny, who shrugged.

'Kenny, Charlie . . .' their mother's voice filtered in from across the house, 'feed those dogs . . . And your father says it's almost time for the morning shake.'

'Either way, hurry it up,' Kenny said.

She clenched her teeth and reached into her jeans for the money.

NINE

BEHR SAT IN his car outside a brown-brick office building. He was waiting for his client, Wells Shipman, accountant, to arrive so he could do something foolish. Behr had called, and buzzed at the door, but had gotten no answer. He'd also entered the building when another tenant had gone inside, and had knocked at the CPA's office door. Going back outside he finally got hold of Shipman on his cell; he told him he'd be there in ten minutes. Behr was anxious to start his canvass of local hospitals, but he needed to square this away first. He also considered calling Susan, but in his current state of mind he wasn't sure what good it would do either of them, so he passed.

He thumbed through Aurelio's address book while he waited. It was fairly organized, with names, addresses, phone numbers and email addresses written in a cribbed hand. Behr recognized many of the names as students from the school. There were a lot of Brazilian names as well, and information that showed they still lived in Aurelio's home country. One thing that caught his eye was about half a dozen entries that weren't names but just initials.

There was a 'CC', a 'D', an 'F', a 'P', an 'R' and an 'LB'. There were corresponding phone numbers he would run down as soon as he could.

Shipman's Impala pulled into the lot. The CPA spotted him and waved, then parked. Behr put away the address book and was getting out of the car when his phone rang.

'Yeah?' Behr answered.

'Mr Behr,' a sixty-ish female with a highly professional manner began, 'my name is Ms Swanton. I'm calling from Mr Potempa's office at the Caro Group . . .' Behr was surprised. The Caro Group was a high-end investigation and security-consulting firm started by a few ex-FBI and Secret Service guys twenty-five years back. Between some early results and good marketing, they had built their business to a dozen offices in the largest US cities, and a bunch of international outposts. Clients liked the way they swarmed in when hired on a case, with their dark suits and the shiny black wingtips that were known as their unofficial signature in the industry. 'Mr Potempa would like to speak with you about a matter. Are you available to meet?' she asked.

'Not now,' Behr said.

'What about this afternoon or evening?' she asked.

'Probably not,' he answered.

'Tomorrow morning then, first thing?' she said with persistence. 'It's a priority matter.'

'Fine,' Behr said, closing his car door and walking towards the accountant, 'fine.'

'Good. Say eight o'clock? Do you know where our offices are?' she asked.

'I'll find it.'

'Thank you, Mr—' Behr hung up, as the willow-thin Shipman fished a briefcase out of his back seat and crossed towards him, head bobbing while he walked. As he drew closer, Behr saw that the accountant had dark circles under his eyes. They'd grown deeper and darker in the two weeks since their last meeting, and it wasn't tax season so that wasn't the reason. Shipman had hired Behr to follow his wife, Mrs Laurie Shipman, whom he suspected of having an affair.

It wasn't the kind of work Behr preferred, but things had been slow. He'd taken a five-thousand-dollar retainer, which would have made it somewhat worthwhile, but now Behr was doing the ridiculous: he was returning twenty-two hundred of it instead of milking it down to zero. If any of his colleagues heard about it, they would laugh him right out of the clubhouse, where the motto was a twist on the old Ernest and Julio Gallo tagline: 'Solve no crime before its time', i.e., before the client has been billed to death.

'Hello, Frank,' Shipman said as he reached Behr.

'Hey, Wells,' Behr said. Over the past two weeks, Behr had confirmed that Shipman's wife, a vivacious brunette, had spent time outside the gym with her trainer, Jake, a buffed-out twenty-five-year-old with a spray-on tan. Laurie was the trainer's last client of the day on Tuesdays and Thursdays, and they would go for a Starbucks after the workout. And it was true those little meetings stretched for close to two hours.

He'd followed each of them alternately when they would separate and leave the coffee shop. The trainer went to the supermarket one night when they were done. She went to the mall on two occasions. Jake went to the movies on the last night. Behr had entered the theatre, sat two rows behind him, but no one had come to meet him. Behr followed the guy home and put him to bed that night, and no one had showed up there either. Especially not Laurie Shipman.

'What's up, Frank? You got something? Pictures, something?' Shipman asked.

'No. No pictures. Wells, I'm gonna have to wrap it up on your case.'

'Really? So no pictures?'

'No.'

'You got a report or – '

'I don't have time to prepare one, and there's not much to put in it,' Behr said. 'I can't confirm your suspicions.'

'Not acceptable,' Shipman said.

'What does she tell you she's doing after the gym?'

'Going out for a coffee with her trainer, then doing some shopping.'

'Well, that's what she's doing.' Behr filled him in on the details.

Shipman frowned. His disappointment seemed to outweigh any relief. 'I need you to keep at it,' the CPA pleaded. 'It's been going on like this for months, and you've only been on her a few weeks.'

'I don't usually take rusty zipper cases in the first place,' Behr said, 'but you've been doing my books for a long time so . . .'

'Is there someone else I can hire – '

'Yeah, plenty. But Wells, let me give *you* some financial advice: don't bother. It's a non-case. Your wife has a friend.'

'So you didn't see anything? Were they holding hands?'

'Not even. Listen, buddy, in instances like this we look for what we call "opportunity and affection". You know what that means? Opportunity is the likely chance for conjugal activity. And affection . . . well, that's affection. Photo or video of the couple in bed—'

'Video?' Shipman blanched.

'Through the curtain or a peephole. A goodbye-kiss at a motel-room door where they've been seen entering the night before. I've witnessed no affection. And "opportunity" doesn't mean a Starbucks.'

Shipman fell silent.

'You want to work it out with your wife? Great. You want to break it off? Then that's what you oughta do. *You* want to be her friend instead of the trainer? Give that a shot. Whatever it is, do it separate from all this.' Behr pulled the cheque out of his pocket. 'This is the rest of your retainer. Buy her a present. Get away for a weekend. I've got to go.'

Behr slid behind the wheel. *Another satisfied customer*, he thought, dropping the car into gear.

Frank Behr stood at the reception station of Wishard Memorial Hospital's emergency room and waited for the attendant to come available. Finally, the burly young man in a hospital-embroidered polo shirt hung up the telephone and swivelled his chair forward. He worked a grape Tootsie Pop around his mouth.

'Help you?' the man said, the sucker clicking against his teeth.

'Yeah, I'm interested in arrivals, either late last night or early this morning,' Behr began.

'What kind of arrivals?'

'Patients sporting certain types of injuries consistent with a fight. Specifically, dislocations – wrists, elbows, shoulders. Broken jaws. Even ankles or knees. Broken ribs.' Behr was aware that the laundry list sounded fairly ridiculous.

'That all?' the burly attendant asked.

His female counterpart finished with some filing and, after listening to Behr, cocked a sceptical eyebrow at him. 'Heath, I'm going on a coffee run. You want any?' she asked.

'Get me one of them mocha javas, Carrie, would ya?'

'The iced ones?'

'Yeah.'

'You all right here?' she said, looking Behr up and down.

'Yeah, we're fine,' Heath said. She left and the man leaned

forward on his elbows. 'I can't be releasing that kind of information to non-police personnel.'

Behr took out his wallet and flashed Heath his old replica shield.

'That's just a three-quarter tin. Your uncle give it to you to beat speeding tickets?'

Behr had to smile. 'Nah, it's mine. I was on the job, now I'm private.' He let Heath see the licence behind his tin – for what that was worth. He also slid a folded twenty-dollar bill across the desk. Heath swept it up, took a suck on his candy and started pecking at a computer keyboard. After a moment he looked up.

'Yeah-hah, we admitted a dislocated knee last night . . . Oh-oh, says it was a motor vehicle accident.'

'*Says* it was a motor vehicle accident?' Behr wondered aloud. *That's probably what one would say*, he figured. 'Is there a police report?'

Heath clicked some keys and started nodding. 'Yep. There is. Other driver was admitted too – steering wheel busted his sternum. Oh well.'

'That it?'

'Sorry, bro. Baby with a fever, heart attack, yada-yada-ya . . .'

'See you later,' Behr said.

'Yeah, funny papers,' Heath said to his back.

Behr spent the day having similar versions of the same conversation at the most likely half dozen other emergency rooms in the vicinity, from Anderson Community to Methodist, all the way up to St Vincent. His wallet was $160 lighter for it, thanks to the fact that one sharpie behind a desk held out for a $40 'tip'.

Behr sat in the Steak 'N' Shake on Arlington chowing down a steak burger, his late lunch/early dinner. Aurelio's assailants either weren't hurt, they were smart enough not to go for medical help in the area, or they were from somewhere else and had gone back there. Whatever the case, running around cloud-seeding for information was not something Behr was in a position to afford for very long, he realized. Especially with zero paying clients currently on the roster. He had wanted his mind to be clean and free to pursue this, but giving back Shipman's retainer might have been a fiscal mistake. He pushed his basket plate away before he was done, leaving an edge of hunger, the way he did when he was on a case, when his cell phone rang and he checked the incoming number. It was Susan, calling from her home. She must've gone straight there after work. Behr took a pull of his soda and answered.

'Hello,' he said.

'Hey, Frank,' her voice came across the line.

'Hey back.'

'How are you?' she asked.

'I'm fine. You?'

'That's funny, you sound kind of effed up.'

'Do I? Must be the connection.' There was a staticky silence. 'Look, I'm sorry about before,' he said.

'Yeah, same,' she said back. It was easy enough to say, but the words changed absolutely nothing between them.

'So we'd talked about dinner and sleeping at my place,' she said, sounding hesitant. 'We were gonna leave early-ish for Lake Monroe, remember? We still on for that?' she wondered.

'Yeah, no, I don't think so . . .' he began.

'No to all of it?' she asked, her back already starting to get up.

'Just the dinner and sleeping over part. I've got some stuff I've gotta run down tonight, and a quick thing early morning.'

'Fine,' she said, her voice tight.

'I could come by late night if – '

'No, thanks . . . I mean, just do what you need to do. I'll go to sleep early and . . .' Her voice wavered between stiff and kind.

'But tomorrow we'll go. You promised your office, right?'

'You sure?'

'Yeah, we'll go.'

'I'm worried about you – '

'Don't be. Look, I got another call coming in,' he said.

'Just call me in the morning when—'

'Will do,' he said, and clicked off. He put the phone down and sat in silence. There was no other call.

Behr drove around burning some gas and thinking. He had zero interest in picnicking on a lake with people from Susan's work tomorrow, but he'd said he would and that was that. He dialled the 'D' and the 'P' from Aurelio's book. The first number yielded a recording that told him the number was not in service. The second wouldn't go through, and as the number was missing an area code Behr suspected it wasn't local. He tried some Illinois and Michigan prefixes, but it wasn't working. He dialled the number listed 'F'. A voicemail picked up after four rings and pop music he didn't recognize played for a few seconds as an outgoing message, then there was a beep.

'My name is Frank Behr, and I'm calling about Aurelio Santos. Please call me back . . .' He left his number and hung up. 'CC' was Commerce Credit, a bank. The other two turned out to be Jiu-Jitsu students he hadn't met. One mentioned the memorial service at noon on Sunday at the Academy.

'I'll be there,' Frank said and hung up, and then drove around until the streets began to glitter under the streetlights in the coming dark.

At about 7.45 he placed a call to his friend Jean Gannon at the coroner's office.

'Jean? Frank Behr.'

'The bad news blues,' she sighed.

'How are ya—'

'What? Which? How much is it gonna cost me?'

'Santos, Aurelio. Late thirties, Brazilian. GSW to—'

'To what's left of the face,' Jean jumped in. 'I heard about it. Didn't catch it though.'

'Damn. Any way for me to get a look?'

Breathing was all that came back across the line.

'C'mon, I'll be your best friend.'

'Position's not open.'

'I'll buy you a year's subscription to *Cat Fancy*—'

'Screw off, Behr. I'm divorced, not a dyke.'

'Ah, what's the difference?'

'Yeah, yeah, I'll let you know when *I* do.' There was a beat of silence. 'Come around nine, night guys will be out at dinner.'

'I'll bring you the usual—' But she'd hung up the phone.

TEN

TERRY SCHLEGEL WARMED up with one eighty-five on the bench while T. Rex played in the back office of Rubber House. The clang of a socket wrench hitting the cement floor out in the garage bay of the tyre change and alignment shop reached him from time to time. After a dozen reps, he re-racked the bar, took a swig of water, and popped a creatine lozenge into his mouth. The shits tasted rancid, like sour orange chemicals, but he was all out of the flavourless powder version. He'd been drinking protein shakes for years to keep the muscle on his light-heavy's frame, but when he'd passed forty-five he'd started to feel the need for some extra oomph. He'd never considered juicing though – nothing that would shrink his liver or his 'nads. No thank you. He'd never do anything to mess with his dick. That was an absolute rule. No Viagra, no Cialis, no MaxiDerm – none of that crap. So far there'd been no need, and he planned on keeping it that way. Maybe he was just being superstitious.

Terry added twenty-five-pound plates to the bar and thought about blood and business. It had been a busy time, and it was soon to be busier still. Then Marc Bolan's voice slid in low and sly over crushed-down guitars.

> *Well you're dirty and sweet*
> *Clad in black*
> *Don't look back*
> *And I love you.*

His mind naturally went to Vicky. It was a big song for them back when they started going out twenty-three years ago. An oldie already at the time, but big all the same. She was nineteen, only a few years younger than he was, but it seemed like a lot. She had a little slip of a body back then. The straps of her bra and panties cut white lines against her taut, flat skin, out in his car at what they all called 'Penetration Park'. She was a bit more of a cruiser these days, but she still looked good, and after all the shit they'd been through and had beat – getting married and raising the boys and all – he felt a stirring even now. *See*, he thought, *some things you just don't mess with* . . .

Terry took down his sets one after another, and getting close to done with the bench he considered the squat rack and whether he should bang out a few. He rolled up his sweatpants and checked his leg. A fat bruise, purple and black, spread over his quad. Maybe he should wait another few days.

The boys. Shit, that thought was enough to take the starch out of him on its own. Raising three wild men, as he had, that was a tricky proposition. It had driven Vicky half to three-quarters crazy already, and they weren't done yet. *You try and look after 'em, shield 'em from the outside elements*, he said to her, *but they need their exposure too, in order not to turn out like all the other soft pukes around in this day and age.* He rolled down the pant leg and loaded the curl bar for skull-crushers.

Kenny, the baby, with his black spiky hair and wise-ass grin, would be in high school for another year – that is if he ever made it to class. Not that he seemed in any hurry to graduate on account of all the trim he wheeled out of there. The place was basically a poontang depot for the kid to dip into every week or so when it was time to refresh his stocks. Vicky had pretty much worn herself out yelling at Kenny about his skipping classes. Terry hadn't gone in for that. *Land war in Asia*, was what he'd said to her on more than one occasion when she'd tried to enlist his help on the matter, *just something unwinnable you don't wanna engage in.*

Then there was Deanie, the middle man, twenty years old already and always in need of a haircut, and Charlie, his big boy, more fair-haired, like his mother, cock diesel at twenty-two, quiet and serious. Time was flying. Hell if it seemed they had any immediate plans to move out again. Why should they? They'd tried it when Deanie had graduated a few years back. They'd gotten a two-bedroom dunghole and filled it with second-hand furniture and beer parties before they realized there was a little thing called 'rent' and it wasn't interested in waiting for hangovers to wear off before being paid. Terry'd had to go have a little chat with their landlord before the Ukrainian sonofabitch went and got the marshal involved with the eviction, so it turned out to be a short-term experiment for the boys.

Now? Room and board, butler and maid, butter and bread. The boys were pretty teed up, of this there was no doubt. Not that you'd know it from the funk Dean was walking around in. *These bitches'll drive you crazy if you let 'em*, he'd told Deano a thousand times. But did Dean listen? Nope, he just kept moping around the house. And Charlie, the gang boss, he was strong as a Mack truck, even though he didn't train much and just stayed in his room most days working the phone and laying plans for God knows what.

Terry didn't mind. Truth was, he liked having them around where he could keep track of 'em. They were damn good boys. That was why he was working so hard to build them a business. They were loyal to him, and they stuck together, even in the shit. Everyone knew the Schlegels were thick on the street and if you messed with one of them, you messed with them all. They kept him young and on fire too, the scrappy bastards. They forced him to stay lean and mean and one step ahead of them. Especially mean. That was his biggest edge these days.

He lay down on the bench and began pressing the curl bar up from his forehead, feeling the burn in his triceps, when the door to the main bay swung open, admitting a hot breeze along with the sound of pneumatic wrenches. He saw the upside-down image of Knute the Newt Bohgen filling the doorframe.

'Look at you there, ripe for a tea-bagging,' Knute said.

'Try it, motherfucker,' Terry grunted between reps. 'See what happens.'

'Don't tease me.' Knute smiled. He found a stool and lit a cigarette.

'Open a window. Shit. I'm getting healthy, you're taking me in the other direction.'

'Sorry.' Knute waved at the smoke and cracked the window a little, blowing out a drag.

'You could pick up a weight some time, you know. Wouldn't kill you,' Terry said.

'Never know. It might,' Knute said. He sucked down another hit and fired his cigarette out the window.

'Probably would.' Terry dropped the bar with a crash. They slapped hands. 'You hear something from Financial Gary?' Terry asked.

'Like you said, I didn't come here for the workout . . .' Knute bumped his eyebrows and wiggled the partial he had standing in for the front teeth that went missing in a bar brawl long ago.

'And?' Terry asked, appraising his long-time partner. Knute was two years older than he, half a foot shorter and forty pounds lighter, which would have made him a super lightweight. He had a droopy moustache and a pink scar on his cheek from his time in ISP in Michigan City, which was where the state sent you to disappear. Up there every trip out of the cell was a chance to get shanked, every visit to the yard an opportunity to be opened up. But Knute hadn't died. Three years in, and now three months back. Those were long, lonely, unproductive years, for them both. A real shit time. But they were getting things back on track. They'd been real eager beavers since Knute's return.

Knute took a scrap of paper out of his pocket and handed it to Terry, who looked it over. It had figures written all over it in no particular order, including one fat number that was double-stroked and circled in felt pen.

'This?' Terry glanced up. Knute nodded. 'Every month?'

'Yeah, but we have to have 'em all good and organized and under control. Not piecemeal. No holdouts. Not just the near Northside, but far Eastside and all the way through Speedway too. Lot more heavy lifting to go—'

'As discussed. We're on our way. We'll have 'em all by winter, wrapped and ready to present to our buyer,' Terry said. He ripped up the scrap, wadded it and tossed it in the garbage can. 'Coupla bandy-bellied pirates gonna carve out a fortune is what we are . . .' Terry smiled. But Knute looked nervous.

ELEVEN

BEHR ARRIVED AT the McCarty Street building that housed the coroner's office and parked. He grabbed the paper bag holding what he'd had to drive around to three stores to find – a box of Lindt truffle chocolates and a bottle of Johnnie Walker Red – and entered the building. It had become a routine between Behr and Jean Gannon over the years he'd known her. On her birthday, and Christmas, and whenever he needed a little access, he'd drop by and they would share a drink and a talk. At first it was just the whisky, but then he'd seen the candies on her desk one time and added them in too. His name was at the front desk and he was allowed back to where Jean worked. The smell of formaldehyde and glutaraldehyde and other chemicals hung in the chill air.

'The candy man can,' he said, entering and waving the bag in front of him.

Jean looked up from her work. She'd put on weight since he'd last seen her and the glow of her computer screen was finding the lines on her face. Divorce wasn't treating her too well, but then it usually didn't.

'Frankie,' she said.

'*Doctor* . . .' Behr smiled, opening his arms.

Jean pushed away her keyboard and came around the desk. She skipped the hug for a squeeze of Behr's forearm and grabbed the sack out of his hand. She glanced inside, then bunched the top of the bag and put it in her desk drawer.

'My spare tyre thanks you,' she said.

'I'll bring you a spirulina muffin next time, you want.'

'That'd be great. Better still would be if there is no next time.' Her tone was harsh, but they shared a smile and she waved him out of the office towards the exam rooms.

'I never asked you, why Johnnie Red?' Behr wondered as they went.

'Because I can't afford Blue.'

'Course.'

'Nah, that's not why. Way back when Greg and I were buying our first house we had this Chinese realtor. At the closing, he gave us a bottle of it, because after a transaction the Chinese are supposed to give something red for luck. Been drinking it ever since.' They walked down a long corridor and Behr couldn't tell if it was actually getting colder as they went or if it was his imagination.

'So you're trying to stay lucky.'

'Yeah, that's it,' she said.

They passed a tall, middle-aged man who nodded to Jean but didn't give Behr a second glance, and then they entered one of the cutting rooms.

It *was* colder inside. Laid out on a slab beneath harsh surgical lights was Aurelio's body. The thing that had made him him was now far away and would never be seen again. The body hadn't been opened up, but the damage to his face had dried into a blackish purple mask. They hadn't bothered topping him with a sheet.

'No relatives scheduled to see the body here, that's why he's uncovered. I can—'

Behr cut her off with a head shake. 'Full autopsy planned?'

'Not unless someone requests it. Cause of death's pretty clear. Pellets have been removed for evidence.' She picked up a tin dish and rattled it, lead shot rolling around inside. Behr took a look.

'Double-aught buck,' she said.

'Twelve-gauge?' Behr asked, pro forma.

'Nope, ten.'

'Damn, a goose gun.' This was a bit of a surprise. A 10-gauge was a lot less usual than a 12. 'Handload or store-bought?' Behr asked.

'Can't really tell unless casings were recovered. Probably store-bought. If you're thinking about fingerprints on the buckshot, forget about it. Not after this kind of cavitation.'

Behr's eyes skimmed over the body. There were old scars covering Aurelio. His knees looked like they'd been gone over with a belt sander, and other patches of skin sported abrasions – mat burns – that would've taken years to heal down completely. His right ear was mostly gone from the gunshot, the left one was a bit cauliflowered. Aurelio didn't generally advocate the headfirst wrestling style that had caused it, but hadn't developed the finer points in his game until he'd already sustained some damage. Behr looked for major swelling or contusions, perhaps a broken bone that would tell a story. He wasn't finding what he was looking for. It was growing increasingly difficult for him to keep his mind clear, so he couldn't be sure he wasn't missing it. The initial notes from the exam rested on a table beside the slab and Behr picked them up, but the words swam in front of his eyes.

'Closed casket for certain,' Jean mused. 'Screw the damn thing shut. Or get him a George W. Bush mask.'

'Bodies don't bruise post-mortem, right?' Behr wondered aloud.

'Right, generally speaking.'

'So if there were any injuries like that, they'd have to have been sustained while he was alive.'

'That's the way it works.' She cocked her head and looked at him. 'First day at the carnival?'

'Sorry, I'm just trying to think straight.'

'What are you doing on this anyway, Frank? You didn't say and I didn't think to ask.'

'He's my friend, Jean. Was.'

'Ah, fuck me uncle Sal!' she said. 'Jeez, that's a real V8 move.' She smacked herself in the head. 'I thought it was business.'

'Forget it. It's business now.' Behr looked around at the white tile and steel surfaces of the room, scrubbed clean and disinfected of germs and meaning. 'What about . . . what about the back of the body? Did he get hit from behind? Was there any evidence of bludgeoning?'

Jean grabbed the exam notes from Behr and threw on a pair of cheaters. She snapped on a latex glove and began going over the body carefully as she referred to the notes.

'OK,' she said, her tone suddenly businesslike, 'posterior side was checked. It's clean. No contusions or skull fracture caused by bludgeoning.'

'What about bruising on the scalp? The ones caused by rod-shaped—'

'Tramline bruises. You think he got hit with the gun barrel?' Behr shrugged.

'That's a special dissection if there's any indication,' she said gravely.

'They'll have to peel the scalp?' Behr asked.

She nodded and continued. 'According to X-rays, we've got

calcification in knuckles, wrists and some toes. This guy was, what, a professional fighter? There are lots of fractures that healed up over the years.' She got near what was left of Aurelio's lower jaw. 'My colleague who caught this one, Dr Rodale, he's real thorough . . .' She leaned in close in a way Behr did not envy. 'He found broken lower teeth and lacerations inside the mouth that bled up. That means before the gunshot.'

'He was hit.'

'Or the gun was jammed in his mouth. Shotgun barrel can do that real easy.'

'But the shot?'

'Not in the mouth.'

Behr nodded. Now he could see powder tattooing, and that the muzzle had been placed beneath Aurelio's chin. After another minute or so of inspection with no talking between them, Jean stripped off the latex glove and put the notes down.

'Come on,' she said, 'they'll be getting back from dinner break soon.' She led Behr down the hall to her office, where she sat him on a stool and poured some of the Johnnie Walker into two lab beakers. She sat behind her desk and they touched glasses over it. Behr drank, but she didn't. He told her the details of the events that had led him there.

'If you don't mind my saying, Frank, maybe you're not the best guy to be looking into this,' she offered when he was done.

'No?' he said, peering over the top of his glass. 'Who'd be better?' She thought about that one for a while, but had no answer. Finally there was just quiet that went on as if it always would. Then he finished up his Scotch and stood. She came around her desk, and this time she did hug him.

'You take care, you got me?' she said.

He nodded. 'Let me know about any tramlines.'

'You stay pro on this thing.'

'Thanks, Jean,' he said, wondering exactly what that meant any more.

On his way home, Behr drove to Aurelio's place. It had been a hell of a day, and he had the Scotch in him, and he knew he should probably shut it down for the night, but he really wanted to get a look inside the house. His feeling didn't change even when he passed by and saw the unmarked police unit sitting on the address, an officer reclined low and just visible over the car door. Behr continued on, turning around the corner on to the next block, where he parked. He sat looking past a small brick cottage, through a line of scraggly trees, at the back of Aurelio's place. In the black of the night, he thought, he could make it over the low chain-link fence, through the trees and to the back door without being seen. He could get in and inspect the place, except for the front room, with his Mini Maglite. He could probably do it all without getting caught. He sat there thinking on it for five or ten minutes.

'Dumb,' he finally said aloud. He dropped his car into gear and drove home.

TWELVE

'SOUTHEASTSIDE MAN KILLED IN APPARENT ROBBERY ATTEMPT,' read the *Star*'s headline. Behr was at the Caro Group, in a waiting room that smelled of fine woodwork, leather sofas and freshly brewed dark-roast coffee. The place smelled like money. He had a cup of the strong, perfect stuff on the table at his knee as he read the account of Aurelio's death. The details were few in the short, vague piece, perhaps because police had nothing, or because that was all they wanted to release. After reading it twice, Behr tossed the paper on the coffee table with disgust and waited.

'Mr Behr, they're ready for you,' Ms Swanton said. She wore heavy make-up, matronly business attire, and had her hair set in an old-fashioned helmet. She was as solid as a Sherman tank, and about as inviting. He sank into the carpet up to his ankles as he followed her down a hallway lined with certificates of civic recognition the company had received from the city. It sure didn't feel like a Saturday in the office, as there were plenty of busy people around. He passed a room, door partially open, that had bakers' racks full of the black, hard-sided cases that protected and transported high-end surveillance equipment. Infrared cameras, hard-line wiretaps, relays, cell phone wiretaps, cell phone scramblers, night vision, voice stress analysers – all the tools of the trade that he couldn't afford. Some of them even worked some of the time.

They neared a corner office that could only belong to the firm's old bull, and when Ms Swanton swung open the door his impression was confirmed. Rising from a large mahogany desk that cost more than Behr's car was a silver-haired man in an expensive charcoal-grey suit. A second man, tall and slim, with curly rust-coloured hair, stood as well. Slim wore an equally expensive navy chalk-stripe suit and held an alligator-skin binder under his arm.

'Mr Behr, meet Mr Potempa,' Ms Swanton intoned. 'Can I get you gentlemen anything?'

'We're fine,' Karl Potempa said in a smooth baritone. Ms Swanton nodded and left and no one spoke until the door closed behind her. In the meantime Behr looked around the office at framed handshake photos of Potempa and other men, including the governor, at various banquets and flesh-presses. Potempa's old FBI badge was in a display case on the desk, which was also full of commemorative clocks and ashtrays from golf outings and law enforcement conferences.

'I'm Curt Lundquist,' the unintroduced man in the navy suit began, 'house counsel for Caro.'

Behr shook his hand and realized he was being hired. It was common practice in private investigation, especially at the higher end, with clients who had money to burn on lawyers as well as investigators. When the lawyer did the hiring, anything the investigator found fell under attorney–client privilege and couldn't be subpoenaed.

'Have a seat,' Potempa hit him with the dulcet baritone again, 'and thanks for coming.' Behr lowered himself into a slick, oxblood-leather chair. 'Do you know anything about our firm?'

'Security. Investigation. I know you charge plenty,' Behr said, evoking no smiles across the desk.

'Crisis and emergency management, executive protection, homeland security solutions, risk analysis, all that,' Potempa went on.

'Colour me impressed,' Behr said. 'What can I do for you?'

'We have two employees, investigators, named Ken Bigby and Derek Schmidt,' Lundquist said. 'They're from our Philly office, put up over at the Valu-Stay Suites while they're in town.'

'It's part of a new programme we've got going where we move guys around for six months at a time, so they develop a national overview,' Potempa added.

'How's that working?' Behr wondered.

'Fine,' Potempa answered, but it didn't sound like the truth. Behr waited for him to continue, already assuming he'd hear of some scam the two employees were involved in that they wanted to investigate with external personnel. Bill padding or misappropriation of company resources or some other kind of fraud was usually the order of the day.

'Anyway,' Potempa went on, 'Ken Bigby and Derek Schmidt . . . we can't locate them,' Lundquist said. 'They're missing.'

'Missing?'

Potempa and Lundquist nodded. Behr waited for them to go on, but they didn't.

'Missing like they stopped showing up for work and went to a competitor with their files?' Behr asked, readjusting his assumptions. Potempa and Lundquist shrugged and shook their heads.

'So you want me to jump in on a case they were working?' Behr asked.

This time neither man moved or responded for a moment. 'It's not the case we need you to pursue at this time,' the lawyer,

Lundquist, said. A moment of silence spread in the room before Behr began to understand what they were looking for.

'You want *me* to track down your people?' he asked, truly surprised.

'That's right,' Potempa said.

'Why don't you all do it?' Behr asked, pointing a thumb towards the outer offices. He had just walked past a bullpen full of shirt-and-tie investigators who looked rough and ready, not to mention a handful of doors that had the title 'Case Manager' stencilled on them. The place was practically an FBI field office.

'We don't want to lose any more man hours to it,' Potempa said evenly, the baritone hitching just slightly.

'Just to find they lit out for Vegas or St Louis or some place?' Behr suggested.

'That's probably not it,' Potempa said, shifting in his seat. 'Though we certainly hope it's that basic . . .'

Behr had been wondering how they had come to choose *him* in a town with four pages' worth of private investigators listed online and in the phone book. Now he was able to put it together – it was a janitor job. He didn't bother filtering his thoughts. 'So while your regular guys are out billing three hundred an hour on real cases, you'll put me on this at seventy-five.'

'Something like that. I hope you don't find it insulting. It's a question of economics,' Potempa said. 'And your reputation is investigative-strong and localized.'

'According to whom?'

'That person would prefer not to be named.'

Behr chewed over whom they'd checked him with and what his reputation might be 'weak' in before speaking again. 'If it's just a question of economics, pay me one-fifty an hour. You'll still be making out that way.'

'A hundred,' Lundquist said.

'Fine,' Behr said, immediately wondering if he'd gone too cheap. Either way, this would be a score for him. A hundred an hour to run down an ATM trail or credit-card pattern that would lead, despite what the bosses thought, to a lost weekend at a riverboat casino or Glitter Gulch hotel with some strippers or bar girls or hookers. And this time he wouldn't be giving back any retainer. Unlike with Shipman, there was no personal connection here. Even though it wouldn't take long, this time around he'd be 'Frank the Milkman' all the way. It could finance him through his Aurelio investigation and beyond. 'So, I'll just need to look at their files and computers then.'

'Sorry, company materials aren't available for view by outside individuals,' Lundquist said.

'OK . . .' Behr said. 'Well, that ups the degree of difficulty.'

'We're also going to need you to sign this,' Lundquist said, taking a piece of paper out of his binder and sliding it towards Behr, who picked it up and looked it over.

'A confidentiality agreement?' Behr said.

'We'd prefer word of us hiring outside didn't get around,' Potempa explained.

'Right,' Behr said. 'Of course. Can I speak to some of their co-workers then?'

'We can't . . . would prefer not to . . . involve . . . other company personnel,' Potempa said, the baritone tightening up now. 'That's one of the reasons we're hiring—'

'Then can you fill me in on what they were working?' Behr said, quickly becoming tired of the game. There was a long, silent pause in response. 'If you don't give me anything, where am I supposed to start?'

Potempa shifted uncomfortably again, tapped his fingers against a crystal paperweight of a size better suited to bludgeoning intruders than holding down documents, then exchanged a nod with Lundquist, who spoke. 'They were checking the status of . . . properties . . . for a client.'

'A client?' Behr asked flatly, already knowing they weren't going to tell him who that client was.

'Yes. A client.'

'I don't suppose you can tell me—'

'No,' Lundquist answered.

'Can you at least tell me what type of property and where the hell they are?' Behr asked as patiently as he could. *The meter's already running, and includes this meeting*, he thought.

The two men exchanged another look, and Potempa nodded before Lundquist went to his alligator binder once more for a sheet of non-letterhead paper, which he fed across the desk. 'Derelict houses,' Potempa said. Behr looked over a list of a dozen addresses. Franklin Street, 33rd, Arrington, a few other streets Behr recognized. Mostly near Brightwood, on the northeast side, and some other shit areas. The parts of town where a real estate speculator of any stature – certainly the kind of businessman who would hire a Caro Group – would not be buying or selling.

Lundquist filled the silence. 'So the gag agreement we mentioned—'

'Curt . . .' Potempa intoned, giving the lawyer a 'take it easy' gesture with his hand.

'Sorry, Karl,' Lundquist whispered.

Behr picked up the page and looked at it, and then at the men. He had more questions but realized they were looking to him for answers, not the other way around.

It was the part of the meeting where he was supposed to say, 'I'll get on it then,' and sign the non-disclosure and start getting paid. But Behr found himself unable to do or say anything like that. The problem, he quickly realized, in taking big dollars from a top shop was that it came with a caveat: you had to deliver. Failing to do so because he had both hands tied behind his back from the start was no way to build that reputation Potempa had mentioned earlier. And then there was the fact that his friend had recently been scraped off his own gym floor, and something needed to be done about it.

Christ, Behr thought a moment before he spoke, *I'm physically unable to make money. It's just not in my DNA.*

'I'm gonna take a pass on this one, gentlemen,' he said, then slid their paperwork back across the desk and headed for the door.

THIRTEEN

I T WAS WEIRD, but her stomach looked flatter in the two-piece than it did in the single. Susan appraised herself in the mirror. She wasn't that religious when it came to the aerobics and gym time in general, but maybe it was time to get some religion. No more 'pour me into it' party dresses for her. She should at least start swimming again. She pictured herself churning up the lanes back in college – it seemed like a long, long time ago, much longer than ten years. She pulled her hair back into a pony and checked her sleepy eyes. She wondered if her mouth had recently started turning down at the corners more than usual, and whether she was on her way to beginning to look old.

She thought about putting on some make-up, but smiled and just rubbed in some tinted sunscreen moisturizer. They were headed down past Bloomington to Lake Monroe, where her boss kept a boat. There would be swimming, tubing, maybe skiing. She checked her top. It seemed secure enough that her business wouldn't go flying when she hit the water. Her phone rang, Frank on the line. A fist of tension knotted around her at the sound of his voice. They'd said their 'sorries' but that hadn't gotten at the issue. Not really, and she knew it was her fault. She pulled up a striped mini and threw on a denim shirt up top. She put a couple of towels in a backpack, grabbed her sunglasses and some lip gloss and headed for the door.

The cornfields formed a corridor of green as they drove down 37. The windows were open and warm morning air blew through the car in place of conversation.

'I'm here,' Behr had said into his cell phone when he'd pulled up in front of Susan's apartment building. 'You need help with anything? . . . All right, see you in a minute,' he'd said before he hung up.

'Hi', 'no' and 'I'll be right down' were all that constituted her side of the conversation. He tried to interpret what kind of day he had ahead of him, but based on that, he'd have done better if she'd sent him a Braille telegram.

'How are you?' she'd said when she got in the car.

'OK, considering,' he answered. 'You?'

'I'm fine.'

'You look good.'

'Thanks,' she said, and then gave a glance at his clothes. 'You're wearing that?'

He looked down and realized the jacket and tie he'd worn to the meeting didn't scream 'day at the lake'. 'I've got some shorts in the trunk.'

She shrugged and then fiddled with the radio before letting it rest on WFBQ playing Jackson Browne.

That had been it for the last half-hour. Then she said: 'So his name is Ed. My boss.'

'Ed Lindsey, right?' Behr nodded.

'His wife is Claire. The rest of my department will be there too, some others from the paper and maybe a few faculty from Indiana U–Purdue, where Ed volunteer teaches.' Behr just looked at the road.

When they'd passed Bloomington, and the signs for Lake Monroe and French Lick started popping up, Susan pointed out the window at a Kroger. 'We should stop and get something.' Behr turned off.

Too many signs in the front windows, place is ripe for a strong-arm job, Behr thought, following Susan through the store. *An armed team comes in and locks the door, and no one outside can tell there's a robbery in progress. If someone does trip an alarm, suddenly you're in a Dirty Harry movie. No clean views or angles from outside for the cops once they did arrive. Most urban stores consider this when they're hanging their specials posters.*

He almost bumped into Susan when she stopped at a refrigerated produce case and he nearly shook his head to clear out the useless chatter in it.

'How does this look?' she asked, holding up a tray of cut-up celery, carrots and either cucumber or zucchini. 'Some crudités?'

Behr shrugged. She put it down. 'You're right, don't over-think it. Beer.' He followed her down an aisle and felt his feet slowing and his head turning. They were in the pharmacy area on the way to the beverage section. There was a shelf full of boxes – pastel pink with maroon script writing – that seemed familiar. He slowed to a stop. He knew why. There was a torn piece of cardboard in his bathroom trashcan – a box flap, which contained a few letters but no full words – that he could swear was from the same product. Looking at it now he saw it was an at-home pregnancy test. Early Response. *Doesn't mean anything*, he said to himself and glanced ahead at Susan, who was just turning the corner at the end of the aisle. He continued walking, no longer feeling his feet. Before long he was holding a twelve-pack of Heineken, then putting it down on the black rubber conveyor belt, paying for it, and they were back in the car.

Lake Monroe glittered like a handful of uncut diamonds had been thrown down on its surface. The trees were bunched thick and green along the shore. The sound of birds was ripped by that of the powerboats and WaveRunners that gnashed across the water. There was a small sprig of dock with a twenty-five-foot Bayliner tied to it, and not far away about a dozen people were clustered around a picnic table loaded down with cold cuts, coolers, grocery bags and a sack of charcoal. Susan led the way in. Behr followed, carrying the beer.

'Hey, y'all,' she said, moving into the group, fake shoulder-bumping a few of them. A round of 'Susan!' went up. It was clear to Behr she was pretty high on the popularity depth chart. Susan turned, making room for him, and he plunked down the Heinekens on a corner of the table, and then she introduced him around. 'Welcome, welcome,' said her boss, Ed Lindsey, head of circulation for the *Indianapolis Star*. He was an older man with curly hair and a pot belly, and Behr liked him immediately. The same didn't go for Chad Quell, a twenty-five-year-old with a big white smile and an expensive haircut.

'So this is your better half, huh, Suzy Q?' Chad said to her as if Behr wasn't there. 'You told him lake not funeral, right?'

'Chad is in ad sales,' Susan said to fill the resulting awkward silence.

'Don't underrate me, I *am* ad sales.' He smiled.

'And modest,' she said.

'It's true, I'm not top dog. Yet. But the guy who is? He's like forty-three, so it won't be long before I run him down.'

'Hard to believe the newspaper business is collapsing with you in it,' Behr said, putting a pretty good pall over the proceedings. But Susan's boss bailed him out.

'You just keep selling, Chad,' Lindsey stated, 'the rest will work itself out.'

'So says the old hand,' the kid answered, before he ripped open the twelve-pack and helped himself to a beer. 'It's cocktail hour somewhere, isn't it?' he said to the group. There were a few takers. He offered one to Susan.

'Too early for me,' she declined. Chad shrugged and started loading the rest into a cooler that already held a good supply of domestic light. Frank said hello to several other men and women from various departments on the paper, and also met the petite Mrs Lindsey, 'Call me Claire,' who appeared from somewhere holding a big bowl of German potato salad.

'Oh, come with me, Frank,' Susan said, pulling him away from the group to where a tall, thin man with salt and pepper hair stood smoking.

'Frank, this is Neil Ratay.'

Ratay turned. 'Hello, Susan.'

'He's a reporter. You'll have tons to talk about,' she said.

Ratay extended a hand and he and Behr shook.

'Frank Behr. I've read you,' Behr said. Ratay was a crime reporter who delivered a steady supply of terse, informative descriptions of home invasions, domestic beatings and drug murders to the *Star*'s readership.

'Pleasure,' Ratay said, putting his cigarette between his lips. 'Have I heard your name?' he asked, breathing out a cloud of smoke.

'Could have. Couldn't have been recent,' Behr said. Ratay just shrugged.

Lindsey, followed by some of the others, all carrying beers, made his way down to the dock. 'First flotilla's leaving. Who's aboard?' he shouted.

'I'm in,' Susan called. She turned to Behr. 'You coming?'

'You go ahead,' he said. 'I'll go change and get on the next ride.' She nodded and went after the group, which included Chad.

Behr went back to the car and took his time about it. He stood behind the open trunk and changed into shorts. He strolled back down to the picnic table where the landlubbers were congregated. Across the way, Ratay was finished smoking but didn't rejoin the group. Instead he sat down on a stump and watched the boats zip back and forth on the lake.

'You're a strong-looking boy, you're drafted,' the nearly sixty-year-old Claire Lindsey said, pointing to a big bag of Kingsford briquettes. He hadn't been called a boy in some time. Amused, Behr hefted the bag, dumped it into a nearby Weber Kettle, and made a pyramid as directed by the hostess. He doused it with lighter fluid, tossed a match and then grabbed a beer. Ratay drifted over and offered Behr a cigarette from his pack. Behr declined. Ratay lit his own by waving the end through the orange flame that leapt out of the grill. Behr sipped his beer, Ratay smoked, and they both settled in to watch the charcoal whiten.

Before long the boat returned and Susan and Chad came up the dock together, laughing over some office joke.

'Holding down the fort?' Chad asked.

'Yep. All taken care of,' Behr said. Susan gave him a 'be nice' look.

'Late enough for you yet?' Chad asked Susan, opening a fresh beer. She shrugged and accepted the bottle, though she didn't drink from it. She set it down in front of her, Behr noticed.

'You've gotta come out on the boat, Frank. It's awesome,' she said.

'OK,' he said, 'in a while.'

Claire was hovering over a cooler pulling out hamburger patties. Susan saw it and went to her. 'Let me help you get those going, Claire . . .'

Chad leaned against the table near Behr. 'So what do you do, dead eyes?' Chad asked. Behr turned and stared into Chad's silver-framed sunglasses, the word 'Armani' stencilled on the left lens.

'I'm a librarian,' he said. Behr felt Ratay smirk over his shoulder.

'Yeah? Interesting work. Dewey Decimal and all,' Chad tried to play back. Maybe he was just making conversation.

'Right.' Behr walked away. He found a spot that looked out over a glen of trees and towards a cove that held a few luxury houses that shared a common dock. He stood there for a while thinking about Aurelio, and how to get a toehold in his investigation.

'Beautiful, isn't it?' Susan said, putting a soft hand on the small of his back. Behr nodded. More than that, he appreciated the gesture. 'Wouldn't be too bad having a place out here,' she said.

'Nope,' he agreed, 'sure wouldn't.' He figured he might as well keep it positive, but that was the ten years between them talking. At her age, he'd have thought why not, just like her. Now he knew why.

'Let's go out on the boat and get a burger when we're back,' she suggested.

'Sure thing, *Suzy Q*,' he said.

'Oh, stop. He's harmless.' She elbowed him.

Behr followed her and a few others down the dock. He felt Chad walking behind them without even looking back, and as they boarded he saw he was right.

'Hang on, my babies,' Ed said, behind the wheel, and he pushed the throttle forward jumping the big Evinrude outboard to life.

Behr could see what looked like a large rubber banana with handles tied to the port side. As they reached the middle of the lake, Ed throttled down to an idle. He moved to the side and untied the yellow float, letting it pay out behind the boat on a long nylon rope. 'All right,' he said, 'who's up for a ride?'

'I'm first,' Susan said, letting her skirt fall to the floor of the boat.

'No thong, Suze? Awwwww,' Chad said. Behr looked at him and considered punching him in the face.

'Shut it, Chad,' she said, jumping into the lake. A moment later she surfaced with a 'Yeow! Cold.'

'How many does it hold, Eddie?' Chad said, peeling off his shirt. Behr saw Chad had a suntan over hairless washboard abs. It looked like he shaved or waxed himself down like a triathlete.

'Four,' Ed said, 'unless Frank wants to go. In that case we should hold it to three.'

'I'm good for now,' Behr said as Chad hit the water with a splash. Jenny, a chunky thirty-year-old from layout, stripped down to a one-piece and lumbered over the gunwale.

'Wait up,' Jenny said, swimming towards them as Susan and Chad slipped and slid over the inflatable, finding their spots.

'Come on, Jenny-girl,' Chad said. Behr tried to spot a look of disappointment on Chad's face at the intrusion, but the glare off the lake was too bright.

'Hold on,' Ed yelled, and powered up. The boat cut the lake. Behind them the inflatable bounced and churned in their wake. The three riders howled and held on.

'Thanks for having me out, Ed,' Behr called over the roar of the engine. 'Real nice spot.'

'Sure thing, Frank. The more the merrier. Been wanting to meet you. Susan always talks about you so—' Ed looked forward and turned the boat and his last words were carried away on the humid summer air. Behr didn't bother asking him to repeat it and instead leaned against a rear-facing seat and looked behind them.

Susan's smile travelled back to him over the forty-foot distance of the towrope. The sun bounced golden off her hair. Behr took a seat in the stern, his beer between his knees, and watched for a moment, then turned his face straight up at the sun until it burned white in his eyes.

FOURTEEN

PEANUT MARBRY SAT in Killah, his stock-to-shock Dodge Neon, and fucked with the bass setting on the Alpine, waking up the Bazooka tube mounted in the back window. The car started to thump and shudder to 'Soulja Boy'.

'When they come, I'm gonna go with them,' Peanut said over the music. 'You follow. You know where we going. Let us back on down first, then you come next. Back on down too, don't front in. Keep it runnin', won't be long at that point.'

Nixie Buncher, sunk low in the Katzkin leather passenger seat, nodded one time. Peanut knew he had the drill. Nixie only needed to hear a play once and he was locked on. That was why Peanut ran with him, even though homey was skinny as a greyhound track dog.

'You notice bad shit always go down when them Schlegels around?' Nixie asked.

Peanut said nothing.

'Hear they walk some dudes out they bar one night and nobody see 'em since?' Nixie said.

'Bad shit happen to good people, yo,' Peanut answered. 'Ever notice we get paid when they around?'

'Shit-talking white boys,' Nixie said, tsking through his teeth. 'What you oughta do is take him out. Charlie. Bim-bam,' he went on, sticking out a left-right combo. 'The minute any one of 'em say shit. Once Charlie Boy's on the ground, them others scatter.'

Nixie reached out a long arm and slapped the crown-shaped pump bottle on the dash two, then three times, filling the car with the scent of Tropical Rainbow.

Peanut shook his head. 'Nah, man, first off that's bad fiscals. Second, them Schlegels'd just keep coming.'

'They only three.'

'Don't forget they daddy. He the worst of the bunch. Who knows, momma prolly too. I bet they got a basement full of 'em – they keep coming like ants out a hill . . .'

Nixie went to hit the air freshener pump again.

'Hol' up,' Peanut said. Nixie looked to him, his eyes red even though he was only a little high. 'Shit's nineteen dollahs a bottle.'

Instead Nixie eased a tiny squirt out on his fingertips and rubbed it on his hands as the Durango pulled up next to them.

The window slid down revealing Charlie Boy Schlegel behind the wheel and that Crazy Kenny across in the passenger seat. No doubt Deanie was in the back behind the smoked window glass.

'Whassup, my negro?' Kenny shouted across the front seat. Peanut's face went granite. Nixie tsked and spat out his window.

'Yo, man, don't be testing me like that,' Peanut said. Kenny just laughed.

'So we follow you, or we gonna do a Chink fire drill?' Charlie asked.

'Yeah, dat,' Peanut said, getting out of his car. More car doors flung open as Nixie went to take the wheel of Peanut's car, Kenny got in the back seat of the Durango and Peanut climbed into the front passenger seat. 'You paying enough for full service—' He stopped talking when he saw the man in the back seat. It wasn't Dean, but an older guy with coal black eyes and a nasty pink rope of scar running down the side of his face. 'Where Dean? Who you?' The man didn't answer, just stared at him.

'Deanie's not feeling too good,' Charlie said. 'That's Knute.'

'Newt?'

'Yeah,' Charlie said, and took off.

The man shot a hand forward, gnarled, hard and small. 'What the fuck's up?' Peanut saw the tattoo on the side of the man's hand, a pale green shamrock. He knew the man had been to prison, and he knew damn well who it meant he was with. Then the dude wiggled his teeth.

Freakshow, Peanut thought, but he didn't say shit.

'Chad doesn't think we're right for each other,' Susan volunteered after they'd said their goodbyes to her colleagues and were well into the drive home.

'Is that so?' Behr said, steering around a chugging tractor-trailer.

'He says you're "too dark" for me.'

'What'd you say?' Behr asked.

'I thanked him for the input. But told him I wasn't shopping opinions,' she said. 'I would've told him you'd just lost your friend if I thought it was his business . . .'

Behr kept driving, trying to keep his hands loose on the wheel.

'He's harmless, Frank,' she said.

'So you keep saying.'

'I wouldn't have repeated it to you if I thought he was right. Guess I shouldn't have anyway.'

Behr grunted a one-syllable response.

'You didn't help things, standing out there like a freaking gargoyle on the shore,' she said.

'I tried, Suze,' Behr said, 'I tried.' That was it for the talking until they reached her apartment.

He pulled up in front of her building and put it in park, the engine idling in the twilight. Their usual practice would have had them going out to dinner, or a movie, or both, and spending the night at one of their places, but this was no regular Saturday. Tonight something bigger than his mood was hanging over them.

'Here you go,' he said.

'Thanks for coming along today. I know you weren't really up for—'

'Listen,' he interrupted. 'I saw you holding those beers, carrying them around all day. And I saw you not drinking 'em. I'm thinking . . . Well, I don't know what I'm thinking. What am I thinking, Suze?'

They looked at each other across the expanse of the front seat for a moment, and then she just said it. 'I'm pregnant.'

He felt like an express bus broadsided the car. The air went out of it, and him too. His mind ran in twenty different directions.

'Did you plan on saying anything?' was what came out of his mouth.

'Of course. I didn't know how. And I was hoping to give what happened to Aurelio some time.'

'I see,' he said, knowing the words weren't enough, and worse, knowing his tone was all wrong. 'How the hell did—'

'How do you think, Frank?'

A cold darkness squeezed his chest so that he was unable to breathe.

'Well, I can see you're pretty excited about—'

'Susan—'

'What?' Silence settled.

'I don't know.' He looked at her, pressed against the door, her arms crossed over her chest. He couldn't tell if she was going to smile or cry. She'd never seemed so small to him. 'Well, we should talk about—'

'I'm not raising a kid on my own. I can't. You know what I'm saying?' she asked.

'I guess so.'

'Does that make me a horrible person?'

'Doesn't make you anything.'

'So. Sorry, but it's on you, Frank. You let me know what you want to do. And quick.' With that, in a blur of smooth speed and action, she was out of the car.

FIFTEEN

'**S**OUNDTRACK,' KENNY SAID, leaning up between the front seats and hitting the CD player. A low swaying beat kicked out of the speakers. Notorious B.I.G.'s voice filled the Durango.

Kenny rapped along:

'I got techniques drippin' out my buttcheeks
Sleep on my stomach so I don't fuck up my sheets—'

'Dude, I've seen Mom dealing with your sheets,' Charlie cut him off, turning the volume low. '*Something*'s dripping out on 'em.' Knute laughed in that silent way of his, while Peanut snorted out loud.

'Yeah, and don't you got any new shit? From some motherfucker who ain't dead?' Peanut asked. They'd followed his directions to Stringtown, past an endless stretch of by-the-hour screw motels, and parked in a little notch on Belmont where they could see the house on Traub Avenue.

'Biggie's not dead,' Kenny said. All three heads in the car swivelled towards him.

'What you talkin' about—' Peanut said.

'He's alive. He knew if he stayed in the game he'd get killed eventually, so he stepped out,' Kenny told them.

'Stepped out?' Peanut asked.

'What the fuck?' Knute said.

'Look at the signs. He practically told everybody he was gonna do it. Albums: *No Way Out*. Even early on he realizes he's fucked. *Life After Death*, he gets the idea. *Ready To Die*, he puts the plan in action. Then he's "killed" in an LA parking garage. No one apprehended in the shooting. He's "dead", but does the music stop? Hell no—'

'Man, they got tracks and tracks laid down in the studio. They only release the best. Then, when they dead, it get valuable so they keep pumping it out. Anyone know that.'

'Oh, sure. But the style changes. It *evolves*,' Kenny said, sounding sure. 'How do you explain that?'

Charlie just shook his head. 'Don't get him started. He can go on for hours.'

'He let his family mourn. He let P. Diddy mourn. Lil' Kim. Where he at then?' Peanut asked.

'Probably Africa,' Kenny answered.

'Africa, shit!'

'He'd blend in. Live like a king. Think about it . . .' Kenny said.

'Look,' Charlie said, pointing to the house. Several cars were now parked in front, and several others were arriving, trolling slowly down the street searching for spots.

'Diddy probably visits him over there,' Kenny added.

'What about 'Pac? He alive too? His music keep coming out,' Peanut asked, seemingly unable to help himself.

'Nah. Music shows no growth. *He*'s really dead. Shot in Vegas for real—'

'Guys, shut it,' came Knute's voice, low and gravelly, and shut it they did. They all watched as people exited their cars and entered the house. From the assortment of race, sex and age, it looked like an AA meeting or a factory shift change. But it wasn't.

'Lookit 'em all,' Charlie said.

'If the Latinos and negroids poured all this money back into their communities it would virtually stamp out poverty in the city,' Kenny said.

'Yo, dead that "negroid" shit,' Peanut warned.

'You a social scientist now?' Knute asked.

'I read it in the paper when I was taking a dump.' Kenny laughed.

'I don't like the approach,' Charlie said. 'Too open. I don't give a fuck about any neighbours,' he went on, referring to the few houses around the one in question. With their broken windows, dirt lawns and wrecked paint, it was clear they were abandoned. 'But it's a dead-end street.'

Knute nodded. 'Car could get boxed in by some late arrival.'

'Uh-uh,' Peanut said, 'this was for looks. They's a back alley. Cut across Belmont over there . . .'

Charlie glanced back at Peanut in the rearview with a look of near respect.

They reached the head of a shared back alley, pocked by tipped-over garbage cans and spilled refuse, which led to the back of the Traub Avenue house. There was a detached garage, but no cars visible on this side.

'Don't front in,' Peanut advised, 'back on down, then you be ready to leave quick.' Charlie jacked the Durango into reverse and backed quickly and smoothly towards the house. Through the windshield they could see Nixie doing the same with Peanut's car. Reaching a place he liked, about ten yards from the back door, Charlie put the Durango in park. For a moment there was only silence in the car.

'Well . . .' Charlie said.

'Hammah time,' Kenny said, drumming on the back of the seat. His was first, and then the other three doors opened. Kenny went to the back and popped open the rear hatch. He handed Knute an aluminium baseball bat, took a length of pipe filled with iron filings and capped on both ends for himself and a six-battery metal flashlight for Charlie. That was in addition to the .40 Smith & Wesson Sigma Charlie usually had in his belt when they did this.

'You sure you don't want in? We'll find you something fun to use . . .' Charlie offered.

Kenny spun his length of pipe like a martial artist and struck a pose out of a chop-socky movie, topping it off with a 'Waaahhh'.

'Just the cheese and thirty seconds to fly,' Peanut said. Charlie pulled out the money – ten crisp $100 bills.

'We'll talk to you soon about the next one,' Charlie said. 'And about that other thing . . .'

'A'ight,' Peanut said, without much enthusiasm. He took the money and hurried to his car. He got in the passenger seat.

'Go on, dog,' he told Nixie. He glanced out the back in time to see Charlie lock the running Durango with a second key. 'Them Schlegels is sick, sick, sick.'

Behr drove as if he could beat the night. After dropping off Susan he hadn't even gone home. The information she'd laid on him was resting heavy and cold in his gut, and he wasn't going to be able to sit around on it. He knew the news was the kind that most people reacted to with much happiness. But he wasn't most people. *This* was an awareness he dragged around with him every day.

He'd had his child. He'd had his wife. He'd experienced the chest-swelling joy that they'd produced. But that had all died, literally and figuratively, and he had been forced to move on to a different kind of life. He knew you've got to be bullish, as the financial guys said, on the world to have a kid, and his days of unbridled optimism were long past. His time with Susan was also pretty close to done, of that he was fairly certain. They'd had a good run, but she was just a kid, and if he stared it down in an honest light, this was the way it had to end some time.

He had a pair of jeans and his laptop in the car, so he'd changed and driven to a coffee place with wireless internet, and parked outside. Using their signal he accessed a pay database reverse directory and ran the phone number marked by the 'F' in Aurelio's book. He got an address on West Elm Avenue, and headed for it.

He came up on the building and pulled over. It was a low-slung two-storey stucco job that looked like it had been built as a motor inn thirty or forty years back but had been converted over to apartments. Behr clocked the unit, 11-B, on the far corner of the second floor. The curtains were drawn and it had no lights on at the moment. He got a look at one of the doors on the ground floor in front of him and it caused him to lean over and root around in the glove box until he found his fish-eye. Then he got out of the car and trotted up the stairs.

Behr tapped at the door a few times, waited, and then gave it a good whack. There was no one home, or no answer anyway. He tried to peer between the curtains but couldn't get much of a look. He glanced around, saw no activity about the building and produced what he'd brought from his glove box: his fish-eye lens peephole viewer. He placed the conical piece of plastic over the peephole on the door and leaned close. The convex lens gave him a super-wide-angle view inside the apartment. The wide lens and the darkness combined to create a somewhat distorted picture, but it was clear enough for him to see that the place was vacant.

Behr heard a thin, raspy cough behind him. He palmed the fish-eye and turned to see a bony, aged black man standing there. The man sported a swollen and blackened eye with a broken blood vessel in it that had spilled red where it should have been white around the iris.

'Who you looking for, officer?' the man asked. He was hunched over a bad leg and supported himself with a cane.

'Who are you?' Behr asked, flat and cop-ish.

'Ezra Blanchard,' the man said. 'I'm the on-site building manager. The real manager works at an office.'

'Then you know who I'm looking for,' Behr said.

'Flavia's gone,' Ezra said, a slight tremble in his voice. *There's my 'F'*, Behr thought. 'Gone on to a nicer place,' Ezra continued, and coughed. Behr tried to read him, wondering if she'd passed away and the old man was being poetic. '. . . that she'd found with her cousin,' he finally added.

'When?'

'Not long ago.' The man gave it some thought. 'Two weeks.'

'Mid-month?' Behr asked.

'She had some paid time left, but she was in a hurry to go.'

'You have an address?'

'She told me she'd send it to me, to forward on any mail and her security cheque. And she asked me not to give it out when I did.'

'I understand,' Behr said.

'But she never did send it. Guess she forgot. Or changed her mind,' the old man said. His posture stiffened up after he spoke.

'I see. What happened to you, buddy? You take a trip down these stairs or something?' Behr asked.

Ezra just stared at him. Behr felt his gaze find the bloody and blackened eye, and willed himself to try and read the man's good eye. 'Not exactly,' Ezra finally answered.

'Who was she worried about getting to her?' Behr asked. Sometimes a simple zigzag was all it took on a person not used to lying. Ezra just shrugged. 'That's fine, but the "I can't tell you" bit isn't gonna work here,' Behr said firmly.

Ezra shuddered. 'If it's police business, I can tell you . . . I can tell you she was trying to keep away from that dude she was seeing . . . if I had my guess.'

Behr just stood there in the night for a moment. 'Is that who did this to you, Ezra?' he asked. Ezra paused, then nodded.

'Now who would he be?' Behr asked.

'Never did get a name. He'd wait in the car for her to come down. Then he'd drive her off. He'd bring her back late sometimes, and go in with her. But he'd be gone before morning,' Ezra said.

'What kind of guy was this?' Behr asked.

'White dude. Young. Six feet, lean and lanky. Had some shaggy brown hair. He'd go stomping up and down the stairs no matter what time of night it was. When she wasn't around, he'd bang on her door and yell all night. He was a real asshole, this dude.'

'And you saw him rough her up, or drag her around? You got in the middle of it?'

'No,' Ezra said.

'But you think she was trying to lose the guy?'

'Oh, she did. 'Cause I seen him show up here a few times looking for her since she gone. Last time he kept banging on the door for twenty minutes until I went and talked to him. I asked him to quiet down. Told him she moved. Told him I didn't have a forwarding address and to leave. He said to get outta his face or I'd "end up down by the river listening to the trains whistle by".'

'What's that supposed to mean?'

'That's what this dude said: "Tell me where she is or you'll end up floating downriver by the m-f'ing railroad tracks." But he said the whole m-f word. Man, he was drunk as hell. I kept on telling him I didn't know, and then . . . Well, like I said, the dude was a real asshole.'

'Did you call the cops?' Behr wondered.

'Didn't have to,' Ezra said, 'they came on their own. Someone else must've called. The guy was long gone of course. And then this lieutenant showed up, real nice fella, and took my statement. Told me they'd try and track the boyfriend down, but if he showed up again I should stay inside.'

'A lieutenant, huh?' Behr asked. Ezra nodded.

'You ever see her with a guy by the name of Aurelio Santos?'

'What's *he* look like?' Ezra asked.

'About five-ten. Solid. Curly black hair. Mid-thirties. Real friendly.'

'No, no . . .'

'If you're on the internet I could show you a picture,' Behr offered.

'I don't do computer,' Ezra said.

Behr was about ready to write out his number for Ezra and walk away when he just asked one more time. Sometimes that worked too. 'Give me her address, Ezra.'

'You're not a cop, are you?' he said.

'Not any more,' Behr said. Ezra shrugged.

'It's in my unit.' Ezra shuffled down to the other end of the apartments. Behr followed and waited at the door, glancing inside at the man's meagre furnishings. Ezra disappeared into a back room for a moment, then reappeared holding a few envelopes and a Post-it with an address on Schultz Park.

'If you're going over there, maybe you could give her these?' Ezra extended a small packet of envelopes rubber-banded to-gether. Behr reached for them, wondering whether he should be careful about opening and resealing them or just tear them apart for information, when Ezra took that off the table, pulling back the mail. 'I should just have the mailman do it. Federal offence otherwise, right?'

'Sure, you do it that way,' Behr said, taking the Post-it with the new address. He'd seen the woman's whole name. It was Flavia Inez.

Behr handed Ezra a business card. 'Call me if that boyfriend shows up again.'

'OK,' the old man said, but he sounded doubtful.

SIXTEEN

HECTOR NOGERO WAS in the den behind locked doors stacking 'peas' and spinner baskets and considering his *suerte*. The last three months had been brilliant. He was making so much money he'd brought his father up from Chamelecón. With an introduction by letter from his uncle, who was in prison for gang activity in Honduras, Hector had taken title to the house on Traub from a man for close to nothing. Foreclosure proceedings had begun on the property, which was why the man had sold cheap, but Hector had earned more than enough to pay off the note and back taxes before the marshals would return to seize the place in the coming weeks. Four or five 'shakes' a day, with a house full of paying customers playing at least one number if not dozens, and his only expenses were a bouncer, a pretty 'shake girl' to pull in players and conduct the drawings, and a cut for MS-13 for his *permiso* to operate. He was like the fucking *lotería*. Even now he had a living room full of them, chilling, drinking a coffee, a beer, watching a race or a few innings of *béisbol*, and handing over their whole paycheques hoping to win a three- or four-number combination that would pay a few thousand. Soon he'd buy the electronic ticket machines and video surveillance cameras. He had his son with him too – Chaco had come on the plane with his father. Hector looked over at Chaco, playing on the floor with some of the peas, which were actually plastic balls. He'd heard they used to use dried peas with numbers written on them back in the old days, when the game was invented, and that was why it was called 'pea shake'. But now the world was plastic.

When the summer ended he would send Chaco to American pre-school. By the time he was four, he'd speak perfect English.

'*Estas bien?*' Hector asked Chaco as he unlocked the door and exited the den. Chaco nodded several times. '*Estas cansado?*' Hector asked. This time Chaco shook his head, and Hector pulled the door shut behind him. On his way to the front parlour, where the sounds of many voices told him he had a full house of customers, he glanced down the hall towards the back door. His father was headed in that direction.

'*Qué haces, viejo?*' Hector called out. Then he heard a tapping at the back door.

'*Quien es?*' his father said, reaching for the doorknob.

'*No, papa!*' Hector called as his father swung the door open and he saw the three men. His father tried to push the door closed, but it blasted open and the first man stepped in. He brought down a black cylinder on top of his father's head with a crack. The old man crumpled to the ground.

'Austin!' Hector yelled. His bouncer appeared in the living-room doorway. He was big, filling the frame, but the man who had dropped his father was almost as big, and harder. The two men behind him – one young and wild-looking, the other older and bad – were no joke either. They were all inside now. The first one advanced, his face speckled with the blood of Hector's father; he could now see that the black cylinder was a metal flashlight, raised to strike. In his last glance back, Hector saw Austin, the fucking *maricón* American bouncer everyone told him he needed to hire to make a smooth transition into the neighbourhood, run back for the living room. And out the door after that, Hector realized with a sinking feeling. Hector turned and lunged at the man who had hit his father, punching him in the jaw. The man's head turned briefly to the side then back forward, his eyes filled with rage. Hector was only a metre sixty-two, his weight under seventy kilos; how much damage could he have hoped for?

Hector felt himself fly into the wall, and then he felt the pain behind his ear. Somehow he knew this must've been backwards and that the flashlight hit was first, the throw second. Before Hector could fall to the ground, the man had him by the neck, had twisted his head sideways and encircled it with an arm. It wasn't exactly a headlock, nor was it a chokehold. He'd have to call it a neck-break half applied. The top of his head was wedged into the man's trunk, his spine arching. He stood up on his toes and tried desperately to keep his balance. He felt the man's forearm crushing into his jaw. His rear teeth crumbled against one another as he was dragged into the front room.

'Shake's over, motherfuckers,' Kenny Schlegel screamed, dinging the person nearest him, a middle-aged black woman smoking a menthol, on her upper back with his length of pipe.

'Oh, lord,' she said, going down; as it was a glancing blow, she then managed to scramble away on all fours.

Knute followed Kenny into the room and used his aluminium bat to obliterate a flat-screen showing a harness race. Then he rang the bat off shins and elbows until a half-dozen would-be pea-shake players were hopping and squirming.

'What the fuck?' said a skinny blonde, in a miniskirt and heavy make-up – the 'shake hostess' – as she emerged from the kitchen holding a cup of coffee.

'Shut up, skank,' Charlie said, pointing to the wall where most of the patrons huddled. 'Get over there with them.'

'Why should I? Who the fuck are you?' she screeched. Kenny approached her, pointing the end of his pipe in her face.

'Shut up and get over there before I kick you in the cunt,' he bellowed.

'Fuck off, tough guy—' she started. Kenny swung his rear leg forward in a vicious up-kick that caught her where her legs met under her brief miniskirt. 'Oah,' she said, going down, rolling and writhing, coffee spilling all over her.

'What the fuck did I tell you?' Kenny loomed over her.

'Oahhh, oahhhh,' she went on and on, curled into a ball.

Knute and Charlie exchanged a look, wondering if the kid, his blood up, was going to cave in her skull with the pipe.

'Take . . . the . . . money,' Hector grunted, barely able to move his mouth. He held up a thick, dirty wad of bills from his pants pocket.

'Shut up,' Charlie said, taking it, stuffing it in his own pocket, and racking him in the head with the flashlight. Then he turned to the assembled players, perhaps thirty people, frozen in front of him.

'Who said you could pea shake here?' Charlie asked them. He punctuated his words with raps to the face and head of the smallish man he held. 'Who said you could shake with this little dirt-bag spic?' Charlie strutted around, feeling like a WWE wrestler, and considered whether he should bash the man's head into something, or if that was too flashy. 'Well?' he asked. There was a bulky, tough-looking Latino with ink creeping up out of his shirt collar standing near the door who wasn't cowering properly. Knute caught it at the same time.

'Door,' Knute said.

'Got it. What the fuck are you thinking, bro?' Charlie screamed, advancing towards the bulky Latino, whacking his captive again and lifting his shirt to reveal the butt of his pistol. 'See that door, motherfucker? Use it. And none of you ever use it again once you're gone. This place is *not* authorized. You fucking get it?'

There was a moment's pause as the gamblers wondered if their release was the truth or some horrible joke.

Kenny flicked open a Zippo with a metallic clink and waved the flame at them. 'It's that or we lock it and burn this shithole to the ground.'

The bulky Latino acted first, hurtling out through the door and into the night. The rest followed, keeping wary eyes on their attackers but receiving boots in the asses and backs and shots across the shoulders all the same. Even the pea-shake girl, dragging herself along like a car-hit dog, made it out. Soon the room was empty and quiet save for the sound of engines starting and tyres screeching.

Charlie straightened Hector up by the head and spoke directly into his face. 'I don't want to fucking see you here again, *comprende*?' Instead of waiting for an answer, Charlie nodded to Kenny who swung the pipe across Hector's stomach like he was lashing a double into the gap. Charlie let the man collapse.

Charlie, Kenny and Knute sauntered down the hall the way they had come. They stepped over the body of the wiry old man, who hadn't moved an inch. They went out to the car. Charlie hit the auto-lock button on his extra key and they got in.

'Let's go to the bar,' Charlie said.

Inside, on the floor, Hector heard the car drive away. After a while he rolled over on to his back and felt around his ribs and organs. Nothing seemed broken. Eventually he got up on all fours, spat out blood and a gritty dust that was his molars, then made it to his feet. One advantage of being his size and growing up in the streets was that he'd gotten used to taking a lot of punishment over the years. He went down the hall and shook his head at the sight of his father lying there in a pool of blood. He couldn't call 911. They'd all be arrested and deported if he did.

'*Vamonos, Chaco*,' he called out, opening the door to the den. '*Rápido!*' Chaco emerged from a low cabinet along the floor where he'd been hiding. The boy's eyes were huge, but he didn't say a word, and he followed as Hector lifted his father and carried him out to the car.

Mierda, Hector thought, *now I have to get a gun.*

SEVENTEEN

DEAN SCHLEGEL WAS in his room crying in the dark when he got their call. It was the vodka and Percocet he was using for his mouth that must've made him this way, because he couldn't remember crying since he was a kid. Then again, things had gotten plenty fucked up over the last little while.

'Yo, D, where you at? We're down at the bar.' It was Kenny. He could hear the sounds of glasses and music and voices in the background.

'I'm home, man,' Dean answered.

'We're down at the bar,' Kenny said again. 'Me and Charlie, and Knute, and Dad too. You gotta come out.' But Dean just didn't feel up for the Tip-Over tonight.

'I don't know, Ken . . .'

'Don't be a puss, brah. Marcus is spinning down here and you know the hos flow where he go.'

Lately it seemed every time that Dean left the house something happened that he either didn't like right away, or after some time had passed he liked even less. He felt guilty for all of it, especially that old man he'd busted up. Still, locking himself away in a dark room wasn't an option that was paying off.

'Come on, meet some *new*, get that scurvy bitch off your mind—'

'Don't go there, dick,' Dean said.

'All right. I'm just saying. Get your ass down here, drink your face off, you'll feel better.' Kenny hung up. Dean sat there for a moment deciding, and then he reached for his pants.

Behr arrived at Flavia Inez's new address, and saw that her old building manager had been right: she'd found a much nicer place. It was a ten-storey brick job with casement windows and a new awning. She lived in 9-F, according to the Post-it. Behr went to the building's outer door and saw the apartments were marked 'F' and 'R', front and rear, only two per floor. It was a real way of life she'd found for herself compared to where she'd been. What Behr didn't find, however, was her name on the list. Instead, the resident of 9-F was listed as 'Blanca White'.

Bullshit, he thought. *White White?* He checked his watch. It was almost ten. Too late for a proper, polite first interview. He hesitated for a moment before he pressed the buzzer. He waited but there was no answer. He tried again several more times. Then he took out his cell phone and dialled the number. Once again he got the pop song, but no voice on the outgoing message. At least it hadn't been disconnected. 'Hello, this is Frank Behr calling about Aurelio Santos again . . .' He left his numbers and asked her to call. He tried the lobby door, which was locked with a solid-looking brass Baldwin. It wasn't going to happen, he realized, not tonight.

The Tip-Over Tap Room's got one hell of an identity crisis, Marcus Daudre, better known as DJ MD or simply 'the Doc', thought. It had the bones of a low-end outskirts Indy pub that should've been full of fifty-year-old rummies and blue-collar factory shit-kickers. But thanks to the Schlegel boys, the fact that Kenny loved hip-hop, and every damn one of 'em loved fresh white females, he'd been hired to spin tunes. Now there were no rummies in sight, and the place was pulling more white shorties than Nicky Blaine's. The little dance floor was currently filled with blondes in belly shirts who were freaking to his mash-up of T.I. and Lynyrd Skynyrd. It was chemical, MD figured, two-parts black music, with a base of redneck, and the white folks just couldn't help themselves. He wound it down and hit an extended mix playlist on his Mac and headed to the bar to take a break.

The Schlegels were generous owners and let him have the run of the place, with no tab, on the nights he worked. It was about the safest place he'd ever DJ'd too. He looked at them there, lying up along the corner curve of the bar: Kenny, Charlie, Papa Terry and Papa Terry's partner. If you thought about throwing a punch in this place, you might as well step in front of a bus – it'd be faster and the results would be prettier. MD slid under the counter and moved in next to Pam, who was pouring Jameson into shot glasses. Half a dozen pints of Guinness were already drawn and settling when Dean Schlegel walked in the door. Now the gang was all here.

'Deanie!' rang out from the Schlegel section in the corner. Dean walked over to his crew, sporting a puffy left jaw and dark circles under his eyes.

MD slid behind Pam and took the opportunity to appreciate her *fine* ass as he helped himself to a Michelob Ultra. She started topping off the Jameson with Baileys Irish Cream, and MD caught some low banter that he did his best not to listen to. What he did hear led him to believe the Schlegels had robbed or otherwise taken off a place, and it even sounded like Kenny had kicked a girl's ass.

'You want one of these?' Pam offered as she doled out the Jameson with Baileys floaters and Guinness to the Schlegels.

'Nah, I'm good,' he said.

'Come on, bro,' Kenny said, dropping his shot glass into his Guinness, 'do an Irish Car Bomb with us.'

'You don't gotta be Irish,' Papa Terry said, smiling. 'We're not.' He dropped his shot into the Guinness as well, and then picked up the pint. He crooked a finger at a young blonde Kenny ran with a little. 'Kathy, get over here.' She broke off from a pack of other white high-school-age chicks.

'What's up, Mr Schlegel?' she said.

He made a big show of looking around behind him, under his barstool. 'Who you talking to with the "Mr Schlegel"? I don't see my father here. *Terry*,' he said. 'How old are you? You got ID?' She reached for her pocket, causing them all to laugh. Terry stopped her. 'Here, try this.' He handed her the pint glass.

'OK, Terry,' she said. The others drank theirs quickly, their gullets moving like wolves' taking down meat. Kathy struggled with hers, but got it about halfway before breaking off.

'Tastes like dessert,' she said. Papa Terry reached out and wiped off her Guinness moustache with his finger, then stuck the finger in her mouth. She sucked the foam off it, and then he put it in his own mouth.

'You're right, it does,' he said. Kenny, his brothers, the partner, they all cracked up. Papa Terry waved Kathy away back to her friends. He turned back to the bar.

'I don't drink that shit either, Doc,' he said to MD, 'unless you're doing one with me, Pammy.'

'Oh, no, Terry,' she said, 'you remember what happened last time? Clean up, aisle six!' They all laughed.

'Give me one of them Michelobs like my man Doc is having,' Terry said. 'He's a man of taste.' MD raised his bottle in return, real friendly. But he didn't kid himself. They weren't his friends, and he wasn't planning on ever getting comfortable around here. He remembered a pair of big, tall, tough-looking white guys who'd recently become something like regulars over the course of a few weeks. The guys were real snazzy – blazers, white dress shirts and shiny wingtips. It looked to MD like they were in the process of getting into some business with Papa Terry and his partner. Then one day MD had heard Papa Terry and partner talking between songs about a meeting they were gonna have that night after the bar closed – one that wasn't gonna go the way those slick boys planned. He hadn't caught the details but he got the gist, and it was nothing he wanted to know. MD cleared out before closing that night. The snazzy white dudes hadn't, and he hadn't seen those snazzy white dudes again.

The Schlegels fell silent as Kathy showed up next to them. She held up the pint glass, which was now empty.

'Good girl,' Papa Terry said. 'You want another?'

'Sure, *Terry*,' she said. He looked at her.

'You like cars?' Papa Terry asked.

'Sure,' she said.

'My shop's right next door. You should come see some of what we got in there,' he offered.

'OK,' she said. Papa Terry got off his barstool and started walking for the door. She followed. The rest of the Schlegel crew acted like they hadn't seen or heard a thing, and that was just the way MD acted as well. He moved down the bar to go back to his faders. He'd be leaving before closing tonight too.

Behr returned home, entered and left the lights off. He dreaded the nights, black and endless, when the work was done and all that was left was time to think. He was fine while there was work. That was when he was at his best. But it never lasted long enough – or he didn't. He needed to shut it down and rest so he could function properly the next day, but that was when things went slippery in his head. He had gotten a chance to forget how bad it could be this last year and a bit, spending most of his evening time with Susan. Maybe he'd let himself believe that things had changed for good. Now he sat for a while with the phone in his hand, considering whether or not to call her. He looked around his place at the evidence of her presence – her organic cereal on the kitchen table, her hairbrush thrown on the couch, a stack of CDs on the coffee table on top of the tabloid magazines she loved. She was probably going through hell, and doing it alone right about now.

He went to dial, but even that simple act felt traitorous. He couldn't do it – any of it. Not to himself, to his past with his son Tim, to his ex-wife Linda, even though there was nothing between them now but dead memories. He stood and dropped the phone on to the cushion from which he'd just risen. He walked down the hall, flicking on a single light as he went. He stopped when he reached the linen closet, which he used as storage since he didn't have much linen, and opened it. There was his one extra set of sheets and a blanket and pillow inside. There was also several years' worth of phone books, hunting boots and insulated bib overalls, camping gear, road salt, coffee cans full of change and extra light bulbs among other household detritus. He pushed some of it aside and found a cardboard box, which he pulled to the front of the shelf. He opened the flap. It had been a long time since he'd done this – a lifetime, it seemed. He peered down into the box and saw them. Tim's old things. A policeman figurine, Thomas the Tank Engine, Matchbox cars, a squishy vinyl football, some lifelike rubber dinosaurs. Behr felt a grim smile burning on his lips. They were Tim's favourites. Nothing would replace either his boy or that time, Behr knew. Nothing. He handled the items for a few moments, feeling for the past, numb and distant between his fingers. Then he closed the flaps. He walked back down the hall with the box in his hands and continued right out the door. He went around back to where the building's trash area was and lifted the lid on the small Dumpster. He heard the toys rattle around as he threw the box in. He slammed the lid down with a hollow metallic clang and marched back inside, his heart empty. When he re-entered his place the phone was ringing, but he didn't answer it. He just let it ring.

EIGHTEEN

BEHR WAS ON his way out first thing in the morning when he saw them. Two men, sitting in a silver Crown Vic that had his car boxed in. He stopped in his tracks when he made out who was behind the wheel. It was Police Captain Pomeroy, his former boss. Last time they had spoken it had not been a pleasant conversation. Now the pair saw him and got out of their car. The second man was a few years older than Pomeroy and was beefier by thirty-five pounds. He was florid-faced already, with the heat of the day still a long way off.

'Behr. Looking quite the winner today,' Pomeroy said. 'Didn't have you for a churcher.'

Behr was dressed in his blue blazer and tie again. 'Memorial service, Captain,' he answered, looking at his old boss. Time didn't seem to change the man. His nose bone was still sharp as a hawk's beak and his black eyes as pitiless.

'The department could use a favour,' Pomeroy said.

'Really?' Behr asked, mainly to check the rough thrill that ran through him at the words. He'd heard of ex-cops doing outside work for the force, at times when it was something so mundane it wasn't worth the department's time, and others when it was a situation so sensitive the cops couldn't afford to be around it. Either way, Behr had never been on the ask list. 'Near Northside stuff?' he guessed, thinking of the amount of drugs and drug violence that existed there.

'Not exactly—' the other man said, speaking for the first time.

'Jerry . . .' Pomeroy interrupted, silencing him.

'Who's this?' Behr wondered of 'Jerry'.

'City attorney,' Pomeroy answered, and didn't add any last name.

'So is this official?' Behr asked.

'Officially unofficial,' Pomeroy said.

'What does that mean?'

'*He*'s having this conversation on behalf of the department,' Pomeroy said.

More confidentiality, Behr realized. He wondered if lawyers were the new must-have accessory around town.

'What's it about?' Behr asked.

'I want you to reconsider the Caro job,' Pomeroy said.

'You want me to help with that?' Behr asked.

Both Pomeroy and Jerry nodded.

Potempa must have reached out, Behr realized. 'But you ran me . . .' he blurted, confused and remembering how it had ended for him with the police years ago. Pomeroy had sighted in on him and pushed and pushed until he was done and all Behr had left was a quarter pension and his old tin. It was personal. The sickening feeling of failure, of being discarded, revisited the pit of his stomach.

'That's right. And now I need someone who knows what he's doing,' Pomeroy said. 'Who can go places where the official asky-asky nicey-nicey won't work. Who doesn't matter.'

'I guess we're being honest this morning,' Behr said. The city attorney made a sound, a half-snuffle, half-cough that connoted both amusement and disgust.

'You weren't incompetent, I just didn't like you.' An early morning silence stretched out for a moment between Pomeroy's words. 'But I know what you were able to do on that thing a while back.'

Behr said nothing.

'I'm hoping for a similar result here. This is a situation you'd be paid an hourly. Off the books. Not by us. Beyond that, it'd be considered a *contribution* to the department. A serious contribution. It'll be noticed and remembered if it's done right. It can change the future of the doer. You want to hear it?'

Behr looked at Pomeroy, then to Jerry. Their faces were scowling and serious. He heard what they were saying, what he was being offered. He knew it was a real chance. 'There's something I'd want up front in return,' Behr said.

'Really?' Pomeroy asked. 'What's that?'

'Flow-through on your investigation into the Santos murder.'

'The judo guy?' Pomeroy said.

'Brazilian Jiu-Jitsu, but yeah,' Behr answered, wondering why he felt it so imperative to be specific.

Pomeroy shrugged. 'That's doable.'

Behr nodded. 'Caro wanted me to locate some of their boys, but they wouldn't even give me a hint. I can't do it unless I know the whole story.'

'Of course.' Pomeroy handed him a folder. 'It's not only about their boys.'

The other man practically lunged into the conversation. 'There's someone out there – some group or crew making jerk-offs out of the department, taking down shake houses—'

'Thanks, Jerry,' Pomeroy cut him off. Then he turned to Behr and spoke more quietly. 'What do you know about pea-shake houses?'

'Same as everybody. Lottery-style betting parlours. Drawings done several times a day with numbers written on balls. There's an editorial every six months calling them the scourge of the city or else suggesting they be legalized and taxed.' That wasn't all he knew. He also knew that the occasional bust of a shake house was the old standby photo op for the police. Department scandal? 'POLICE RAID PEA-SHAKE HOUSE' would be on the front page of the paper. Teen gang violence? 'SHAKE HOUSE TAKEN DOWN' would be the lead story on the evening news. It was like a joke that everyone was in on. But this was a whole different approach.

'You know how much illegal gambling money they represent?' Jerry piped up.

'How can anybody?' Behr wondered.

'We *know*—' Jerry said.

'That's not the point,' Pomeroy cut him off again. Jerry fell silent, tugging at his collar, which had irritated his neck to the colour and texture of tenderized meat. 'The point is, by tomorrow night, the next morning if we can't hold it off, there's gonna be a story in the news about a city inspector looking to condemn a place and turning up a few bodies in a shake house out on Everly.'

'Who are they?' Behr asked.

'Couple of Peruvian fellas running it. And let's just say they weren't fresh.' Pomeroy sighed and took a pause. 'It's not the first time it's happened.'

'How many times?' Behr asked.

'One other body, two months back. And seven or eight instances of players getting terrorized and the guys running the shakes getting beat down. Bad. In the past three months. Those are the ones we've heard of. There must be more we haven't.'

'Christ. You've sat on houses waiting for the crew?' Behr asked.

'The shakers move their locations, so does the crew. We never know which one will be next, so we keep missing,' Jerry said. Behr turned to Pomeroy, who looked annoyed but nodded.

'Seems like CIs could be developed who would—' Behr started.

'That's been tried. We never even get a reliable description. No one's talking,' Pomeroy said.

'Someone always talks.' Behr had never seen a case when a confidential informant couldn't be developed or paid or leveraged into giving up a key piece of information.

'Everybody's scared shit. That's the problem. You'll see.' Pomeroy sniffed and then spit. 'I want this crew, and I want it before we have a war, or the Feds, up my nuts. It's what Caro was after, they just didn't say it to you.'

Behr took it in. 'And if I find something – a who, when or where?'

'You let us know,' Pomeroy said.

'Simple as that? These guys are leaving behind corpses, so if I stumble into something and I need a little help and have to call for back-up?' he asked.

'Don't,' Pomeroy said. Jerry just shook his head and fought with his collar some more.

Don't stumble or don't call for back-up? Behr wasn't sure. But the point was clear: there was no room for fucking up in this.

'You still wear that wheel gun?'

'Sometimes.' Behr shrugged.

'Start carrying it.'

This gave Behr pause. A police captain telling him to carry while pursuing an off-the-record case was no small deal, but then again the comment fell under attorney–client privilege so it couldn't come back on Pomeroy. After a long moment Behr nodded.

'Keep our communication limited and outside of regular channels. That means don't call my office,' Pomeroy said.

'Got it,' Behr answered. He watched as Pomeroy and Jerry climbed back into their car.

'And those Caro boys – Bigby and Schmidt?'

'Let me know if you find 'em,' Pomeroy said, and then drove away.

So that was it. Behr was suddenly standing there alone thumbing the folder he'd been given. He was back inside the ring ropes. He might only be on the undercard, but at least he had a new chance at the main event.

NINETEEN

THE ACADEMY WAS usually a place of joyful, spirited effort. Today it was hushed and sombre. Behr had arrived early, right after his little chat and long before the memorial was to begin. He had glanced in the window and seen that the mat had been cleansed of Aurelio's blood. He had also seen a few people with dark hair and caramel complexions moving around inside, setting up coffee and pastries. The family, he surmised. But he wasn't ready to go face to face with them yet, and he walked away from the window. Instead he visited the rest of the businesses in the strip centre. The cheque-cashing place was closed, and would be until Monday at 9 a.m. according to an hours sign hanging on the door. He visited the dry cleaner, the sandwich shop and the shoe store, which were all open despite it being a Sunday. The current economy was not one that allowed many businesses the luxury of a day off. He ran his questions with the owners and employees: was anybody at work here that morning? Did you see anyone suspicious in the area in the days before it happened? Do you have exterior security cameras? Do your interior security cameras pick up anything outside through the windows? All he got in response was 'no', 'no' and 'no', as well as 'we already told this to the cops and who, exactly, are you?'

After a while Behr noticed cars showing up and a stream of people, some of them students and instructors he recognized, heading into the Academy. It was time.

Behr entered to find the place four times as crowded as he'd ever seen it. Besides the regular members of the school, many others were arriving. Aurelio was something of a legend in mixed martial arts, and lots of trainers, aficionados and fighters, past and present, some even famous, were entering. Behr could only wonder at the attendance had the memorial been held in Las Vegas or Los Angeles. Things were more cramped than they would have been because the mat where Aurelio had been found was taped off, and the proceedings were held in the waiting and warm-up area.

Snuffling, coughing and wiping of tears had already begun even though people were only milling about and speaking informally. A framed and prominently displayed 30″ by 30″ photo of Aurelio in his prime, smiling, his hands raised in victory as he straddled the cage wall after a fight, was enough to break them all down. A ring of votive candles burned around the photo and soulful Brazilian guitar music played softly out of a boom box. Behr walked past the massive and impressive display of Aurelio's trophies, belts and awards. He felt awkward, attired as he was in blazer and tie. Most of the others, especially the Brazilians, were dressed much more casually. He greeted several instructors and a few of the students he knew.

He also noted the IMPD detective on the case, there clocking those in attendance, based on the old saw that the killer often can't stop himself from going to the funeral, Behr supposed. He didn't know the guy, who was trying to blend in by the coffee machine, but it was clear enough who he was – after all he was wearing a blazer and tie just like Behr. Behr gave him a nod across the room. Nothing came back.

Despite today's turnout, the school was still small, Behr realized, perhaps three more years from really starting to grow and needing a larger space. Aurelio had left Brazil a decade ago, but he had first gone to New York, where he had trained out of a cousin's gym. After he had finished the main body of his career as a fighter, he had decided to find a new city in which to establish his own training centre, and had moved to Indianapolis. This was the way Brazilian Jiu-Jitsu spread: families and friends built their schools in loose association with more established ones. They used their reputations to make inroads into new markets. Eventually, when the original students, the ones who hung in, started to earn their brown and black belts, took on some of the teaching duties, and began competing and winning in local and regional matches, a school really sank its roots and grew. Aurelio's was just on the cusp of that kind of success. Now there was a real question as to whether or not the place would survive without him.

As he moved through the crowd, Behr lightly grabbed elbows of the locals and doled out business cards, asking people to email him so he could be in touch. Those who knew him, and what he did for a living, asked him if he'd heard anything. This was a bad sign. A lot of the time people didn't know how much they actually knew and he believed there must be something out there, but he already felt like a jackal scavenging for scraps of information during a time of mourning. He couldn't take it much further at the moment. The other bad sign was that the police had turned the location back over to the family after only a few days. After their initial processing of the crime scene, they must not have felt there was any more hope of physical evidence.

Behr steeled himself and moved through a maze of folding chairs and a din of English, broken English and Portuguese, towards the family in its place of honour.

'Mr and Mrs Santos? Frank Behr. I was a student. My condolences.' He wasn't sure if they spoke English, and after they nodded their thanks he still wasn't. He moved past them to two men in their late twenties or early thirties. Curly-haired, heavy-featured and fit, they were clearly Aurelio's brothers. They flanked a dark-haired, grief-stricken young woman with red-rimmed eyes whom Behr had pegged as a sister.

'I'm sorry for your loss,' Behr said to them, shaking their hands between both of his.

'You train with my brother?' the older one asked. 'I'm Alberto.'

'Yeah, Frank Behr. I was taking private—'

'Oh, sure, 'Elio told us about you. He say you will be a pain in the ass to submit one day soon. He say you forget you only training.'

'I'm stupid like that,' Behr said. He glanced over at the other brother, who seemed to be listening.

'Rory don't speak English,' Alberto said. Then Alberto spoke Portuguese and Behr heard his name. Then Rory said a few words including *'detetive'*.

Alberto turned to him. 'You are a detective?'

Behr nodded.

'The police say there is nothing so far. You can maybe find something about what happened?' he asked. The desperation Behr saw in such a strong man's eyes made it all the more unbearable.

'I'll try. I am trying,' Behr said.

Rory, who'd been following the exchange in silence, stood up. He crossed to a table where perhaps a dozen Brazilian flags were folded. Rory took one and handed it to Behr and then spoke in Portuguese.

'These are the flags he wear into the ring,' Alberto translated.

Behr knew that Aurelio's practice was to drape one around his shoulders when entering, and he waved them and held them aloft to the crowd after a win. 'We want to give them to the special students. To remember.'

Behr felt the green flag, smooth and shiny under his fingers, and stood there for a moment unable to speak. He finally nodded his thanks and scratched out an '*Obrigado . . . obrigado.*' He looked up and saw that Alberto's eyes were moist, but he wore a smile so close to Aurelio's they might have shared the one.

'Your accent is good,' he said. 'So tell me, I don't see the new girl. You know her?'

'Girl . . . ?' Behr began.

'The one he start with maybe six weeks ago,' Alberto said. 'I don't speak to him much in these days, he so busy. So busy with her. He don't tell me her name, just that there is a new girl.'

Five hours a week alone with the guy, and he didn't know something as basic as his new girlfriend. Behr marvelled at his own anti-people skills, his ability to *not* connect. Before the conversation could continue, Aurelio's father stood and cleared his throat.

'We talk again after, I translate for my father now,' Alberto said. Behr nodded and moved towards the door where there were still one or two empty seats.

Aurelio's father began in halting, emotional Portuguese for a time and then allowed his son to speak his words to the room. 'My son Aurelio love the Jiu-Jitsu. My father taught me. I teach Aurelio. And even though he don't have a son, he love the people he teach. He do it from when he was five year old and it is his life . . .' The father spoke again for a few moments and Behr's mind ran back over some of the many things Aurelio had taught him, and taught him the hard way – by using them on him. The guillotine, the reverse guillotine, front headlock choke, omaplata, gogoplata, knee bar, ankle lock, the western, the stocks, kimura, *jujigitame* – arm bar – of all stripes, triangle choke, arm triangle, bolt cutter, a nasty one called the crucifix. The list went on and on. The variety and combination of the moves was an endless and fluid stream from Aurelio, but then it had stopped in the abrupt, graceless way that only death could bring.

Behr had a reason for choosing his seat near the door: as inappropriate as it was to walk out on a friend's memorial, Behr knew it was his last best chance to get into Aurelio's house. The family, if they were staying at his place, as he assumed they were, would all be at the school for the next little while. When the ceremony was over it was likely they would go back and begin packing his personal effects and Behr would lose the chance for good. He only hoped the police wouldn't still be sitting on the house, or that he'd have the good judgement not to go in anyway.

The father paused in his words and then Alberto took over once more. 'My son have a special way with the people. He always compete with the most respect,' he said. 'He never try to make someone feel small, he always try to lift up when he teach.' Behr raised his eyes and scanned the room. Several of the fighters were nodding. 'Even the many that he beat, many become his friends after. And some of them here today . . .'

But some of them aren't, Behr thought, as the words bored into his gut, *and it's not just because they don't live nearby.* He glanced towards the door, about six steps away. He hoped his taking French leave wouldn't be too conspicuous. He made his move.

Luck was raining down on him. There was no cop posted on Aurelio's house. Behr had parked around the corner and was approaching from the rear, in case anyone on the street happened to be watching. And now he had an open window. As he cut across the backyard he saw it right away. He could've beaten the locks

– which were bargain-basement Schlages he remembered from his last visit – but he wasn't the type to look a gift horse in the mouth. He figured he had forty-five minutes before anyone would be back from the memorial, so there was no time to waste and he had the blade on his Leatherman tool out before he reached the house. He slid it quickly behind the frame of the screen, which came out of its track with a pop. The other side went even easier, and he raised the window and slid through.

The inside of the house smelled delicious. He had entered in the kitchen and he saw a large pot of meat and rice on the stove that he imagined Aurelio's mother had cooked for the group. The aroma made him hungry, but he moved on into the living room. There were a few open suitcases on the floor, as well as two large half-packed duffel bags. A sheet, blanket and pillow were on the couch, which was likely being used as a bed by one of the brothers. He saw that the wires of Aurelio's stereo had been disconnected and the components were ready to be boxed up, the same with a 42″ flat-screen television. The cable box and remote rested on the coffee table bundled up in the power cord. Behr checked along the bookshelves for any photos or loose papers but didn't find any. He feathered the pages of several likely hardback books, but found nothing stashed. He considered continuing on through the hundred-plus paperbacks, but abandoned the idea as too time-consuming with too little expectation of reward. As he walked towards the bedroom he hoped he wasn't mistakenly leaving a lead undisturbed.

The moment he entered, he saw that the bedroom was a problem. There were four large cardboard boxes, three of them already sealed with tape. *Damn*, Behr breathed and crossed to the closet. He pulled a string lighting the bare bulb. All he saw were wire hangers and dust balls. The family had been thorough and quick with the packing. He opened the only box that wasn't closed up and found it full of shoes – dressy ones, sneakers, flip flops, and a pair of low rubber winter boots that Aurelio must've despised. Behr closed the flaps and scanned around the room. It was not heavily or particularly well furnished. Aurelio wasn't the kind to care. Behr dropped to his hands and knees and looked under the bed. He found nothing there but a yoga mat and a massage stick for breaking up fibrous tissue.

Back on his feet, Behr went and took a cursory glance at the bathroom. He examined the toiletries in it. Some were women's, and he tried to deduce whether they were the mother and the sister's or if they could belong to the 'new girl'. Some of the products were Brazilian, others American. But a Schick razor and Suave shampoo weren't much of an indicator. He noted that there was a half-empty green box of Trojan Twists in the medicine cabinet.

Behr was feeling he'd used up all his good fortune on getting inside when he continued on through the last door in the house and discovered the guest room. It held two twin beds that had clearly been slept in and two carry-on-size roller suitcases with luggage tags from Brazil. And tucked in the corner was a desk. Behr practically leapt at it. He started with the laptop that rested in the centre. He supposed it could have belonged to one of the brothers or the sister, but for some reason, maybe because of its placement, it seemed like Aurelio's. Behr tried to remember if there had been a computer in the office down at the school, and believed there hadn't been. He pressed the power button and the machine turned on with a mechanical chime. After a moment it booted up and, to his dismay, Behr saw that both the keyboard and the desktop were in Portuguese. He tried to double-click on some documents, but a box came up asking for what Behr assumed was a password. He considered stealing the machine and taking it to his IT connection to unravel. After a moment Behr abandoned the idea and turned the computer off.

There were two drawers on either side of the desk, and he found them full of various papers – paid bills, solicitations, an outline for a book on Jiu-Jitsu handwritten in English with crudely drawn diagrams of the moves. There were snapshots taken at the school and in Aurelio's home country, menus from local restaurants. Then, in the second to last drawer, Behr hit pay dirt when he found Aurelio's chequebook.

A quick glance told him the stubs went back almost a year and a half. He started the long process of thumbing through them, from most distant to most recent. The cheques painted a picture of the mundane. It was Aurelio's personal account, so there was nothing having to do with the Academy, but there was a rent cheque each month on the house, same with the cable, and gas and electric. Aurelio had two credit cards on which he paid between two and six hundred dollars a month total. His car insurance was paid quarterly. The balance on the account hovered around six thousand in the beginning, but over the following year or so it had grown up to a high of sixteen thousand. Then two months back there was a cheque for four thousand made out to cash.

Red flag, Behr thought. And three and a half weeks later, another was written for seventy-five hundred dollars, again to cash. *Flashing red light.* Erratic banking often meant erratic behaviour. But Aurelio was solid. He'd seemed solid anyhow. Drug use would often be the first thought, but surely Behr, even with his limited social skills, would have noticed the physical changes that drugs on that scale would have wrought. Gambling was his next thought. Gambling wouldn't have left any physical traces. Behr had never heard him mention online poker. And as far as Behr knew, Aurelio never cared about American football or basketball. He was a soccer fan, and Behr supposed he could've got in deep over that even though local bookies weren't that exotic and might not have taken big action on those games. There was also the possibility he was betting on MMA fights. Aurelio was no degenerate cowering over losses, Behr realized; someone showing up to strong-arm Aurelio into paying would've found himself in a rapidly deteriorating situation. It could've gone to guns . . .

Behr tossed the remaining drawer for the bank statements that would contain the cancelled cheques with endorsements that might fill in the picture, but he couldn't find them. He looked all over the room, coming up empty, before he wrote down Aurelio's account number and the numbers of the two big cheques. He glanced at his watch and chewed the inside of his mouth. It'd be pretty handy to find those cancelled cheques, but he didn't know where else to look and time was getting tight. He got up to go, made one last cursory sweep and let himself out the back door. He paused to replace the screen before hustling low across the lawn towards his car.

'Tommy? Frank Behr,' he said into his cell phone as he made a short cross-town drive.

'Hey, Frank-o' came back to him. Tommy Connaughton was the IT connect he'd thought of earlier. Connaughton's day job was as a computer repair and data recovery specialist, but that was not how Behr had met him, or how he made the bulk of his money.

Some years back, just after Behr had gotten off the force and gone private, he'd received a call from a student at Butler. It seemed the young man was having problems with the Taus, the football fraternity. He'd had the temerity to show up at their party and talk to the wrong girl or some such bullshit. The kid said he was from up Carmel, and his parents had money, and he was interested in hiring a bodyguard temporarily. Behr figured this was what happened when your name started with a 'B' and someone went yellow page hunting, but he'd had precious little work back then – even less than he currently had – so he'd gone and met with the kid, though he had no real intention of taking the bodyguard gig. Behr was sitting across from the pale, skinny Tommy Connaughton in the student union, talking over coffee, when the kid went stiff. Behr glanced over and saw half a dozen strong-looking athletes enter. They ranged from stout and solid to tall and lanky, as the positions they played dictated, and one, a thick-necked lineman, stood out.

'That's Molk. He plays nose tackle and he's like the lead prick,' Connaughton said. The nose tackle had longish greasy yellow hair in the Bob Golic mould and looked over at Connaughton with malice. It was probably only Behr's presence that kept him from approaching.

'I tell you what,' Behr said to Connaughton, 'I'm gonna help you. I'm not gonna bodyguard you, I'm just gonna make this go away.' They agreed on a five-hundred-dollar price.

Behr walked over to the athletes, and rested his fists on the table, leaning down over the now-silent ballplayers. They might have been carrying a lot of gym-made meat on their frames, but he was pure gristle.

'You see Tom Connaughton over there?' Behr said. 'You give him a twenty-five-foot buffer zone from now on. You don't say anything to him. You don't say anything about him. You sure as hell don't touch him. Otherwise you're dealing with me. Got it?' The ballplayers all just nodded. Behr looked into Molk's eyes and saw fear there. He also saw a distinct lack of intelligence, and that was to become a lesson for Behr. Behr left with Connaughton, who promised him a cheque.

Two days later Behr received a call to come get his cheque and he showed up at Connaughton's apartment. When Connaughton opened the door, Behr saw the place was a dump, not the dwelling of a well-to-do kid from Carmel, even if his parents were keeping him humble. He also saw that the kid had been roughed up.

Connaughton had a big, nasty shiner with greenish-yellow edges that had purpled into the hollow of his nose bone.

'Molk?' Behr asked.

Connaughton nodded and handed him his cheque. The way the kid paid him anyway was what really got Behr. If it was calculation on Connaughton's part, it was the perfect one.

'Crap, I'm sorry, Tom,' Behr said, realizing that the dimness he'd seen in Molk's eyes was what had allowed the ballplayer to do this, despite the consequences that had been promised. Behr vowed to himself never to underestimate the combination of stupidity and malevolence again.

'You hold this,' Behr said of the cheque. 'I'll be back.'

Behr went directly over to campus and found the Tau house. He parked out front and slipped on a pair of zap gloves – tight-fitting leather gloves with eight ounces of powdered lead sewn across the knuckles that caused punches to land as heavy as falling cinder blocks. Behr went right through the front door, which was open, as fraternity house doors always are.

A half-dozen frat brothers and ballplayers sat around a big television that played *The Jerry Springer Show*.

'Molk?' Behr demanded when their heads had all turned towards him.

'Who the fuck are you?' a tall black kid who looked like a free safety asked, standing.

Just then Molk came out of the kitchen holding a bottle of beer. His eyes flashed scared when he saw Behr, but he tried to hide it.

'You want something?' he said to Behr, attempting to act casual. He took a sip of his beer and Behr didn't hesitate. He struck with his palm, jamming the bottle back into Molk's mouth. Molk went down, his face a mess of broken teeth, glass and blood.

The free safety stepped around the couch towards Behr, ready to front. Behr crushed him with a body shot. The zap gloves did their work, folding the big kid over and dropping him next to the couch.

Behr stood over Molk, who tried to writhe away, expecting a kick. 'Don't make me come back,' Behr said. The nose tackle nodded. Behr saw a new level of understanding in Molk's eyes and knew it was over.

When he returned to Connaughton's place it wasn't long before the kid admitted he wasn't from a rich family and he'd used his computer skills to order some stuff – a big-screen television – that he'd sold to raise the five hundred dollars. They argued for a moment over who should keep the cheque until Behr shoved it into Connaughton's pocket. A year and a half later Behr needed some tax information for a background search that wasn't coming up on the regular databases. Connaughton was happy to help him out, and that was the way it started.

'So I almost had a big job for you,' Behr said into his cell phone, shutting off his car. 'Laptop from Brazil.'

'Fun,' Connaughton said.

'But instead I have something less far afield,' he went on. 'I've got an account number and a few cheques I need you to run. They're made out to cash, but I figure you can trace who cashed 'em.'

'Hmm,' Connaughton breathed. 'The laptop might've been easier . . .'

'Ahh—' Behr began.

'I don't work at the bank, man. You know? I'm not a teller. I'm gonna have to hack it. It's gonna take some time.'

'How long?' Behr wondered.

'Three, four days. And I'm gonna have to charge you, you know? Real money. I'll give you the friendly rate, but still—'

'Do it.'

'Do it? That's it? You don't even ask me the price?' Connaughton said.

'You'll be fair, and I'll pay. If I don't, you'll probably hack *my* bank account. And if you aren't fair, I'll hack your front door,' Behr said.

'Right . . .' Connaughton said, sounding a little uncomfortable.

Behr read him the account and cheque numbers. 'Call me when you have something. Soon as you can, Tommy.' He hung up.

Behr was parked outside the house of someone who should have been at the memorial but wasn't. He got out of his car and went towards the house, which was dark, with the blinds down despite it being afternoon. Behr knocked anyway. Pounded was a better word for what he did to the door. After a moment it swung open revealing Steven Dannels, a man of about Behr's age, half a foot shorter, but thick through the chest and arms, and with longish brown hair.

''Lo, Steven,' Behr said.

'Frank,' Dannels said, his Australian accent present even in the single word. He shook hands with the light grip of a fighter whose knuckles were perennially sore. 'C'mon in.'

Behr followed as Dannels crossed his dim, cave-like living room. He walked with a ginger, swinging gait close to a limp that revealed long-term injuries from ankle to knee to hip and shoulder. It was no surprise: the guy practically lived on the mat. In fact, Behr heard he rubbed Preparation H into his sore spots before workouts on the theory it would shrink swollen tissue. Behr had asked him if it worked. 'Fucked if I know, mate,' Dannels said, 'but my joints sure don't have haemorrhoids.'

'Have a seat, man,' Dannels said, and Behr found a spot on the couch. The room was filled with books and the air rank with sweaty workout clothes and the menthol of Thai liniment. Dannels was the senior instructor at Aurelio's school, an equal, nearly, to his former mentor in both knowledge and application of Jiu-Jitsu, despite his not having had a storied career in the ring. Dannels's day job was as an engineer at Navi-Gen, a company that built next-generation heavy and medium trucks and buses, and he held a PhD in physics. Because of that, or his technical approach on the ground, or both, most people referred to him as 'the Professor', though Behr didn't.

'Missed you down at the memorial,' Behr said, as Dannels sat across from him in an armchair. Dannels had started with Aurelio soon after the school had opened. He had arrived from California, where he'd worked for Lockheed, with two black belts already – one in tae kwon do, the other in Japanese Jiu-Jitsu.

'I spoke to the family, but I just couldn't face it. Know what I mean, mate?' Dannels said.

'I do,' Behr said, and it was the truth. He didn't suspect the man of anything but grief. Dannels had summarily claimed his black belt in Brazilian Jiu-Jitsu a short time after undertaking his training with Aurelio. That was close to five years ago, and Behr could only imagine the extent of the man's knowledge now. Soft-spoken, with an educated, unassuming manner and an easy smile, he was what Behr classified as a basic bar nightmare. If Dannels got a drink spilled on him, *he*'d probably be the one to apologize, but if the spiller decided to push it, he'd find himself in a disastrous situation – broken or unconscious or some combination thereof.

'You have keys to the school and the lease won't be flipped for a while, I imagine. You shouldn't take too long before you get back on the mat,' Behr advised.

'You neither,' Dannels said. 'Your game was coming along.'

Behr nodded. He'd had the opportunity to roll with Dannels a few times and equated it with grappling a boa constrictor. Attacks didn't seem to work against the man, and submission, usually by choke, was a steady process executed smoothly and inexorably. When discussing the fine points of a technique, Dannels would often begin with 'Of the hundreds of men I've choked out . . .' and there was absolutely no bravado attached. It was more the tone of a mechanic referring to the brake jobs he'd done.

'Maybe you should pick up teaching some classes if you can,' Behr suggested.

'Some crap state of affairs, eh?' Dannels said, as if talking to the walls, which it seemed he'd been doing for the past few days.

'Yeah . . .' Behr said, and then launched in, hoping Dannels's subtle mind possessed a detail that would help him. 'You knew Aurelio as well as anyone, inside and outside the ring. You hear anything about a girl he'd been seeing?' Behr asked.

'Man, since Maria,' Dannels said, 'he'd seen a couple of chicks, but he was taking it slow and they weren't lasting. Maybe he'd met someone lately – matter of fact I'd seen him on his celly having some quiet convos the last few weeks – but we'd both been busy, just passing in the locker room and talking shop on the mat, so I don't know fuck-all about it. Sorry, mate.'

'I know less than you, don't worry about it,' Behr said, trying to keep his subject confident. 'So who was he beefing with? Who wanted to take him down? Who could've?'

Dannels paused, but it wasn't to think because he'd already done his thinking on it. Behr had asked the right question. Dannels got up and crossed to a desk where there was a laptop. He booted it up and Behr moved around behind him as he opened an internet video clip.

The screen played rough footage from a mixed martial arts website that had been shot at an event in Chicago. After a winner was announced in a lightweight bout, a large bull of a man with a brush cut stepped into the cage and took the microphone from the announcer. 'Who's that, Francovic?' Behr asked.

'That's right,' Dannels said. Dennis Francovic was a well-known fighter who'd been champion at light-heavy up until about two years back when he'd fought and lost to Aurelio. Behr knew he was a ground and pound specialist with good stand-up and wrestling and enough submission experience, in combination with his unusual natural strength, to build an impressive career in the sport.

'There's a guy here who's got something that's mine,' Francovic growled into the microphone. His eyes searched the crowd. 'Come on, Santos, let's do it again. The first time was a war. But you know we've got unfinished business together. Show me what kinda man you are. Let's do it again!' The audience ate it up. The camera jerkily panned the crowd where Francovic was looking. It was like something out of a WWE show, but the fight he was asking for would be for real.

'When was this?' Behr wondered.

''Bout a year ago.'

'Is Aurelio even there?' Behr asked.

'Nah, man. Not even in the building,' Dannels answered. The camera shot returned to the ring and found a burly young man wearing a bad suit and sporting a faux-hawk who was clapping and smiling in the background.

'And him?' Behr wondered.

'Promoter hoping to get it going.'

Francovic continued using the microphone to call out the absent Aurelio.

'How good is he?' Behr asked.

Dannels nodded with respect. 'If Jiu-Jitsu and MMA had been popular in this country when he'd been a kid, he would have been one of the game's all-time legends,' he said. 'But there's no substitute for time, man, and when Aurelio moved to the area and they fought, he became second best.'

'Huh,' Behr grunted.

'Not by much. But second all the same, ya know?' Dannels asked. Behr nodded. He did know. It was the kind of thing that ate at a fighter, at a man.

'So there was an issue?' Behr said. Dannels hit a key on his computer and the grainy footage paused. 'Was Aurelio pissed about that?' Behr pointed at the screen. 'He was retired. Was he going to come out and give him another fight? He never mentioned anything like that to me.'

Dannels just shrugged. 'Fucking Francovic showed up at the Academy with a camera crew a while after their fight. This was a bit before you started training there. It was a pretty big deal around the school apparently. Aurelio hadn't been there that day, but the advanced students were up in arms that he'd been disrespected. Aurelio was pretty stoic about it. That kind of posturing is par for the course down in Brazil. You know what he said?'

'What?'

Dannels mimicked Aurelio's Portuguese accent. '"I would have run over and kick his ass for free, but I already do that in the ring and got paid."' They both laughed at the memory of their friend. 'So I don't know if he was gonna come out. Doubt it, mate. Retiring with the belt worked for him, and that last fight was a gem . . .' Dannels said.

Behr remembered the affair as a five-round classic and made a mental note to watch it again. 'Francovic trains out of Muncie, doesn't he?'

'He's got a fighter factory up there. He turns some damn fine grapplers out of his gym,' Dannels said.

Behr nodded as he took in the information. 'Guess I'll go pay him a visit.'

'I showed this to the cops when they came to interview me, but I didn't tell 'em this: you figure out it's definitely him . . .' Dannels said '. . . let me have ninety seconds with him before you put the cops in it.' That was the fighter's mindset – even a guy who gave someone better and more experienced than you all he could handle in an epic battle, and you still wanted him for yourself.

Behr thought about it for a moment, then said, 'Hold on,' and went out to his car. He came back to the door and handed the folded flag to Dannels, who knew exactly what it was.

'The family asked me to give it to you.'

'Did they?' Dannels said, his eyes on the shiny green fabric.

'I mentioned I was dropping by, and that's what they asked me to do,' Behr told him.

'Thanks, Frank.' Dannels stuck out a hand. 'Thanks.'

Behr left and got in his car. He had a new direction.

TWENTY

BEHR CUPPED HIS hands around his eyes and peered through the window into the darkened interior of the Francovic Training Center. A dozen heavy, Thai, uppercut and speed bags hung dormant in the darkened space inside the brick building. There was a low wooden platform in front of a mirror for skipping rope and shadowboxing. There were free weights, benches, squat racks, dumbbells and such in a corner. A pegboard was mounted on the rear wall. A regulation octagonal cage centred several hundred square feet of mats. Factory indeed. Late on a Sunday afternoon, however, no one was there. Behr had called before driving up and had gotten no answer but had made the trip anyway on the off chance he'd run into Francovic training or doing some cleaning or maintenance.

He should have headed home to get to work on the Caro case, but he couldn't seem to make himself leave. Instead he hung around for half an hour, then left and cruised the rust-belt streets of Muncie killing time. He drove past the chain stores on McGalliard and stopped in at a Bob Evans for coffee, where he burned another half-hour, and then went back to Francovic's gym, where this time he was in business. The lights were on inside and there was movement on the mat. Behr opened the door and immediately caught a whiff of the heavy, musty sweat smell common to all the serious gyms and dojos he'd ever frequented, the kind that never had time to air out fully before the next workout, where the rank moisture built up over the years into a cloud that became another part of the challenge of attending. A small group of grapplers dressed in board shorts and rash guards were going through warm-ups, lunge walking around the mat like a line of circus elephants. At the head of the pack, leading, was the human equivalent of Jumbo. Every school or gym has its resident heavyweight, its monster. This young guy went a good 6'8" from the tips of his massive toes to the top of his blond dome and weighed three bills easy. He was one big boy.

'Let's go, get down and deep, the way your girlfriend likes it,' Big Boy called out in a bass bellow.

Behr moved into the room but stayed well away from the mat as he was wearing street shoes. When the line made it around the corner, Big Boy saw him there.

'This isn't a class. Team workout,' Big Boy called out. 'Schedule's on the door.'

'Not here for a class. I'm looking to talk to Dennis Francovic,' Behr said, stepping closer.

'No shoes on the mat!' Big Boy shouted.

'That's why I'm staying off the mat,' Behr shouted back.

Big Boy broke off his lunge walks. 'Keep 'em going, Tink,' he said to a middleweight who was next in line. Then Big Boy crossed to Behr. The kid sported a high and tight haircut without side-burns that made him seem like a dimwit from the Middle Ages. He already had a sheen of sweat going that made Behr wonder how deep into a fight Big Boy could take all that bulk.

'Dennis doesn't come in on Sundays. What do you want?' the kid said. He seemed to enjoy rising up over Behr. Behr didn't experience the sensation often – certainly not since his football days – and had to admit he didn't much care for it. He took a glance over Big Boy's shoulder and was struck anew by just how many tough young bastards there were out there pursuing the fight game. Here alone, on a Sunday evening, in a little corner of nowhere, were eight rugged bucks spanning the weight classes. Most of them had short, spiky hair or were shaved clean. All of them wore ink. Some sported tribal tats, or barbed wire rings around their biceps, colourful pictures, or professionally done prison-style black Gothic lettering, like the jacked, shirtless kid on the end with 'RTD' on his upper chest. And the thing about the game now was that it promised big money to those who studied the science. Most weren't *just* brawlers any more, though they were that too. Besides striking and kicking, they also worked takedowns and takedown defence and could go to the ground and apply submissions. It was a nasty business indeed out there with the kids these days.

'When's Francovic in?' Behr asked.

'I'm not his secretary,' Big Boy said. 'What's it about?'

'I want to talk to him personally,' Behr said, already tired of the interaction.

'Whyn't you tell me who you are and I'll let him know you came by?' Big Boy said, rolling his shoulders and loosening his neck.

'I'll cover that when I see him,' Behr said, not wanting to tip Francovic to anything in advance, hoping to get a cold reaction from the man when they spoke.

'You come walking in here asking questions, and you won't say who you are?' Big Boy said, his eyes going flat and angry.

'Pretty much,' Behr said, causing Big Boy's eyes to flare outright this time.

'All right then, spiffy, have it your way,' Big Boy said, flipping Behr's tie up in the air.

Now Behr felt his own eyes flicker in anger. He seethed for a moment but reined it in. 'I'll come back,' Behr said when he could unclench his jaw.

'You do that,' Big Boy said. They turned from each other to see the team watching the exchange.

'I said keep 'em going, Tink . . .' Big Boy called out, turning to rejoin them. 'All right, frog hops, motherfuckers.' Behr saw them begin the exercise and then as he neared the door he heard something muttered, at his expense no doubt, and then there was laughter. Behr got outside, took a big suck of the cooling evening air, and got in his car.

TWENTY-ONE

DARKNESS HAD FALLEN gunmetal blue over the city by the time Behr reached Donohue's. It had been a long day, a long weekend, a long week, but it wasn't going to be over until he worked his Caro case at least a little. He wanted a beer and he needed information, and he didn't know a better place to get those things than Donohue's. He cracked the door and the amber light spilled on to him. Business was quiet and the half-dozen drinkers at the bar kept half an eye on an Indians game playing on the elevated corner television. Behr saw Pal Murphy, crisp in his white dress shirt and gold-framed shades, sitting in his owner's booth and going over some paperwork. It would've been bad form for him to go rushing over there, so Behr pulled up at the corner of the bar and raised a finger to Arch Currey, who nodded and moved towards the taps. During the fall and winter that finger meant Becks Dark; since it was summer it meant Oberon Ale.

'Thanks,' Behr said, feeling the ale's cold bite. 'I could use a minute with the man when he's ready.'

'Sure, hang out,' Arch said, then crossed out from under the bar to Pal. They had a muted exchange and Pal nodded before Arch returned to his post.

'He says, "Sure, hang out,"' Arch said, as he climbed back under the bar.

'Will do. How're things?'

'Quiet enough,' Arch said, and then began wiping down bottles.

Behr nodded hello to Kaitlin, with her pen behind one ear, wispy strands of dyed blonde hair behind the other, who stood on the service side of the bar leafing through a tabloid magazine.

Behr had just received his second Oberon when he glanced over at Pal, who pushed aside his papers and gave him the nod.

Behr slid into the booth across from Pal Murphy and they shook hands. Pal's exact age was difficult to determine – Behr pegged him somewhere between sixty-five and eighty. Pal's skin had a desiccated, parchment quality to it, and laugh crinkles cut deep at the corners of his eyes, though they must've been pretty ancient because in the twelve years Behr had been coming to Donohue's he couldn't recall Pal laughing.

'So, Frank,' Pal said, grit under his voice.

'You need a drink?' Behr asked. Pal preferred small batch whiskey, if he recalled. Behr wasn't offering to buy, it being Pal's place, but merely get it for him.

Pal raised his half-full coffee cup in response, so Behr got to it.

'I'm working a thing,' Behr said, 'and I don't have the luxury of time.'

'Who does?'

'Someone's making a run at the shake houses,' Behr said.

'Robbing 'em?' Pal asked.

'Not sure. Robbing 'em, squeezing 'em. Something. I need to know who, or to be at one *before* they get to it, not after.'

'Why's it your problem?' Pal asked.

'It just is,' Behr said.

'Course. Dumb question, forget I asked it.'

'You didn't. If there's something you hear, and it's something you can tell, I'd appreciate you passing it on,' Behr said. 'For some reason it's not information that's been previously available.'

It was tricky with Pal. He was one of the most wired guys in the city. There were plenty of rumours about what he was into, and more about what he'd done when he was young. In a world with immigrant gangs showing up in the city each week, and truckloads of meth and weed rumbling by on the interstates, an old-world gent like Pal, with his patronage and hook-ups, wasn't often bothered by the cops. And he kept it that way by playing his every day like a chess master. Behr merely hoped his request fell into the fabric of Pal's larger plan.

The older man's eyes pinched, causing the skin at the corners to wrinkle, and Behr realized they were lines of thought, not laughter, and that he'd done plenty of that over the years. 'OK' was all he said.

'I hate asking,' Behr said, 'but I'll owe you—'

'You've done for me. And if I can . . . you know, we'll keep it going.'

Behr nodded his thanks and stood.

Terry Schlegel sat behind the wheel of his Charger and peered at the broke-ass house. It was astonishing, but half a dozen cars had arrived over the last fifteen minutes. He looked over at Knute. 'You believe this motherfucker?'

Knute just shook his head. It *was* kind of incredible, but then again, since he'd been inside and certainly since he'd been back out, nothing about human behaviour really surprised him any more. 'People just act in their own self-interest, man,' he said.

'Sometimes they get it right, sometimes they get it wrong.'

'Well, this taco's got it all the way wrong,' Terry said. 'This was supposed to be simple. But we need to step it up, so we step it up. This is how we step it up.' He was really just tossing the words around in his mind, trying to keep his thinking linear and efficient, which was hard to do considering the dirty sonofabitch was still open for business and farting in their faces.

Terry tried to force out the rage and focus on where he was at, and on the future. He remembered when he'd sat with Knute and Financial Gary – who was also known as 'Numbers' – a few weeks after Knute's release and presented the idea.

'I want to get into pea-shake houses,' he'd said.

'Mice nuts' was Numbers's response. And he was right, the take from an individual pea-shake house was meaningless on its own.

'I don't want three of 'em, man. I want 'em all,' Terry said. There was a moment's stunned silence, as Numbers calculated.

'All of 'em rounded up and operated together? Now that's a huge business,' he said.

'Right,' said Terry.

'How huge?' Knute asked.

'Millions. Tens of millions. Maybe a fucking hundred,' Gary said. Terry just nodded. He was no whiz like Financial Gary, but he'd roughed out a general idea. 'You want to be Starbucks . . .' Gary continued, with admiration.

'Fuckin'-A,' Terry said. 'Except I don't want to round 'em up and operate 'em.'

'No?' Numbers asked.

'No, because we'll get skimmed and beat and ratted on. It just won't work. What I want is to close 'em down, kill the business city-wide—'

Numbers nodded, excited now, 'Create a vacuum—'

'That's right, create a vacuum, and then open our own to fill it,' Terry finished.

Knute shook his head wearily, the practical little bastard. 'That's gonna be a lot of work. A *lot* of work.'

'Yep,' Terry had said. 'You think you were gonna get out and relax? You were supposed to rest inside.'

So they'd gotten started. The pea-shake houses run by white dudes had fallen like dominoes. They knew half the guys operating those joints, and they were willing, if not happy, to close for a while and agreed to let the Schlegels take over later rather than face the alternative. A roughneck out by Speedway held fast but reconsidered after he'd had his dental work rearranged by Terry's boys. That turned out to be good advertising anyway.

When they moved into the Latin market, word was already spreading. A pair of hard cases out by the fairgrounds had stood up and had to be dealt with – fucking immigrants had a lot more sack than real Americans these days – but that was it. The gangs supposedly had a piece of some of the houses, but they hadn't come forward to claim them. And if they had, the Newt had some connections from Michigan City he could work out a deal with. The converts and closures started coming fast. Before long, any houses that were still shaking were too small to get on their radar. One place was so accommodating when they showed up that they decided to just leave it open to get a better idea of the take. 'Beta testing,' Numbers Gary had called it. But that had turned to shit in its own special way, for Dean anyhow. Maybe showing a little lenience and mercy had been a mistake, because now there was this current stubborn prick . . . But that would be ending tonight. Once the Latin ones went, they'd start hammering the black-run houses. They expected some opposition there, which was why they'd saved them for last. Terry wanted them to feel like the odds were stacked against them, like they were in the Alamo and surrounded.

Then, when the darkies had gone down *they*'d reopen big time to fill the void. The players would come in droves once word got out that it was safe. Between him and Knute and the boys, and other guys they knew, they had all the right personnel to operate fewer but more profitable houses city-wide.

'It can't last for ever,' Knute had said.

'Don't have to. We only need to be up for a month or so, show some returns, before we sell,' Terry responded, and the others had gotten it.

Now, Knute nodded in the car. It was easy enough for him to follow the disjointed statement. After they were open and they *were* pea shake in town, for all intents and purposes, buyers from Chicago, or maybe Campbell Doray locally, would take them out lump sum, buying the infrastructure for cash, and the Schlegels would stay on in management for a cut, and under the umbrella of protection of course. It actually mirrored standard mergers and acquisitions procedure, according to Numbers Gary.

An electronic beep punctured the quiet of the car. Kenny and the boys had just arrived, and his voice blared over the walkie-talkie feature of his phone. 'You believe this dumb fucking cholo?' Kenny said.

'Shut your phone off,' Terry answered, trading a look with Knute, and then shut off his own. A moment later the back door of Charlie's Durango opened and Kenny came running back to the driver's window.

Terry lowered his window. 'You want the cops to be able to triangulate our whereabouts by cell records—' he began.

'Sorry, Pop—' Kenny cut in.

'Why don't you send 'em a text message while you're at it?'

'All right. Good idea. I'll set up a web cam too—'

'Enough,' Terry said, and Kenny shut up. 'Where have you been?'

'Training. So what's the play?' Kenny asked. 'We go in storm trooper?'

'Not this time,' Terry said. 'You guys tried to make your point, and this fucker missed it. Get back in the truck and wait till all the players leave. Tell Dean to come over here.'

Kenny's eyes went serious. He nodded and walked back to the Durango.

Behr left Donohue's and was headed home when his car seemed to develop a mind of its own and he found himself parked in front of the building on Schultz Park. He went to the door and buzzed, but got no answer. He had turned and was walking back to his car when an early nineties silver Honda Accord rolled down the street and parked. A tall, black-haired woman got out and started for the building. Behr felt himself hitch and process something unconscious. He slowed his step as he reached his car, turned and moved quietly back for the door. She was putting her key in the lock when he spoke.

'I've been trying to reach you,' he said, noticing her shoulders jerk upward in surprise. 'I think . . .' He let her face him before he said more, and when she did, he was struck by her beauty. Her skin was creamy and mocha-coloured, her lips full, her eyes dark. 'Flavia Inez, right? My name is Frank Behr,' he said.

'Frank Behr?' she asked.

'I'm a private investigator. I left you messages regarding Aurelio Santos,' he said, flat and sure, leaving her no room to manoeuvre. She processed it quickly and nodded.

'Yes, of course.' There was the slightest of Latin accents under her words. 'Would you like to come in?'

I found the girlfriend, Behr thought.

*   *   *

139

Her apartment was dark, and when she flipped the switch it was still mostly dark, because all the lights were on dimmers. There was a faint whiff of sandalwood incense in the air. A large piece of batik fabric functioning as a shade flapped in the slight breeze coming through an open window. There was a white slip-covered couch and chair that appeared to have come in a set, and a dark wood coffee table covered with crystal figurines of dolphins. The kitchen was new – a stainless steel fridge and range, granite counter-tops and cherry-wood cabinets. Even if it was a rental, the place cost some money.

'So you heard what happened to Aurelio?' Behr said as she tossed her keys on the counter.

'I did. How terrible,' she said plainly. 'Would you like some water?'

'No thanks,' Behr answered. 'How come you weren't at the memorial?'

'I couldn't make it. I really wanted to, but I had an appointment.'

'I see,' Behr said, wondering at the cool temperature of her voice.

'He was such a nice guy . . .' she said, as if recalling a grade-school friend she hadn't seen for years.

'You were his girlfriend . . . ?' Behr half-asked.

'Me? No.'

'No?' There was a moment of silence as she shook her head. Her smooth hair shushed over her shoulders when she did. Behr forced his eyes from her and glanced at some framed photos on a shelf. He saw none of Aurelio. There were shots of Flavia out with girlfriends, and others of an older couple – her parents, it seemed – and one of an even older couple, likely her grandparents.

'He was a good-looking guy, but I just got out of something and wanted a break.'

Behr thought of Ezra's condition back at her prior building. 'I think your ex roughed up your old building manager.'

'Ezra?' she said, concerned, her hand coming to her mouth. 'Is he all right?'

'A little banged up, but OK.'

She pouted over it for a moment and then moved on. 'He told you where to find me?'

'Let's just leave it at I found you,' Behr said. 'How'd you know Aurelio?'

'He was my teacher.'

'He was teaching you Jiu-Jitsu?' Behr asked. She didn't seem the type. But that was the thing about martial arts, especially a grappling style; it brought in all kinds. 'I never saw you at the school. What class did you usually take?'

'I was taking private lessons. I don't like to go to classes in a group. I learn better on my own,' she said, and Behr felt himself nodding in agreement.

'Nice place you've got here,' he said.

'I've been doing pretty well lately.'

'What do you do? You don't mind my asking . . .'

'I'm a hair stylist,' she said.

'Must have some good clients.' He did his best to sound light.

'Yeah, a lot pay in cash. Don't tell the government on me.' She hit him with a mischievous smile.

'I won't,' he said. He found it difficult to imagine anyone acting against her wishes. But even she had managed to find some sonofabitch who had caused her to run for it and cover her tracks when she went. 'So how did you meet him, by the way?'

She made a scissor-cutting motion with her fingers.

'Of course,' Behr said. 'When was this?'

'A couple, three months back,' she said, and then she unzipped and peeled off her sweatshirt down to a tight-fitting tank top that revealed her inviting figure. She carried an extra five pounds down by her hips where her velour pants sat. Somehow the extra weight suited her though, and the colour of the thong panties that rode up at her lower back made Behr think of mangos before he realized his mind had wandered.

'He came into your shop?' Behr asked, racking his brain for any recollection of Aurelio sporting a memorable haircut. *How good a job would she really have to do to keep you coming back?* Behr thought.

'I've been between places for a while.' She smiled. 'It was a referral. It must've been.'

'Who?' Behr asked, not pleased at all by the bald interrogatories he was tossing around.

Her shoulders went up and down in an *I don't know* and she yawned in a way that made Behr feel old and lame for concerning himself with such trivialities. 'Mr . . . ?'

'Behr,' he said. 'Call me Frank.'

'Frank. I'm tired, can we . . .'

'Yeah, sure, I'll get out of here,' he said, heading for the door, then pausing. 'So, nothing between you and Aurelio?'

'We joked about going out after all the rolling around on the mat. It didn't happen. Like I said.'

'Right. Your ex.'

'Yeah. Never happen now.' A slight shadow of sadness passed over her eyes, and Behr found himself on the other side of the door. 'I don't know if you write reports or who else you'll be talking to, but could you leave my name and address out? I'm in a place in my life where I just want to be under the radar, you know?'

That ex must be some peach, Behr thought, then nodded. 'OK, shouldn't be a problem,' he said.

'Give me a call if you want a haircut.' She treated him to a last, heavy-lidded smile.

'I will,' he said, and the door closed.

They went in through the front door loaded. Terry was first, then Knute, Charlie and Kenny. Dean was already inside. The dude running the place didn't know him, so he'd slipped in as a player. Deanie was to spread fifty dollars and, when the shake was over and the other players were leaving, go into the bathroom. When it sounded quiet, he was to emerge and unlock the front door for them. They had seen the people exiting the house and the cars starting to leave the street. When everyone had gone, they pulled in close, pointing their vehicles east, the direction they wanted to go when it was done, and left them running. Then they went around back of the Durango and armed up. Kenny took his pipe, and Knute the bat. Charlie had his gun and offered the flashlight to Terry, who passed on it and instead chose a machete that had been sharpened on a grinder at the shop and had duct tape wrapped around the handle until it was as comfortable to hold as a tennis racquet. Then they went single file towards the house.

As they reached the door they heard the muffled pop from a small-calibre handgun from inside.

'Is your brother carrying a piece?' Terry asked, moving quickly.

'Uh-uh,' Charlie said.

Terry tried the knob. It turned and the door swung open. Deanie had done his job. They stepped inside to see him wrestling with the little spic pea shaker, numbered plastic balls rolling all over the floor around them.

Terry crossed the living room in two steps and grabbed the Latin man by the hair, wrenching his head back.

'He's got a gun,' Dean yelled when he saw them.

'Are you shot?' Terry asked.

'No,' Dean grunted. Terry saw that Dean had both hands locked around the Latin man's wrist, immobilizing a piece-of-shit silver

.32. Terry hit the man in the side of the head with the butt of the machete and wrenched the gun out of his hand.

'You little fucking asshole,' Terry seethed. He stepped down on the man's back with most of his weight, pinning him to the floor and allowing Dean to get up. 'Good job, Deanie,' he said.

'Fuckin'-A, bro,' Charlie said.

Dean climbed to his feet, a little shocked, and rubbed the powder burn on the underside of his wrist. 'Shit,' he said.

They all grabbed a part of the pea shaker – his arms, his legs, his neck – and gang-carried him towards the back bedroom.

How had things gone so malo *for the Nogeros so quickly?* Hector wondered, fear surging through him like a current. He'd been in the hospital all day with Chaco, sitting beside the bed of his father who lay in a coma. Then he'd bought the gun in the alley behind a Criolla restaurant, and when he'd returned for the evening shake and found Austin was a no-show he'd had no time to replace him. So when the tall, shaggy-haired man he'd never seen before showed up, there was little he could do to stop it short of pulling his new gun and clearing the house. Instead he'd let him in to play, taken the fifty-dollar bill and set up the shake. Hector was doing it all on his own now, since the girl also hadn't come back after the attack. When the drawing and the payouts were finished, all the players started to leave and he'd lost track of the new man. Then, when the house had gone quiet, Hector saw him emerge from the bathroom and move towards the front door. Instead of leaving, the man turned the lock.

'What the hell?' Hector said, wasting no time in pulling his new gun.

'Whoa, whoa, whoa,' the new man said, raising his hands. 'I was just taking a piss . . .'

But when Hector came close, to throw him out and lock the

door behind him, the new man lunged at him and tackled him to the ground. Hector managed to fire a shot, but it must've gone into the floor because the new man didn't lose strength. In fact he was strong as a bull, Hector realized with dismay. Then he heard footsteps and voices inside the house and felt the blow to his head. Hector saw the ceiling rush by as he was carried down the hall, before his vision went black and blurry from what he knew must be blood running into his eyes.

Hector felt himself tossed down on to the sheetless bed, and managed to get a hand loose. He wiped his eyes to see them. He recognized three of them from the last time. And there was another man, older than the rest, but resembling them – the father, he felt – leaning over him. He thought of Chaco and knew his boy would be hiding in his cabinet in the den. The thought gave him the force to fight, and he ripped a foot loose, kicking up into the face of the youngest. The young man barely flinched.

'Cocksucker,' he said, and spat down on Hector.

'All right, hold him,' the father said, the cords in his neck standing out like high-voltage wires, and Hector felt himself held still. The air went thick with the finality of it, even before it happened.

'No,' Hector said. Then he felt his head jerked back by the hair and his throat exposed. He saw the father loom over him and raise a machete, his black eyes devoid of light. *Chaco*, flashed through Hector's mind, *Papa*. The blade came down towards him.

TWENTY-TWO

I T WAS A NIGHT of cataclysmic mash-ups for DJ MD. 'Crazy Train' and '99 Problems' were joined in a mad creation that had the dance floor packed. Then the Schlegels and Knute came in and their corner of the bar cleared without a word. They all sat and Pam served them Jameson poured to the top of rocks glasses with no rocks, and beers back. Dean said something to her, and Doc saw her use the speed gun to soak a bar towel with water, wring it out and hand it to him. None of them spoke to each other. They just drank and stared at themselves in the mirror, although their gazes were fixed on the far beyond. Doc's tracks ended and he switched up to 'Black Dog' mashed with 'One Time 4 Your Mind' from Illmatic and kicked it to top volume.

The sound didn't touch them. The Schlegels were in some kind of bubble. And it didn't help Doc escape those faces either. Newt looked grim, almost like he was in pain; Charlie appeared pissed off. Terry wore a flat stare that was all business. Kenny's mouth curled up at the edges. And Dean, with the wet bar rag wrapped around his wrist, he looked like he might cry. Something about them all there in a row made Doc stay as far away as he could without attracting attention to himself. When the songs ended, Doc put a mix CD in the house system and packed out his gear the minute he felt he could get away with it.

TWENTY-THREE

WHEN BEHR OPENED his door Monday morning there was a green folder waiting for him next to his daily paper. The paper's lead story read 'CITY INSPECTOR DISCOVERS PAIR OF BODIES ON EVERLY'. It was just as Pomeroy and his attorney had previewed. There was an account of an inspector who entered an abandoned house near the fairgrounds and discovered the bodies of two forty-year-old Hispanic males. Dead and decomposing, they were thought to be brothers or cousins, by the name of Restrapo. No one knew how they had come to be there or why. Vermin, including rats, had overrun the house and the bodies appeared to have been there for at least several weeks. One man had been beaten to death, the other stabbed – but that was only speculation, as the rats had gotten at them. It didn't sound pretty.

The article was tight and well-written and Behr noticed the byline belonged to Neil Ratay, the reporter he'd met out at Lake Monroe. Behr thought of Ratay at the crime scene, his experienced eyes knowing and fixed as he took down the particulars in his notebook before going outside for a smoke. Behr wondered if it was right then and there that Pomeroy, or someone else on the force, got him to leave a few details out.

It was no day on the lake, that was for sure, Behr thought. Then his mind drifted to Susan, not out at the lake but for some reason in the shower in the morning, rinsing shampoo out of her hair while he stood at the sink and shaved – their usual morning routine. It had been only thirty-six hours since he'd seen her last, and he'd almost called her a dozen times, but they seemed a great distance apart. He pictured her face through the steam, her chin tipped up, her eyes closed to the water in an expression of purity. The image hurt him in a place deep in his core.

He shook it off by browsing the contents of the folder. It was a photocopy of Aurelio's case file. The news, such as it was, was bad. No legitimate prints had been developed at the Academy. The department's witness canvass had come up as blank as his own. There was a bland, uninformative interview with the bread-truck driver. He didn't need a call from Jean Gannon either, as no tramline fractures came up in the medical; Aurelio hadn't been hit with a shotgun barrel. There was a blood alcohol level of .01 and the food in his stomach had been from the night before, which led Behr to believe Aurelio hadn't arrived at the Academy in the morning after a night's sleep and his customary light breakfast of fruit but had come there or been brought there at some point during the night before. The police had collected Aurelio's cell phone from the family at the house and accessed the records. There was no activity after nine o'clock the night before. There was a thick sheaf of papers listing past calls that Behr would have to go over in detail.

He closed the folder and set it on the passenger seat, putting aside his thoughts on the matter for the moment. He had to. Earlier in the morning he'd run backgrounds on Ken Bigby and Derek Schmidt. Both men were in their early forties, neither was currently married, though Schmidt had been at one time, which must have suited the Caro bosses when they assigned the case. Bigby had been Philadelphia PD, right out of high school, and had gotten his twenty by the time he was thirty-eight years old. He took his detective's shield and his full pension and went to work at Caro. Schmidt was from Virginia, the Falls Church area. He did college at University of Maryland, combined criminology and law degrees in six years and joined the Bureau. He'd spent twelve years in various East Coast field offices including New York and Boston, specializing in forensic accounting and tracking the ill-gotten gains of drug dealers, smugglers and counterfeiters, before ending in Philly and making the jump to Caro. Both were members in good standing of the World Association of Detectives, and both were currently nowhere to be found. This fact was confirmed over the phone by the manager of the Valu-Stay Suites, where neither man had been seen in or around his studio sleeper unit for the past four or five days. Behr would need to check their accommodations in person, and it was something he should do right away. After the background on the men, he'd gone on to run the properties on the list that Pomeroy had given him. That didn't turn up much besides nondescript owners' names – White, Fletcher, Menefee, Bustamante, Skillman, Minchin – and dodgy tax-lien situations. What he really needed to do in order to pursue the Caro case properly was to go out and recon the properties in person. Instead he put the car in gear and shot back out to Muncie.

Behr nosed his car over to the side of a driveway in front of the large, well-kept clapboard house that had come up on his data-base search. It was Francovic's home address. Fighting had been good to the man, that much was clear. The house was probably six thousand square feet, undoubtedly featuring one of those finished basements with screening room, video games and poker table.

There was a three-car garage, an outbuilding that had once been a barn but now looked like it had been converted into a guest or caretaker's cottage, and his land – fifty acres according to the county database – spread out past green fields to a distant tree line. He could see the edge of an in-ground swimming pool poking around the side of the house. Behr shifted in his seat feeling the handle of his Bulldog .44, the one that Pomeroy recommended he keep handy, press into his kidney from where it sat, snug in its Don Hume DAH small-of-the-back holster. He opened the window and listened closely for the sound of dogs, which often roamed properties like this one. If there were any, they weren't around at the moment. At least he couldn't hear them. He got out of the car and trod carefully towards the front door.

Behr knocked and rang the bell and waited, but there was no answer. He peered in through the window and saw a quiet, clean, nicely furnished home. There was a family room dominated by a leather sectional and large plasma television. A case holding several championship belts was on one side of the television, a gun cabinet on the other. There were several long guns behind the cabinet's glass, and Behr wondered if a 10-gauge was among them. Even if Francovic owned one, even if he had used it on Aurelio, what were the chances it would have been put back in its place? Zero, Behr figured, but he sure wanted a look. After knocking again, he tried the knob. It didn't turn. The door was locked. He had to admit some relief as he walked back to his car, as he wasn't at all sure he could've stopped himself from going in had it been unlocked.

The door to the Francovic Training Center was wedged open, Behr saw as he approached. It was just a matter of time – or timing rather – until he caught up with and got face to face with the man, and Behr wondered if this was the time. As he stepped inside, there was the must in the air, acrid and familiar. The fluorescents' glare was blunted this time by the daylight spilling in through the windows. Behr heard grunts and muttered instructions and saw that an advanced gi class was under way. Half a dozen black belts, including Behr's old buddy Big Boy, were in white gis practising throws.

As Behr crossed the weight area, he realized he'd have to walk past the edge of the mat to get to the office and locker room towards the back, and there was no doubt the black belts would notice him doing it. He continued on his path, not breaking stride, when he heard it.

'Ho! Where the fuck are you going, spiffy?' Behr stopped and turned. It was Big Boy, broken off from the class and moving in his direction. Behr was far from dressed up, but the nickname, as it were, had stuck.

'Like I told you last time, I'm here to talk to Francovic,' Behr said. He suddenly had the sensation he was in a schoolyard or college bar.

'Like I told *you* last time, what the fuck for?' Big Boy said. 'And it's *Mr* Francovic until you have one of these.' Big Boy thumbed his black belt.

'Why don't you go back to your training and stick to things that concern you, Garfield?' Behr said. It wasn't much of a zinger anywhere else, but to go through life carrying some extra pounds in the town where Jim Davis, the creator of the cartoon cat, lived, it was a pay-dirt shot.

'Why don't you take a suck on my cock?' Big Boy said and pushed him, hard.

Big Boy's hands thumping off his chest sent Behr white hot with anger. The momentum of the shove took him a step backwards, but he caught himself and moved to push back and it was on. Big Boy caught his wrist with one huge hand, and the other fed up under his triceps and jerked him forward with a short-arm drag.

The question with a big guy isn't whether he's powerful – they usually are – but whether or not he can move. Upon locking up, Behr saw, or felt rather, that this dog knew how to hunt.

Big Boy stepped in smoothly and went to wrap an arm around Behr's waist for a body lock, but Behr managed to catch the arm in a whizzer – his own forearm hooking deep under Big Boy's armpit, and ripping upward. Behr dropped his weight and swivelled his hips around, going low, as he would to hip throw, but then allowed his weight to pull down on Big Boy and collapse them both to the edge of the mat.

Behr needed to keep the arm and turn and fully face his opponent, but the kid was remarkably quick in taking the opportunity to jerk his sweated-up gi sleeve free and go for Behr's back. Behr tried to sit out and square up to him, but Big Boy flattened out on top of him when he was midway through the move. He was heavy as hell, and Behr collapsed down to the mat on his right side, Big Boy on top of him.

The kid attempted to gain side control, going for a modified headlock around Behr's neck and arm, but Behr framed up, using his forearms like the skis of a forklift to push Big Boy up and over his head and escape. Behr felt the young man's hipbone impact with his face as he slid out from under him. He heard the crack and realized he'd broken his nose again for the countless time since the inaugural incident during freshman-year football at University of Washington, when a senior slapped his helmet down during two-a-days.

Behr was free, but only for a second. He flipped on to his hands and knees to get up, but Big Boy swung on him and he was forced to turtle in order to avoid it, and the blow rattled harmlessly off the back of his head. Before Behr could rise, though, Big Boy got an arm around his waist and threaded the other past his collarbone and looked to join his hands around Behr's chest.

Shit, Behr thought. It was four moves away, but he was headed for something called a rear naked choke, which was every bit as bad as it sounded and would render him unconscious, and there was very little he could do about it.

'Do him, Brody! You got him!' the others in the school shouted, seeing the progression as well. Behr was vaguely aware of the other black belts standing around the edges of the mat cheering their buddy on, as Big Boy – Brody, he now knew – succeeded in joining his hands in a lock around Behr's chest, and then rolled over, in a tight, economical spiral, taking Behr with him. Brody ended up with his own back against the mat, sitting up somewhat, while Behr was in front of him and lodged between his legs. Brody got his hooks in, his heels digging past Behr's inner thighs, immobilizing him. Brody's arms were still locked across Behr's chest in a control position that would only last for a moment more before it was improved and Brody's bent arm would form a V around Behr's carotids. He reached back and raked for Brody's eyes, getting a piece of something but not a direct hit. The move failed, but Behr felt Brody's head pull away from his just slightly. Behr didn't immediately realize what a fluke it was, as he was busy trying to duck his chin and get a hand against his own throat in order to thwart the strangle. He wasn't able to execute in time, though.

Behr felt Brody apply the hold. When a choke is sunk deep, it's not about air but blood. A person can last thirty seconds or a minute without air, but if the blood flow to the carotids is cut off, unconsciousness is abrupt. This one didn't quite cut the blood flow completely, but it was just a matter of time until the large man's arm wriggled in and found a true seat around his throat. Behr couldn't get his shoulders to the mat, which was the first step in the escape, and had about three seconds before it was hello darkness. The lights on the gym ceiling were bright and stark in his eyes. He smelled the stink coming off Brody. He heard his own heart beating in his ears.

Things were getting dire in a hurry. Behr went for the eyes again. Brody pulled his face back slightly once more. Then Behr moved his hand around the back of his own head and found a crack of space. Brody's head should have been pressed tight against his in a vice-like seal, but instead there was just the tiniest bit of room. Boxing may be known as the 'sweet science' but Jiu-Jitsu is considered the 'subtle science', and neglecting the smallest detail can make a large difference. Behr's hand slid through and he found the hand of Brody's non-choking arm.

In knife fighting, in the absence of a clean killing stroke, the object is to cut the opponent repeatedly until he weakens from blood loss and opens himself to a vital strike. It was a theory Aurelio had mentioned as having a parallel in Jiu-Jitsu – the idea of going joint by joint, from smallest to largest, breaking them, until the man was immobilized. He hadn't gone into much detail as full breaks didn't really apply in a controlled setting, but the thought had stayed with Behr over the past year, and it echoed deep in his subconscious mind now. Brody wasn't wearing hand wraps or practice gloves; if he had, there would've been no hope. There were no words, or coherent thoughts, or lofty concepts in Behr's head now. Only desperation fuelled him. His vision closing in as if he were entering a narrowing, unlit tunnel, Behr saw black spots in front of his eyes, but he got a hold of Brody's pinky finger and snapped it like a breadstick.

Brody jolted and released his hooks in the onrush of panic that the pain of the damaged finger brought on, but he didn't let off the choke. Behr moved on to Brody's ring finger and broke that one clean and deep too. Now the man wailed and Behr felt the strength go out of Brody's mangled hand. The choking arm let off next. Oxygenated blood rushed back into Behr's brain. He rolled face to face with Brody to counter the next attack. But there wasn't one. Improbably, Brody began patting Behr's shoulder with his good hand.

'Brody, no!' Behr heard one of the black belts yell. Brody was tapping out. He was *too* well schooled, it seemed. Under stress, most men do what they've done repeatedly in training, and when it was over and one was beaten in the civilized confines of the gym, everyone stopped and reset. Now that response had taken over in Brody at the worst possible moment, for Behr wasn't operating under those rules of engagement. And he sure wasn't feeling sporting. Behr caught Brody's gi in a cross-collar choke and slammed him down on to the mat. He reared up and drove his knee, piston-like, into Brody's skull, two then three times, blanking him out. It was an illegal move in organized competition, but that was not where he was. Behr sucked air and jumped to his feet. He spat right on their mat, in disgust and disrespect, as he faced the rest of the school. The black belts paused for a moment, seeing the biggest of their lot laid out. Then they began to move slowly towards him. Behr considered the consequences of reaching for the Bulldog .44 jammed in the small of his back and then did it, keeping the muzzle pointed down. They stopped as a unit when they saw the gun. There was a long, tense moment of quiet while everyone decided on what they would do next, and then stepping out of his office came Francovic.

Thick-necked, with veins popping, he walked out on to the edge of the mat and stood between his black belts and the gun, which Behr had to admire.

'That's not how we settle our beefs here,' Francovic said in a sandpaper voice. He approached Behr, another few steps, rolling that bull neck, ready to fight. Behr raised the gun and Francovic stopped.

'Don't try and save face with me now. I'm a private investigator and I came here to talk, until this fuckwad started in.' Brody was flopping around on the mat now, coming out of it.

'So let's talk,' Francovic said, showing some real Jiu-Jitsu and taking a confrontation in which he was at a disadvantage in another direction. He gestured to his office. After a moment Behr nodded and Francovic started walking towards it. Behr lowered the gun and followed.

They sat across from each other, Francovic's desk between them. Behr had moved his chair so his back wasn't to the door. For the moment, though, it seemed the other fighters had forgotten about him. One of the black belts had brought a bag of ice to Brody, and another, the jacked kid with a wise-ass spiky haircut whom Behr had seen there before, had helped him out of the gym. To the doctor, Behr supposed. The rest of the group had gone back to training.

'Sorry about Brody,' Francovic began. 'He's a good kid. He was just being loyal.'

'Stupid is what he is,' Behr said.

Francovic nodded slightly at this. 'Nasty move with the fingers – there goes his piano career. He needs to clean up his technique. Should've had his head tighter on yours.'

'Yeah,' Behr allowed, sick with himself for drawing his gun, for the fight, for ending up in the situation, and not much in the mood for a post-mortem review.

A moment of charged silence stretched between them before Francovic spoke. 'What's this about?'

'Aurelio Santos.'

'What—'

'Don't fucking say, "What about him,"' Behr said.

'Take it easy—' Francovic started.

'You take it easy,' Behr flung back, the residual adrenalin from the confrontation washing through him.

'*You*'ve got the gun.' Francovic shrugged and sat back.

'I'm looking into what happened to Aurelio,' Behr said after a moment.

'You trained with him.' Francovic figured it. Behr nodded. 'That makes sense, the way you handled yourself with Brody.'

'Tell me what you know.'

'I don't know a thing. Don't know what he'd been up to, don't know with who. Hell, all I do is teach and train and fight.'

'You managed to find time to do some talking too, didn't you? You and your camera crew . . .'

Francovic folded his arms. 'It was no crew, just one guy with a video camera. The promoter suggested it, said it'd be good hype for a potential rematch. So I did it. You ever do anything stupid?'

'Yeah, plenty,' Behr said.

A picture of Francovic was coming together quickly, and it was different from what Behr had expected. Behr had watched the clips of the man wresting the microphone from ring announcers to call out other fighters after a win, and storming around the ring roaring like a rabid beast after delivering a brutal knockout, the black mouth guard across his teeth making him appear inhuman. But here he was, fairly soft-spoken, almost thoughtful. That very morning Behr had gone on YouTube and rewatched the footage of Francovic's fight with Aurelio two years earlier, in which he'd been choked out with thirty seconds to go in the fifth round. The fight was a bit before Behr had started training and turned out to be Aurelio's last before he retired. Despite being around the same age, Francovic hadn't shut it down. He'd fought three or four times since, laying waste to all his opponents, mostly with ground and pound knockouts, and had been talking a lot on his web page about going again with Aurelio.

'So you weren't done with him.'

'No, we weren't done. Not by a long shot. He caught me in that choke . . . But, hell, anybody can get caught. You know that.'

'Sure,' Behr said.

'But I hadn't shown what I could really do against him. I was going to if he agreed to it . . .' Francovic drifted away, deep in thought. 'A loss like that . . . they just don't shake off. I learned him in that first fight. The next one was gonna be a war.' Behr tried to imagine it – the *first* one had been a war.

'But he was done. Maybe you got frustrated with that. You couldn't live with the loss, so you showed up one night to call him out, with some guys, with a gun . . .' Behr said. Francovic shook his head. '. . . And it went wrong. It went wrong and now we're here.' It was a hell of a suggestion, and Behr gripped the handle of *his* gun, which was still in his hand. He knew Francovic wouldn't go tapping out with a few broken fingers.

'You think it was a battle between sensei, like *The Karate Kid* or some shit?'

Behr shrugged. 'I don't know how it was. You tell me.'

Francovic shook his head again. The resignation in the gesture persuaded Behr of his innocence. In order to be this convincing, Francovic would have to be in the lying business. Instead, like he said, he was just in the fighting and teaching business.

'Only thing you're right about is not being able to live with it,' Francovic said. 'But he would've come out and given me another one. I know it.'

Behr looked at him doubtfully. As far as he knew, Aurelio was actually retired, not just temporarily like most fighters.

Francovic caught the look. 'I'm telling you, he would've come out and given me another one. Eventually. I know it in my bones. You spend twenty-five long minutes with someone like that – it's a lifetime. You get to know him all the way through. I threw everything I had at that mother for five rounds and he was right there with me. He was a warrior. He understood . . .' As Francovic's words trailed off, his eyes got watery. 'I'm not saying I would've won if we did it again. I think I would've. I'm just saying I would've gotten a chance to . . . answer those questions. For myself. Now, I won't ever have the chance.'

Behr let that clear before he spoke.

'While I'm here, why don't you tell me where you were the night before and the morning it happened?' Behr said.

'I'll tell you what I told the police: I was camping with my kid's Cub Scout troop. They checked it.'

'You were camping with fucking Cub Scouts?' Behr said, incredulous, but also pleased the police had been thorough enough to check Francovic out in the first place. The fighter just lifted and dropped his shoulders.

Behr looked at him through narrow eyes. 'So you got any idea who might be responsible?' he asked.

Francovic, in his own world now, thinking about a rematch that would never happen, shook his head. 'No. I don't know nothing about that.'

'Call me if anything occurs,' Behr said, putting a business card on the desk. Then he stood, holstered his gun and draped his shirt over it. He walked through the gym towards the exit and no one said a word to him.

TWENTY-FOUR

VICKY SCHLEGEL STOOD in front of a window-unit air conditioner that was losing in its valiant effort to staunch the heat. She was taking a cigarette/iced coffee break from rearranging the knick-knacks and photos on the living-room shelves. It wasn't easy to concentrate on her task though, considering the problems and the noise. The noise was the music, mean and ominous, coming from Charlie's room. A singer wailed about having a 'ball and a biscuit', and then blaring guitar erupted and shot through her head.

The problems were Deanie's. She held a picture of him, standing on a softball diamond, sweet and unfettered only a few years back. Now her boy was hurting and Vicky knew why: it was that mocha-skinned bitch he couldn't get over. Vicky had met her a few times – she'd only been to the house on a couple occasions since she had a place of her own – and Vicky had seen her in action, turning not just Deanie but Charlie and even Terry all drooling and stupid. Only her Kenny-bear seemed immune to the girl's skanky Latin charms. It was bad enough when they were together,

161

but now she'd gone and met someone else and left Deanie a mess. Vicky didn't know anything concrete, but she was sure of it. A girl disappears like that, and that's what it means. Her mother's intuition told her that much. And it made Vicky want to pluck the broad's smoky-brown eyes out.

Then there was the fact that Terry was working the boys too hard. She looked at another framed picture of them, the three boys and Terry, about seven years back out at the fairground. Kenny was just a kid and hadn't had his growth spurt yet. Charlie and Dean were teenagers, gangly, awkward and unformed. It was hard to imagine them all then the way they would become: tough and funny and thick with muscle. They were doing well. It was an unbelievable plan Terry had. Sure, they'd had to do some rough stuff, that was how it was in business. And who, really, had more grit than her men? No-fucking-body, that's who. But they'd been at it all times of the day and night these last few months and she could see the effects. Terry's complexion had gone a little grey from fatigue, especially under the eyes. And all of them had grown a bit grim as of late. Except for Kenny. He'd kept his colour and his bounce. But the snuffling and crying coming from Dean's room, the mass of empty bottles she saw in there when he finally let her in to change the sheets, and the snorting she heard coming through the door every hour or so had her practically grateful for the distraction of Charlie's music. *Practically* but not completely. And what the hell was he always doing on the phone in there? With all the racket, no less? Thousands of minutes per month. She'd seen the usage on his cell bill. A relentless, skin-peeling guitar solo leaked through the walls. She banged on the door to his room.

'Charlie! My ears are bleeding!' she yelled. The result? The 'music' got louder.

Something needed to be done for Deanie and she wondered

what *she* could do. She grabbed her cell and went outside into the heat and quiet and dialled her brother.

'Larry Bustamante, please,' she said to whoever answered, and then she waited a minute.

'Bustamante' came through the phone.

'Hi, Larry, it's Vick. Can you find someone for me?'

Dean was feeling skinny, scared and off his game. He was brain-fucked completely. He'd been sitting in his room with the lights off all day and the only thing he'd left for was to piss and to get more to drink. He couldn't shake the other night. It kept playing back in his head like a grind-house movie. He'd felt a wave of adrenalin and dread hit him that was unlike anything he'd ever experienced that night when he was in the bathroom waiting for the shake house to empty. He knew there was going to be trouble when he stepped out. Of course he knew there was going to be trouble in general – that was what they were there for – but somehow he knew he was going to see a gun. He'd just felt it. It was like he had developed fear-based ESP. And instead of that knowledge fuelling him, causing him to be so pissed off that he crossed the living room right at the little spic and put him down before there was any question, it made his limbs hang like wet towels, like fucking boiled noodles. He had gripped the edge of the sink and held on as his breath came in furious stabs and he felt like he was going to yak. He thought of what his father had said a few years back, when he had quit wrestling – that he was truly happy he had such a sweet daughter in Dean. The memory of that insult was the only thing that got him out the bathroom door.

Even then, once he was in the living room, he hadn't moved quickly because his feet were stuck in fear cement, and he had almost fucked up the whole thing beyond repair. It was only last-minute self-preservation and the spic's unpractised gun handling that saved his ass. And even then, when he'd gotten the guy down, instead of taking the risk of controlling the guy's gun wrist with one of his hands, which would have allowed him to punch and elbow with his other, Dean had grabbed on with two and settled for rolling around, hanging on for dear life until the others showed up and bailed his ass out.

I'm in the wrong line of work, Dean thought. *If 'work' is what you could call it. And nothing's been right since she left.*

Charlie's tunes were giving him a headache. He needed to get some air. Suddenly he knew where to go. He put on his shoes and grabbed his keys. He paused at the door for a moment, listening for his mom over the music, hoping to miss her and her laser eyes on his way out.

Charlie saw Dean, slump-shouldered and shuffling, slide into his Magnum and drive off. *God knows to where, the poor bastard*, Charlie thought. *At least he's going some place for a change.* Charlie poked his head out his bedroom door and saw his mother outside through the sliders; she was on the phone, facing away, smoking a cigarette, and he decided to make the most of the opportunity. He moved down the hallway and turned up the stairs to the walk-in attic. All the family's storage stuff was in the basement and one of the garage bays, so it was a part of the house that no one used – no one except him. There was a doorknob lock and the key for it lived in the utility drawer in the kitchen, but that key no longer worked should anyone try to use it, because Charlie had changed a pin on the lock and had his own new key. He used it and entered.

Fuck, he thought to himself, as the smell hit him: good thing he was close to the end of the cycle. The hot, poorly ventilated space was redolent with the scent of thickly budded marijuana that he had grown under six banks of high-intensity-discharge mercury halide lamps, better known as grow lights. It was a good thing the

DEA's use of infrared spotting planes had been ruled illegal search, because if one had passed over the house its scanning screen would have registered like a volcano was erupting in the attic. The lamps threw off 3,000 lumens per square foot and a lot of heat came with that, more than the exhaust fan could properly handle. And if they found the weed, they'd then find the blow and the oxy and he'd be carted away in bracelets and the house probably seized.

It hadn't been easy getting the apparatus upstairs – someone was always home – and wiring the ballasts from diagrams he'd found online, and cultivating the plants when he wasn't even a weed head, but he'd eventually managed.

That was the ole American entrepreneurial spirit, he supposed. Mom, since she wrote the cheques for the household expenses, might have been bitching about their running the air conditioners night and day, her understanding of the insane electrical bills, but the old man would skin him plain and simple if he discovered the grow op and the rest of it. He'd *try* to skin him anyway. It was debatable whether Terry could take Charlie any more. He wouldn't say his father had gone soft, that wasn't accurate – more like he'd just lost some force lately, probably due to his getting older. His age, that was what had to be behind their latest piece of work as well. The old man was getting all *Godfather II* and shit. Trying to prop up his ego with grand designs, cloaked in the idea that it was for Charlie and his brothers. What else could explain something like trying to corner shake houses city-wide? For profitability nothing could beat drugs. If he wanted to secure their future, Terry should've supported his, Dean and Kenny's efforts in that department.

'You want to lose everything, dealing drugs is the prescription,' was what Terry always said though.

Sure, there was risk, Charlie understood, but so was there reward.

Guess that's why it's a play for the young, he practically said aloud, locking the door behind him. *And it wasn't like the current project was risk-free, for fuck sake.* He thought, with a grimace, of the other night in the house on Traub. The little man had cried and cried when the first two or three chops hadn't done it yet. And then he'd shit himself when it was finally over. What a fucking mess.

The attic space was dark, the lamps dormant now, as he was in the curing phase. The cut plants hung upside down and had dried to a smokeable state. Charlie found his scale and set about bagging the stuff into z-bags. It wouldn't be long before he moved it all. Then he'd take a break, cut the risk profile and decide what to do with his cash.

If Sheila Fleck, the middle-aged manager of the Valu-Stay Suites, where Ken Bigby and Derek Schmidt had been lodging while in Indianapolis, had any reaction to the abrasion across the bridge of Behr's nose, she wasn't showing it.

'I need to get into the rooms of a pair of our operatives,' Behr had said to her when he arrived and identified himself as a Caro employee. She was more interested in his clothes.

'Thought you boys always wore suits,' she said.

'Yeah, we do. It's my day off, they just asked me to swing by,' he said.

'Follow me,' she said, surprising him with her pliability. 'You folks are paying the bill, so I'm happy to open the door . . .' She used her master key card to open the first door with a swipe, and then she asked: 'Your co-workers forget something?'

Behr saw immediately what she meant. Caro had already been there. Schmidt's belongings had been packed up, and rested on a dinette table in unsealed cardboard boxes. 'Yeah, they forgot something important we need down at the office,' Behr said.

'Schmidt and Bigby got reassigned to something new out of town,' he added lamely and unnecessarily.

'That's what the other boys said,' she observed, stepping back into the kitchenette to wait as Behr began looking through the boxes. All they contained were folded clothes, shoes, toiletries, newspapers and magazines. It was clear the room had been totally sanitized. Whatever had been there by way of files, notes or a lap-top had been removed by those Caro assholes, who sure liked to make things difficult.

Behr stopped what he was doing and stepped back.

'Can't find it?' Sheila asked.

'No,' Behr said. He couldn't see anything of use at all. He fished around in a large plastic cup from Burger King. It held about a pound of change and matchbooks from various places – Indy Dancers, Big Daddy Rays, the Tip-Over Tap Room, the Red Garter – that told him Schmidt didn't mind spending time in a bar.

'Maybe your co-workers got it after all,' she suggested.

Behr nodded.

'You want to check the other room?' she wondered.

He didn't feel the need to bother with another sterile room that wouldn't say much of anything about the men he was looking for or where to find them.

'Sure,' Behr said anyway, a slave to method, and trudged after her towards Bigby's room.

Kenny Schlegel pulled into the lot of Nick's Chili Parlor and saw his pop's car was already there. He walked inside to find Terry and Knute sitting over a feast that turned his stomach. The sign outside announced the special of the day, and that was what they'd ordered: FOUR CHILI DOGS OR A HALF-POUND OF FISH FOR $5.94. What a deal. They also had bowls of chili in front of them.

'No wonder you're fighting the spare tyre-age,' Kenny said, sitting down.

'This one's for you, funny man,' Terry said, sliding the paper basket of fish and chips towards Kenny. He looked down at it, a fried golden mess, and started picking the batter off as he spoke.

'So I was out in Muncie . . .' Kenny began.

'The kid drives forty miles to roll around on a mat with a bunch of guys. Probably burns two tanks of gas a week,' Terry said.

'Can't you find a boyfriend here?' Knute chimed in.

'Good one,' Kenny said, eating a piece of the white fish.

'Look at my sweet little girl, eating his fish fillet,' Terry said, causing Knute to snort out a laugh.

'Some shit went down at the gym today,' Kenny said, spitting out a fine translucent bone. 'Brody got into a real brawl. Big-time knockout.'

'Yeah?' Terry said, half interested. He turned to Knute. 'This kid Brody is a real monster.'

'He dust another student?' Knute asked.

'Nope. Brody got wasted.'

'What do you mean?' Terry said, truly surprised, which was a rare thing. 'Francovic?'

'No.'

'Who?'

'Some raw motherfucker, his jits was all rough but he got it done.'

'What happened?' Knute asked.

'They beefed. Brody got in his face, took him down and had him in a rear naked choke but the guy busted a few of Brody's fingers, got out of it and punched his ticket. Knee strikes to the head.'

'He knocked fucking Len Brody out?'

'That's what I'm telling you.'

'Who is this guy, Randy Couture?'

'A guy who came in asking around about some shit, and it just developed,' Kenny said.

'Cop?' Terry said, concerned, but keeping it out of his voice.

'No. Those bastards can't wait to flash their badges around. This guy came back two times and didn't do that. Afterwards, I heard he was a private investigator asking about Santos.'

'What'd you do about it?' Terry asked. He didn't bother hiding the concern any more.

'Stayed out of his way,' Kenny said. 'Heard he went in and talked to Francovic for a while. Then I heard he left. I'd already powdered out of there, took Brody to the doctor. Figured whatever was up, that was the best bet.'

'Yeah,' Terry said, and then thought about it for a long moment. When he finally spoke again he said, 'So what you gotta do now is, you gotta go ask Francovic who he is.'

'Yeah?'

'Fucking-A right. Just go in there wide-eyed, all "Hey, Mr Francovic, or "Hey, Master Francovic" – whatever the hell you call him – "who was that bad, bad man who hurt Len Brody?"'

'OK,' Kenny said, not feeling too sure about it.

'Do it. Don't make a special trip. Your next workout,' Terry said.

'All right,' Kenny said.

'Then bring back the name.' Terry tore a chili dog in half with his jaws and spoke through the meat and bread. 'Tell your brothers.'

Kenny just nodded.

TWENTY-FIVE

A DEAD END WAS what Behr had. *Two dead ends and a headache, more accurately*, he thought, as he sat in his car on Pennsylvania outside the red-brick building that housed the *Star*. And worse than all that was the ruined situation with Susan he had on his hands. He knew he should've called her, or emailed her, or texted her many times over the past days. He'd wanted to, but he didn't know what to say, and all he seemed able to do was witness his own glacial drift towards silence. He hoped to change that now, although the dark clouds that hung low in the sky masking the summer sun echoed his mood. Fishing through the packed cartons in Bigby and Schmidt's rooms, a realization had settled on him, grim and unassailable: he was on some kind of autopilot, executing what seemed like sound investigative moves on one case, but he wasn't thinking straight on another, and it had gotten his face smashed and it could've been worse. Brody could've broken his arm or choked him out or he could've been gang-stomped. Or he could've shot someone in that gym and he would've been done – off the streets and serving time for it.

He'd allowed Dannels's suggestion to dovetail with his own loose theories, then added the desire for easy revenge and let it steamroll his intellect towards a conclusion, rather than seeing it for what it was – conjecture. Jean Gannon's words about staying pro echoed in his mind. He suddenly knew what she'd meant.

He checked his nose in the rearview mirror. It had sounded worse than it was. It hadn't bled, and there was only some swelling across the bridge, discoloration and darkening beneath his eyes. The subsequent breaks are never as bad as the first one, and since that day in freshman football he'd experienced too many to remember.

He was nowhere with the Aurelio matter, and now he had the new baffler on his plate. He badly needed information and facts. The thing was, it was never easy to tell which piece of a case was most important. They were all time-consuming, necessary. And it wasn't even the need to discover all of the pieces but to assemble them into the proper picture that was the hard part. It took external pressure to get it started. Threat pressure, ask pressure, desire pressure, all applied in the right ways at the right time to those who had the answers, until something popped loose. In order to do it, he needed to get clear. And to do that, he needed to talk to Susan, because she was a big part of his clarity, or lack thereof. He'd seen enough movies, read enough books and heard enough country songs to know he'd done everything about as wrong as he could with her when she'd given him the news that he'd already suspected. Things were broken between them now, and it had him feeling like he had a hacksaw blade wedged in the middle of his chest. Or it could have been Brody's knuckles driving into his sternum during the body lock that caused that.

A knocking on his window brought him out of the reverie. Behr turned and looked into the black eyes and glowing cigarette tip of

Neil Ratay, the crime reporter. Behr lowered the window. 'Hey, Neil,' he said.

'Frank.'

'Been reading you,' Behr said.

'I thank ye,' Ratay said with a nod.

'What're you leaving out?' Behr asked. It was a question that used to be pro forma when he was on the force and would run into a reporter at a bar. Ratay shot out a little laugh. He'd heard the question plenty in his day too.

'All right,' Ratay said. He took a last drag and fired the butt across the hood of Behr's car into traffic. 'The abandoned house with the bodies. It wasn't really a derelict. It was a pea shake.'

'Really?' Behr said, allowing himself to sound surprised. 'How do you know?'

'Well, for one, it wasn't stripped.' He didn't have to explain to Behr that it didn't take long for a truly abandoned house in certain parts of Indianapolis to be set upon like a carcass in the Sahara. Urban vultures descended, removing sinks, tubs, radiators, ductwork, appliances, moulding and wood flooring. They even tore out wiring and copper piping for sale or use elsewhere. 'And they've found other evidence.'

'Gambling instruments?' Behr asked.

Ratay nodded.

'What's it about?' Behr wondered. 'Turf war?'

'I don't know.' Ratay shrugged, leaving Behr sure that he did know more. 'As always, we will see . . .'

'Guess we will,' Behr said. It must have been some bargain that Pomeroy had struck for the reporter to sit on what he knew. Behr could only guess at what future 'get' Ratay had been offered. It was a hell of a chit for him to hold. Behr used to have a few like it a long, long time ago.

'So, here to pick up Miss Susan?' Ratay asked, and looked at him in a way that made him wonder if the reporter knew the specifics or was just a reader of situations in general. Either way, Behr felt like he was on a slide under a microscope.

'Yeah,' Behr said.

'I'm headed in. Take 'er easy,' Ratay said.

'Any way I can,' Behr answered, and with a knock on the car's roof Ratay moved towards the *Star* building with long, unhurried strides.

Twenty minutes later Susan exited the building. Her hair flashed in the evening sunlight, but it looked like she bore a weight across her shoulders. She turned left, walking away from where he was parked. He started up the car and rolled up beside her at a trolling pace.

'Take you for a Ritter's?' he asked. She looked over and saw him and stopped.

'I'll follow you,' she answered.

They sat down outside Ritter's with their frozen custards as the twilight settled around them. The cars going by created a steady, soothing drone.

'Didn't have dinner yet,' she said.

'Better than dinner,' he responded, working the top scoop in his waffle cone with a spoon.

'Yeah.' They shared a smile, the first one in a while.

'You look beautiful,' he said, and she did. Despite a slight shadow across her eyes, her skin shone and he thought she looked like she'd been bathed in milk.

'Thanks,' she said, though simple compliments weren't going to do it for her. She ate more of her custard, the plastic spoon scraping softly against the side of the container. 'Have you been working Aurelio?'

He nodded. 'And another thing.'

'You making any progress?' she asked. He grimaced and left his spoon in his mouth for a long time after a bite, unwilling to speak, and she figured the rest. 'But you got this working it?' She ran the back of her finger over the purple and swollen bridge of his nose. He just shrugged. 'Oh, Frank.' It seemed part of her wanted to reach out for him, another part of her wanted him to reach for her, and something else in her wanted to get far, far away to where she'd be free and easy. She stayed though. She sat there on that bench next to him and ate her ice cream.

'It's nothing,' he finally said. 'What about you? How you feeling? You all right at work . . . considering?'

'Yeah. Just a little tired.'

'You want another custard?'

'Nah, this one's making me nauseous as it is.'

'Something else then? A proper meal.'

She couldn't stand the concern oozing out of him. It made her feel silly. 'It's just because it's so sweet. Forget it.'

'OK,' he said.

She wished things were normal between them, so they could just talk, and after another moment that was what she went ahead and did. 'Frank, I'm sorry, and don't take this wrong . . . but how good a friend was he?'

Behr didn't answer for a long while. He looked into her eyes and saw she wasn't trying to insult him, or diminish Aurelio. She was trying to give him perspective, which was what he needed. She was wondering when she would have him back. He thought about her question. How could he answer it? What constituted a friend? Aurelio wasn't his oldest friend, or his closest or best. That would've made things clear. They hadn't gone to school together, or been on the force together. He had none of the usual markers, just a feeling. He saw other questions behind her first one: could he walk away from it? Could he leave it to others? To no one?

But something about Aurelio's death had pierced him. The man was no saint, he wasn't saving orphans, he was just a regular guy who'd earned a living the way he saw fit. But in another way he was a pilgrim for strength and good, a missionary spreading his art. And someone had chosen to take his existence from him.

'It just seems like there's a line that needs to be held,' Behr said.

She nodded, and neither of them spoke for a moment.

'Can we talk about us for a second?' Susan said.

'Sure,' Behr said, then her face pinched as if her custard had gone off.

'Uch, listen to me, I sound like one of those annoying ladies on *Oprah*.'

'No you don't,' Behr told her.

'Things feel bad,' she said, her voice flat and grim.

'Yeah,' he agreed.

'We've got some decisions to make. I shouldn't have run out of the car like that, but we've got to deal with this thing.'

He nodded.

'When I'd just graduated college and was dating some meaning-less guys my mother used to say to me, "You'll never be younger or prettier or more wanted than you are right now."'

'Sounds more like a madam than a mother.'

'Don't talk that way about my mother, Frank,' she said, without anger.

'Sorry,' he said.

'She was trying to steer me to the "eligible" guys. But you're right, it never meant much to me. I was looking for what *I* wanted, not for what someone else wanted for me. And then, later, I wanted you.' She stopped for a moment, and put down her spoon before continuing. 'But I've gotta know if this is how it's going to be.'

'You know I don't make a big living, Suze,' he said.

She shook it off with a toss of her head. 'We both do OK. Better together,' she said. 'But that's not what I meant. I'll admit I found it romantic or exciting, in the beginning, when we first met and you were fifty feet deep on that thing. But I mean, now, is this how it's going to be when you're on a case?'

He blew out a lungful of air. 'If I'm doing background checks and asset searches and crap like that, no. But if it's something real . . . this is how it gets. How I get.'

She nodded, and stood. 'Then I guess you've got to ask yourself . . . is life something you've got to face essentially alone, or can you share it? Really share it? 'Cause I won't do it like this.' She tossed her ice-cream container into the gaping mouth of a trashcan.

TWENTY-SIX

A GARGOYLE. THAT WAS what Susan had called him coming back from the lake, and she was right. He'd apparently turned to stone and lost his ability to speak – or to speak about things of importance anyhow. The rest of the conversation at Ritter's hadn't gone very far or well. Susan had said her piece and he had found himself looking down at his feet, trying to answer but doing a poor job of it. Resolution was a long way off as they separated. They had mumbled a pledge to speak again soon but there was neither force nor commitment coming from either side, and he had driven off towards Lafayette Street.

Behr parked under the illuminated sign that read 'DON'S GUNS – I DON'T MAKE THE RULES, I JUST FOLLOW THEM'. He reached the door just as the clerk, a fortyish man with a salt and pepper moustache and a similarly coloured buzz cut, was locking up. He wore a stainless .357 on his hip.

'Just want to pick up some shells,' Behr said, showing his three-quarter tin. This time it actually had some effect. The clerk waved him in and followed him towards the ammunition shelves, spinning his keyring on his finger, past the sign bearing Don's well-worn motto: 'I DON'T WANT TO MAKE MONEY, I JUST WANT TO SELL SOME GUNS'.

'What you need?' the clerk asked.

'Forty-four special,' Behr said. The clerk gave a nod that was not quite devoid of interest and pointed to the small area stocked with the slightly unusual calibre. Behr grabbed ten boxes of wadcutters for the range, where he pledged to put in some time since he hadn't for a long while, and one box of Winchester Special Super X 200-grain Silvertip hollow points for carry. He followed the clerk to the register.

'Which will make it easier for you, cash or credit?' Behr asked.

'I closed out the drawer already, so credit,' the man said, and took Behr's charge card.

Dropping the heavy plastic bag in the trunk and getting in his car, Behr wasn't sure exactly for what or whom he needed the shells, he just knew he did. He felt like he was entering the dark tunnel of the flume ride at Kings Island – things were dark and all he could expect was a big drop and a splash. Then his phone rang.

The Ritter's tore it. Sucking down a container full of creamy milk fat alongside her misery was no answer. She'd gone straight home to get her suit and goggles, and had called Lynn Budusky, a friend whom she used to swim against in college, to meet at the IU Natatorium, where they had privileges and there were open lanes for free swim. Now she stood on the edge, bathed in blue fluorescent lights and the familiar chlorine smell, the long pool stretching out before her in perfectly organized geometric lines. She tucked her hair up under her cap as Lynn hit the water in the lane next to her with a hard splash and started eating up metres with her powerful chopping stroke. Lynn's nickname had been

'Mule' back in college, because she could pull like one in distance races, and the intervening years hadn't changed that. Her shoulders and glutes were still thick and powerful. She'd been swimming a lot more than Susan lately, that much was clear. Susan launched herself into the water, slick as a dolphin, the one aspect of her swim game that she never lost, no matter how long a layoff she took. She started with 1,000 metres freestyle, feeling her shoulders getting loose and finding more travel in their sockets.

It had all come out wrong with Frank today, an ultimatum instead of a conversation. And he hadn't helped matters. She usually liked the fact that he wasn't the nervous, gabby type like so many guys these days. They seemed like they needed shrinks more than they needed a woman most of the time. But it was only a positive when things were going well. When things were going badly, Frank's taciturnity took it all the way to terrible. She shut her mind for the remainder of her freestyle laps, reached for the wall, readjusted her goggles and started in on backstroke. She'd been a multi-event swimmer back in the day at DePaul, and in high school before that. Her favourite had been individual medley way back when. She'd had all the strokes back in her late teens. By college she'd had to cut down her events to the 400 freestyle relay and the 50 and the 200 fly, due to the level of the competition. Specialization always brings loss.

Now she could have killed herself for letting her training dip to such a horrifying level. Getting it back was always the hardest part. After gutting out 1,000 metres of backstroke, she dropped her heart rate and breathing with a medium-paced set of breaststroke. There was a time when a 5,500-metre training session was just her morning, and only one component of her workout. She'd also do dry-land training, core work, the occasional run. She cut through the water, paying attention to her technique, trying to draw on smoothness to minimize effort. Ten more laps of freestyle, moving more quickly through the water now, kicking off each wall, alternating her breath smoothly side to side every fourth stroke, she seemed to be alternating what she should do about her *situation*. In one moment she was sure she would keep it, have the baby, that Frank would come around, that she'd help him come around and pull him out of the black hole he was in, and even if he didn't, she'd do it herself. She could do day care, or move nearer to her parents in Chicago. Then after a flip turn, she knew what she had to do, because a child, a family, was serious business and you didn't toy around with a responsibility like that alone, and certainly not with a brooding dude with major issues.

She felt her heart hammering and gauged that she had another 1,000 metres left in her, maximum, and transitioned into butterfly. This was her wheelhouse, her dominant stroke. She felt her arms windmilling above the surface, plunging in and carving a keyhole shape beneath her, while her legs thumped as one. She was like a mermaid or some amphibious mammal. She ran down her last laps as fast as she could manage and reached the wall to hang on. She stripped off her goggles and cap and looked over to see Lynn had just wrapped it as well.

'Whew,' Lynn said, 'good one.'

'Please, I'm disgusting. Don't try to make me feel better,' Susan said, pulling herself up on to the pool deck.

'You're still a fastie,' Lynn said, following.

Dripping, Susan grabbed her towel and realized she'd decided exactly nothing.

Behr walked into Chubby's, the toasted sandwich joint, and didn't see the guy he was looking for. Pal Murphy had called and said his nephew knew somebody who knew something that might have gone down in the pea-shake world, and Behr should go meet him and pursue it. But the only customer in the place was a greasy-looking black-haired dude just under thirty with a slightly pointy nose poised over the second half of a delicious-looking toasted sandwich. Behr didn't have him as a relative of the natty and crisp Pal but there was no accounting for family, he supposed. He crossed over to the guy.

'You Pal's nephew?' Behr asked.

'You the PI?' the guy said, looking up at Behr with shiny black eyes that were a little bit off.

'Yep.'

'Fuck, you are big,' the guy said. 'You been scrapping?' Behr ignored both the comment and the question. 'I'm Matt McMurphy,' the guy finally said. 'Everyone calls me Kid.' Behr sat down and they shook hands.

'You a Murphy or a McMurphy?' Behr wondered.

'McMurphy's a stage name,' the guy said. 'Pal is my dad's brother.'

'You're the musician?' Behr asked. He remembered hearing the guy's roots-rock music on local radio, and he thought he'd seen a flyer a while back about him playing Donohue's on St Paddy's Day too.

'Yeah,' Kid said, and stuck his nose into the wrapper holding the sandwich half. It looked bigger than he could possibly finish, especially with the nibbling bites he was taking, but he stayed after it until Behr was convinced. After a while, he finally took a break.

'You gonna get something?' he asked.

'Nah,' said Behr. It wasn't because he didn't like Chubby's, but he'd become aware, upon sitting down, of a certain wet-mop smell that didn't make him want to eat. The smell wasn't coming from the floor either. 'Whenever you're finished.'

Eventually McMurphy wrapped the remains of the sandwich in

its paper and took a suck on a large cup of soda and belched. 'OK,' he said, looking nervous.

'So you know something that can help me?' Behr said.

'I know lots of things. Meth scene, E scene, blow scene, vike scene – ' Kid McMurphy stated with some odd pride.

'That's not a help to me. You know something pea shake?'

'Not really. But I know a guy who used to work at one, and he said he saw some crazy doings go down. It might have just been bar bullshit, but you know . . .'

'What kind of doings?' Behr asked.

'I don't know.'

'Who's the guy?'

'Maybe I shouldn't say.' McMurphy winced. 'I mean this guy could really fuck me up.'

'All right,' Behr said. He noticed the kid was getting a little twitchy. The eyes, which looked like they might have been ringed with a coat of black eyeliner several days prior, shot from side to side. He wore a dusty black suit over a burgundy vest, and a black shirt open at the throat revealing several rawhide necklaces and a Celtic crucifix. It was the outfit of a dandy after all, so maybe that did run in the family. But this kid didn't look too dandy at the moment. He looked like he'd been sleeping in the suit, on a long stagecoach ride.

'So how do you want to do it?' Behr asked. 'You want to slide me his name and I'll bump into him and leave you out of it?'

'Well,' the kid said, sucking on his soda straw but coming up empty and casting a longing eye at the refill machine, 'I don't think that'll work. But my uncle said to help you. So maybe I should go to this guy, see if he's willing to tell it to you, then give you a call.'

'OK,' Behr said, 'that sounds good. Offer him money.'

'Uh, I don't have any money,' McMurphy said.

'I didn't say *give* him money. Offer it to him if he'll talk to me. I'll give him a little if he's helpful,' Behr told him.

'Oh, cool. Cool, cool,' McMurphy said. 'That's totally cool, cool, cool—'

Behr, fearing he'd go on indefinitely, slid him a business card. 'Call me the minute the guy's ready to talk.'

Behr stood up and left. This flume ride was going nowhere but down.

TWENTY-SEVEN

SOME NIGHTS WERE hurtling locomotive engines, others just wheezed along the tracks. This night at the Tip-Over Tap Room wasn't going anywhere fast. DJ MD was spinning but they'd just called him down last minute, it wasn't a night he'd promoted, so the crowd was thin. There were still a few girls worth doing, but Charlie Schlegel wasn't there for fun. He checked his watch. He had Peanut coming for a meeting, and no doubt that fucked-up, silent, slit-eyed partner of his, Nixie, would be along with him.

Charlie pulled at the corner of the bar across from where MD was spinning. He raised his eyes at Pam, who started drawing him a Stroh's from the tap. She delivered it with the shy smile of the once banged and seemingly forgotten. But he hadn't forgotten her. They'd had a couple of fun nights after closing, but the way things worked in the family was to ring up the numbers and keep the attachments to a minimum, or a little more neatly put: *bros before hos.*

'Thanks, Pammy,' Charlie said. Besides, she was a bit of a 'butter face', and his mother would mock the shit out of him for it if he showed up with her like a proper girlfriend.

'Sure thing.' She smiled again, and moved away, giving him a chance to admire her rock-hard ass.

'*Thanks, Pammy,*' he heard in a derisive sing-song at his elbow and looked over to see a chick named Raquel, who was the older sister of some little blonde Kenny and he had just done up an ID for.

'Hey, Rocky,' Charlie said.

'Chickie,' she said, 'got any sniff?'

Before he could even answer he felt an arm, strong and hairy, wrench tight around his neck. 'No, *Chickie* don't have any sniff,' his father's rough voice sounded, ''cause he knows if he fucks with that, Daddy will bust his head.' The girl went wide-eyed with fear and beat it. Charlie just shrugged, done with it. But Terry wasn't done.

'Why the hell's she even asking that, Charlie?' Terry demanded.

'I have no fucking clue,' Charlie said, grabbing his father's wrist and unwinding the arm. 'I don't hardly know her.' There was some truth to what Charlie was saying – he had no idea why she was asking him for blow. He hadn't advertised his upcoming move, and he certainly never sold to neighbourhood schoolie girls. 'She's just someone's sister who's got it wrong,' Charlie added, as his father's black eyes stared into his.

'Uh-huh,' Terry said, 'better be the case.'

'It is,' Charlie said, cool, and not trying too hard to sell it, though he couldn't help wondering how his dad had jumped him like that with the bar all empty and with mirrors around them too. *Maybe he didn't cast a shadow.* Sloppy shit on his part, Charlie concluded.

'Better fucking be,' Terry said and headed on towards the front

DAVID LEVIEN

door. The old man could still move like a wraith when he needed
to. It was disturbing. Then Charlie saw Kenny appear at the back
door and give him the nod. Charlie looked around to make sure
that his father had left and that the room was clear, and then he
went on out the back door.

Peanut Marbry and Nixie Buncher were waiting for them behind the building. The night glowed gold from the sodium-vapour
street lamps that hissed in the near distance. That silly-ass car
Peanut was so proud of idled ten feet away, shaking slightly from
the bass thumping inside it.

Handshakes and half-hearted chest bumps were exchanged
before any words were spoken.

'A'ight, a'ight,' Peanut said, 'now it's time to do some real
commercializing. You gots the vegetation?'

'Just under five pounds. Call it four and a half libs, pure hydro.
Two hundred oxys. A few eight-balls too,' Charlie said, a little
smile creeping up. 'A whole party kit. Here.' Charlie extended a
thick, tightly rolled spliff, which Peanut took.

'How much for it?' Peanut asked. He sniffed the joint and lit it.

'Five thousand,' Charlie said. 'You got the cash ready?'

A silent moment passed, along with a look between Peanut and
his partner. 'Will have it, in a couple-few days,' Peanut said, blowing out the smoke. 'But how 'bout this: start me off with a pound
on consignment, then in two days I re-up for the rest and give you
all the cash.'

'Fuck that,' Kenny said.

Nixie sucked at his cheek audibly.

'Nah,' Charlie said, then repeated, 'nah.'

'A'ight then, it's gonna be a couple-few days.'

The group of them seemed disappointed at the forced wait, then
Charlie remembered their other business. 'It's time for us to be
moving into the 'hood.'

At this Nixie sucked his cheek again, then spat.

Kenny looked to him. 'All politics is local, bro. You got a problem with that?'

Nixie was about to say something when Peanut said, 'Chill. 'S'all chill.' His eyes lit and he turned to Charlie. 'I's thinking, how's about you front me the shit and then don't pay me for the next house I take you to?'

Charlie and Kenny looked at each other. It made perfect sense. Better than perfect sense. Transition their old business into their new and more profitable business. He could pay for the information with the weed and keep the money his father gave him to pay for the information. But the thought of those black eyes and that coarse wedge of arm scraping around his neck came to him. His father would bury him for even having this conversation.

'Nah, man,' Charlie said, 'we can't commingle that shit. Like I said: next house you take us to is in the 'hood. You get paid for it. When you get the rest of the money together we'll meet and do the other thing.'

After a moment Peanut nodded, took another hit off the joint, and he and Nixie headed for the car. Charlie turned to his brother. Kenny was smart enough to be anything he wanted to be; that was why Charlie had cut him in on his side action. But the kid was a stone wise-ass, way worse than Charlie had ever been. '"All politics is local."' Charlie shook his head. 'You gotta stop reading the paper.'

Kenny just laughed and they went inside.

Getting into his car, Peanut stopped. 'That's some broke-ass chronic,' Peanut said, and flicked the joint away into the night.

TWENTY-EIGHT

'**H**OMELESS ASSAULTED IN SQUAT HOUSE' announced the *Star*'s head-line. The piece was written by Neil Ratay, and told of an attack by several unidentified males on a house in The Meadows, near where the Mozel Sander Projects used to be, where a group of 'the homeless' had assembled and were 'thought to be residing'. Two of them needed to be taken to the hospital with blunt trauma injuries. The rest had scattered. No deaths. The victims were unidentified at 'police request due to ongoing investigation'. Details were thin. There was no electricity in the house, and a few battery-powered lamps had been upset at the start of the violence, so the victims couldn't even pinpoint the race of their attackers or how many had been involved. Behr read it and reread it, and couldn't decide if it even smacked of another pea-shake hit, with the reporting tamped down and manipulated by the police. He was tempted to reach out to Ratay and ask for the real deal, but he was concerned his questions would only serve to place a bigger story about the missing Caro detectives than the one he was confirming, so he didn't. He figured he'd just check it out on his own.

There was no reason not to: things had gone quiet the past four days and August had arrived, crawling slowly in on a trail of thick heat. Behr's anger boiled, low and bilious, at the base of his throat. Frustration clutched at him. He was feeling abandoned by his sources, unoriginal in his thinking, without skill or drive. He had no live angles to work, and had resorted to pursuing background on both his cases in a futile attempt to stay busy. His experience told him that if he kept at it he would discover a mistake or a connection that would lead him to answers. No one could commit ongoing crimes without leaving some residue. So he ran interviews, by phone, email and in person, with Aurelio's students. He'd been out to Eli Lilly to see some executives and a guy from one of the warehouses, all of whom trained at the Academy. He'd been to a fitness club where some other students worked as personal trainers. He'd been to a car dealership, a supermarket and a bank. People from all walks of life trained in Jiu-Jitsu now. Nothing of particular interest turned up. He had even gone and sat outside Ben Davis High School, where he waited for summer football practice to end, to talk to Max Sanchez and Juan Aybar, two juniors he knew vaguely from around the studio, kids who cleaned the mats and did errands for Aurelio in exchange for taking classes there.

He saw Sanchez first, looking bigger and stronger than when last he'd seen him, and called out, 'Hey, Max.' Sanchez stopped putting his key into the door of an old Volkswagen Passat and turned.

'You doing summer school, man?' Sanchez asked.

'Yeah, exactly, studying up,' Behr said. 'Wanted to talk to you and Juan about what went down. Didn't see you at the memorial.'

'We had two-a-days. Coach said we could miss for family only. He's a hard-ass mother—'

'They all are,' Behr said.

'I'm grabbing Aybes at the side door. We just lifted. Come on,' Sanchez said, and got in the car. Behr crammed himself into the passenger seat and they drove around to where a few ballplayers straggled out of the weight room. Juan was sitting outside, his back against the building, drinking a Gatorade. He got up and came towards the car carrying both of their gym bags as Behr unfolded himself from his seat.

'Hey, Behr,' Aybar said. He looked like he'd grown four inches in the past month, but his weight hadn't kept pace.

'Hey,' Behr said, 'wanted to know if you guys had seen or heard anything that might have a connection with what happened.' Both kids shrugged and shook their heads.

'When was the last time you saw him?'

'Besides class and cleaning up?' Max asked. Behr nodded.

'Nothing really. Picked up a bunch of cases of water with him at Wal-Mart,' Aybar said. 'Oh, and the NAGA tournament.'

'In Chicago. We rode up there with him, a few weeks back,' Max added.

'How'd you do?' Behr wondered.

'Submitted my first guy, then got triangled,' Sanchez said, and Behr looked to Aybar.

'I submitted my first guy, then lost on points,' he said. 'But that judge was totally tripping. He missed, like, two of my takedowns and a reversal. I totally had that shit.'

'Was anyone there from Francovic's school?' Behr asked, though he felt it was pointless.

'Nah, don't think so,' Sanchez said, 'not in the under-eighteens. Maybe some adults were there, I didn't see 'em.'

'Was Francovic there? Did Aurelio talk to him?' Behr asked. Both kids shook their heads.

'Other than that, just the usual picking up boxes, moving around furniture and shit.' Sanchez shrugged.

'The whole thing really sucks,' Aybar said. Behr nodded his agreement. Then Aybar continued, 'We got nowhere to roll now.'

'We can do it in the wrestling room here, but we got to find another teacher,' Sanchez added. Behr looked at them, young and strong, so full of life and maybe because of that so unattached to it. Any sadness they might have felt competed with the inconvenience of not having an instructor in a way that was so completely genuine and without malice he almost laughed.

'Yeah,' Behr said. 'Maybe the Academy will open back up.'

So four days had passed, and while he searched for an angle to pursue, Behr went to the tyre. It was a training technique he used from time to time. He had a large tractor tyre stashed down at the track of the nearby middle school that was closed for the summer. He'd go down there and rope it to an old weight belt he strapped around his waist. Then he'd run, the heavy black-rubber circle bouncing and dragging behind him as he went around the track and up and down the hill next to it. When his lungs and legs gave out, he'd unbuckle the belt and go after the tyre with a sixteen-pound sledgehammer. He'd slam the thing, controlling the rebound of the heavy hammer, until his core and his extremities were quaking and his mind was blank, even mercifully so of Susan. The idea was to continue on, session after session, until the tyre had worn away to nothing, then get a new tyre and do it all again. Then Behr would drag his hammer home enveloped in a sense of hollowness. He was hitting it hard, literally and figuratively, but there was no longer a sense of purpose to it for him. While he had previously trained to support his efforts in Jiu-Jitsu, so that the physical fitness component wouldn't hinder his progress, that was gone. His motivation had been replaced by a grim but increasingly vague sense of payback.

Then there was the Caro list. Behr ground it out nightly, driving by every last damn one of those miserable properties in his rapidly-becoming-a-piece-of-shit car. He glanced at the passenger seat, which, while it wasn't new, was still in pristine condition. Testament to how few people rode in it, and for how little time, compared to the leatherette under his ass and behind his head, which was cracking and peeling – disintegrating really – under his weight and sweat and the fact that he practically lived in the car at times. But the answers were out there, somewhere, in a morass of meaningless information and blank faces and seemingly disconnected facts. It was just a question of him finding them, so he went.

And as for the properties themselves, paint was nearly non-existent on the houses, as were intact windows. Rotten siding was the rule. Foundations and eaves sagged. His expeditions stretched into the nights, when he would cross paths with the SLED team – the Street Level Enforcement Detail – an aggressive roving tactical unit that was supposed to turn the tide, or at least survive, in the high crime areas – and they would eyeball him, silently urging him to get on his way.

As he visited the addresses on the list, he was able to enter them all. The abandoned houses were easy targets, with broken windows and rotted jambs and sashes, and weak locks – when the locks and knobs and even doors weren't missing altogether. None of it was going to keep him out. But once he was inside, there was very little to inform him. Save for feral cats, used crack vials, spent malt liquor cans and even human faeces, the dwellings were all empty in a way that seemed a reflection of his own being at the moment. The gleaming commercial and municipal structures of downtown, like the one that housed Caro, and the immaculate parks and public spaces that surrounded them, filled with lunchers, strollers and joggers, were a world away and seemed built to mock him and the neighbourhoods he was exploring.

Among the worst of them was the house from Ratay's latest story. Behr made his way past some fallen crime-scene tape and through a loose piece of plywood into the darkened cavern of the busted-out dwelling. As he made his way through a living room he shined his Mini Maglite and stepped around empty bottles of Alizé and Martell in his path. He was headed towards the bedrooms when he froze and killed the light. He heard noises, a voice, and recognized that he wasn't alone in the house. He moved silently in the direction of the sound. Stepping into the doorway, Behr raised his light with his left hand and pressed his right against his gun's handle, ready to draw it if necessary. Jacked-up eyes, glowing red in the flashlight beam, peered back at him. There were three of them, two men and a woman, all African-American. They looked old and weathered at first glance, but upon closer inspection Behr saw none of them was close to thirty yet.

'Oh shit, you po-lice?' one of the men said. 'We won't run.'

'I'm not,' Behr said. 'Don't run anyway.'

One of the men nodded and finished what he was doing, which was handing a glass pipe to the woman.

'Were any of you here the other night when that thing went down?' Behr asked.

They all shook their heads no. 'We come after the police are done, nobody's around for a few days,' the woman said, 'and we have us a place.'

'I get it. Was this a pea-shake house? You know anything about it?'

'Nope,' the woman said. They all shrugged and shook their heads again, and then just sat there looking as fearful as newborn rodents. Behr stared at them for a moment. Then he clicked off his light and left the way he'd come.

Upon his return home he ran property searches on the addresses that told a story of foreclosures, city seizures, building department condemnations and cases of flat-out abandonment. A few of the houses changed hands via sale, but the owners' names meant nothing to him and didn't form any discernible pattern that he could see. Pilgren, Craig to Stavros, Mr A. Had it been a dream home purchase? In that neighbourhood it seemed unlikely. Or was it a bad play before the real estate bubble burst? Rodriguez, Raul to Bustamante, Victoria. It could have been a Latin-to-Latin transfer, or Latin to Italian. Her name was on a few transactions. She must have been a low-level speculator. Same with Snopes, C. to Kale, Maurice. Mr Kale owned five properties but had lost three to foreclosure within the past eighteen months. He made a note to run a p-check on those names.

And then, finally, there was nothing else to do. Originally Behr had gone into police work and then investigation in order to wrestle with the *not knowing*. He had imagined himself uniquely built to explore the dank, murky corners of crime, where lacking the coordinates of hard information the ordinary person might become lost and panic. But that had been near twenty years ago, and lately the state of things had gone beyond the intriguing, past the irritating and was approaching the maddening. The thought of another twenty years of it stretching out ahead of him was daunting. Especially when he considered he might be at the height of his powers, or worse, that the high-water mark was already behind him. He had the sensation he was up to his shoulders in cold, wet mud, and he was sinking. What good was what he was doing anyway? Regardless of what he found out, Aurelio was going to stay dead, and this crew wasn't his problem in the first place. Was he going to feel satisfied if he found something out? What did *that* mean anyway?

It made him want to give it up, and not just these matters but maybe the profession as a whole. He didn't know how to do anything else though, and shining his flashlight on the doors of a Costco in a night watchman's uniform didn't seem like much of an alternative.

His mind was chewing itself into a pulp, and perhaps that was why he found himself, in the fading light, driving through the gates of South County Municipal Landfill. He was desperate, and this latest hit on a house was in the 'hood, and no one he knew knew the 'hood as well as his friend Terry Cottrell.

Behr parked and got out of his car to see Cottrell standing on a dirt mound pumping an air pistol, which he then raised and fired. Satisfied with his shot, he turned and saw Behr.

'Huh-heh, Large,' Cottrell said.

'Big-game hunting?' Behr said.

'Rats around here qualify,' Terry said, and spat some steel pellets, the extra ammo stored in his cheek, on to the ground. They shook hands and chest bumped. It was a silly action, and not something Behr engaged in with anyone else. They began walking through the low stink. The refuse was well spread out at South County, but the heat intensified the odour into a potent cloud of fecund rot that surrounded them. Behr wondered if getting Cottrell the job overseeing the facility years ago, which had moved the man off the streets and out of a life of larceny, was going to hurt him worse in the long run due to the exposure to carcinogens.

'Let's get inside,' Cottrell said, seeming to read his mind, 'I got the AC kicking.' Behr followed him to a doublewide.

It was air-conditioned cold and dark in the trailer, the only light coming from a too big flat-screen television freeze-framed on a black and white image of a man in a trench coat lighting a cigarette.

'What you been up to?' Behr asked. He cast his eyes about as they adjusted to the low light and saw that several stacks of books had been moved from their shelves to accommodate a large DVD collection.

'Been *watching*,' Cottrell said. 'I'm on a New Wave and noir kick: *400 Blows, Rififi, Le Samouraï, Le Cercle Rouge, ça va*?' Cottrell blazed a Newport in the disaffected way Behr had seen in the few French films he'd caught with girls back in college. 'You know *Elevator to the Gallows*? Cottrell asked.

'That what this is?' Behr asked of muted, soulful trumpet music that was playing in the trailer.

'Yeah, Miles Davis did the soundtrack. Brother laid it down live to picture. He had a flap of skin that came loose on his lip but kept playing. That's what gives it that muted quality.'

'That's fascinating, buddy,' Behr said. He would've been mocking Cottrell if it weren't so interesting. He'd tried listening to jazz a few times, but it made him feel like he was eating dinner at an airport hotel, and today he just didn't have the time. 'I'm on something that has to do with pea shake and was wondering if you knew anything about that?'

Cottrell's eyes narrowed for a moment, then relaxed and filled with mirth. 'No, but I heard there's some broad-ass shit being pulled over at the Flackville bingo game—' Cottrell cut himself off with his own harsh staccato laugh, 'hah heh-heh-heh-heh-hey.'

'Come on, man,' Behr said.

'OK. You don't want to know about a major league skim, don't matter to me . . .'

'Do I look like I'm playing?' Behr said.

'You never do.'

'So tell me what you know.'

'Folks in the community still like the numbers, that's all I can tell you,' Cottrell said.

'When Grandma has her dream you gotta put your dollar down on it.'

'Damn skippy, you Richard Pryor motherfucker . . .' Cottrell shook his head. 'But there's plenty out there playing pea shake too, I guess. Then there's your folks, but they mostly play Cherry Master, don't they?' Cottrell was referring to the legal video gambling machines that licensed, mostly white-run and -patronized bars were able to install. The inequity and potential racism of the system was an oft-debated topic in the paper and on the web.

Behr saw a few days' worth of the *Star* sitting on a side table. 'You read about that shit over by the fairgrounds?'

'I mighta glimpsed it,' Cottrell said. 'Angry Latinos.'

Behr shook his head.

'No?' Cottrell blew out smoke.

'Some kind of a move on a shake house,' Behr said. He looked at Cottrell, almost thirty now, still lean and wiry, pulling away from his youth out on the corner with grace. Despite his distance from that world, and working the straight job for the last several years, Cottrell still seemed to know most everything that went down in the projects and their surrounding strata.

'Someone's running a Trafficante play, huh?' Cottrell said. Behr knew he was well read in crime, both fictional and true, and recognized the mobster's name but he didn't get the reference. 'Old Santo rounded up the *bolita* business down in Tampa – the Cuban and Sicilian part of town, Ybor City. Made himself rich off it.'

'Is that what's going on here?'

'I don't know what all's going on here. I didn't know shit about it until you just told me.' Cottrell stubbed out his cigarette in a half-full ashtray. 'Just saying it's a traditional way to build a power base, at least for La Cosa Nostra, ha-heh-heh-heh-heh-hey.'

'Glad you find it such an interesting social study. And so amusing,' Behr said. There was no Indianapolis Mafia as far as he knew, so it wasn't much help. 'Could you work it for me?' he asked.

'He-ll no!' Cottrell said. 'I don't do that.'

'Would you be so kind as to let me know if you hear anything about it then? I'm looking for a pair of missing investigators – they were working it for an outfit called Caro. Could be big for me if I can locate 'em.'

'Yep, I'll go 'round the way asking a bunch of questions, and when the homies ask why, I'll say, "Some ex-cop I truck with wants to know." Cool?' Cottrell said, and Behr rode a fresh wave of his laughter out the door.

Behr crossed the lot to his car. As he got in he glanced back at Cottrell, framed in the doorway of the trailer, lighting a fresh cigarette, and could swear he saw his friend's face pinched in concern, or maybe it was just thought, but he was too far away to be sure.

Night had come and Behr was near home and debating whether or not to get something to eat when his cell rang with a number he didn't recognize.

'Is this Behr?' came a voice.

'Who's this?' he asked back.

'Kid McMurphy. Pal's—'

'Where you been?' Behr asked.

'That guy, you know, the one I told you about. He was away for a while, but he's back,' McMurphy said.

'He ready to tell me something?'

'Well . . .' McMurphy said, then seemed to drift off mid-conversation.

'Where is he? We'll figure it out,' Behr said.

'Can you, like, do it without me? I'll just tell you what he looks like and—'

'No. Where are you? I'll pick you up,' Behr said, and stepped on the gas.

TWENTY-NINE

McMURPHY WAS SITTING alone in a booth in the dark rear corner of Vic 'n' Vitos. He had a gigantic half-eaten thin-crust pizza pie cut into diagonal slices resting in front of him. Behr slid into the booth, and saw that the guy was still in his dusty black suit, but now he wore a white shirt under it with two different shades of lipstick smeared on the collar. He was using his slender musician's fingers to pluck spicy homemade *giardinare* from a massive jar and arrange it on a slice of the pizza. McMurphy gave him a nod hello and started in on the slice with small, mincing bites. He was skinny as a rail but seemed to eat full-time, not to mention that Behr had tried the *giardinare* at Vic 'n' Vitos, and just a taste of the pickled vegetables was enough to burn a hole clean through a stomach.

'So this guy, his name is Austin. He actually worked – fricking *worked* – at a shake house. You believe that man? He seemed pretty interested in the money-for-info aspect.'

The whole 'snitch on the payroll' concept was not one that Behr was in a position to afford. 'Let me know when you're ready,' he said, leaning his elbows up on the table.

McMurphy nodded again, this time to himself, like he was steeling himself to do something unpleasant. Maybe he was just sorry to be saying goodbye to what was left of his pizza. The nodding continued on, growing in energy until it seemed like the guy was turning into a bobble-head doll.

'You all right?' Behr asked.

'Yeah, yeah,' he said, 'you know, just geeked.'

'Geeked over what?' Behr asked, but got no answer, save a nervous giggle from Kid. A tremor-like sideways twitch of the head was starting to develop in him too. Behr looked deep into his eyes. There was a lot of sparkle, but not enough coherence. 'What are you on?' Behr demanded.

'Nothing,' Kid said.

'No?'

'No, man,' Kid pleaded, looking hurt. 'Just geeked to be helping—'

''Cause I won't deal with you if you're on something,' Behr said flatly, trying to figure out what it was – coke, meth, pills – or whether he was just a freak.

'I had a few Beam and Cokes and a few of these.' He pointed at a half-killed pint of the black that had lost its head.

'What's a few?'

'Just a few. Don't worry, after my last tour I could probably drink a gallon of Beam and not even feel it.'

'Congratulations,' Behr said, standing and lifting a diamond-shaped piece of pizza, half of which he ate with a single bite. 'So where are we headed?'

The answer was Fionn MacCool's, an Irish pub out in Fishers. The brick building tried to recreate the Dublin effect and housed a bar, tables, a dance floor and a small stage where live music and toe dancing were performed. The place was popular with the young smart set, and around St Patrick's Day was sure to be full of 'DRUNK ME I'M IRISH' T-shirts and green beer puke running in the street. Behr wasn't a regular. Tonight there was no live band, but he and Kid McMurphy entered on loud music playing from the sound system and a pretty good crowd of drinkers, and Behr quickly saw that he was with a local celebrity. McMurphy greeted about three-quarters of the patrons with handshakes and hugs for the guys and double kisses in the European style for the girls. Behr heard more than a few requests for McMurphy to do some shots, play a song on the stage or come 'smoke up later'. What they didn't encounter was the guy they'd come looking for. After scouting around for a while, McMurphy flagged down a passing waitress.

'Yo, you seen Austin around?' he asked.

'Austin Tuck?' she wondered.

'Yeah.'

'He's out on the deck with Davey Veln,' she said. McMurphy led the way towards the side door that gave on to the outdoor space.

'He's probably playing cornhole,' McMurphy said. 'He's freaking awesome at cornhole.'

The deck was more crowded than inside. Music was pumping out there as well, and groups of drinkers, mainly blonde-haired post-college girls, were standing jammed around tables, while players, mainly big-boned farm boys, were clustered around two cornhole pitches. Slanted wooden boxes were placed bottom-up about ten yards apart while two-man teams tossed fabric bags filled with corn kernels at small holes cut into the tops of them. It was the kind of game that was only likely to catch on in agricultural country, and copious drinking certainly enhanced its amusements. Three points were scored for every bag that went in the hole, and one point for every bag that landed on the board but didn't go in, if Behr recalled. He'd only played once or twice. It just wasn't in his blood, he guessed.

'There he is,' McMurphy said, and pointed at a pair of young men standing by the far rail. One was tall and husky, with a shaved head and the sloping shoulders and over-developed traps of a college wrestler. The other was mid-sized but showing some lean muscle under his tank top. He had several tattoos covering his arms and creeping up his neck, and also sported some big gauge-hole earrings in his earlobes.

'Which one?' Behr asked.

'Guy with the shaved dome.'

'Well, come on.'

'Right, right,' McMurphy said, and walked towards the pair, who each held a pint of beer and flipped around a beanbag while they waited for their turn at the game.

'Hey, Austin,' McMurphy said, and the big man turned and tried to focus.

'What up, Kid?' Austin said. The other man, Davey Veln, nodded as well. They didn't seem to notice Behr.

'This guy needs to talk to you,' McMurphy said. Only now did the pair register Behr's presence. 'Remember the thing I mentioned, about the money . . . ?'

'What about?' Austin said, turning towards Behr. He might have been a big guy, gym-muscled, but there was no will in this Austin. Behr could see that right away. Behr could also see he was powerfully drunk. His eyes were glassy and distant.

'About your old job,' Behr said.

'No thanks—' Austin began, trying for defiant cool but just sounding hesitant.

'Look, bro, we're next up for cornhole, so you can either wait . . . or better yet, buzz off,' Veln said, squaring with Behr. So Austin was the bigger of the two but Veln was dominant, Behr realized.

'I'm not talking to you,' Behr said, then angled towards Austin. 'You'll play later. Let's go.'

'You don't get it, dude. These are the qualies for the big tourney, so he can't play later,' Veln said with menace, '*and* he's also not fucking interested.'

Behr's hand shot up and his finger found its way through the gauge in Veln's right ear. He grabbed on tight and yanked down, doubling the man over.

'Ahh, shit!' Veln yelped in surprise and pain.

'I said I wasn't talking to you,' Behr snarled, grabbing the man's hair with his other hand and cocking his head. 'Now if you want to keep your goddamned ear – and I'm not talking about the lobe, because I'm not gonna pull down, I'm gonna pull *up* and take the whole damn thing – you'll head to the bar for another drink and get the hell out of my face,' Behr said, and twisted hard for good measure.

'Fuck! All right, all right,' Veln almost whined. Behr let him go and he straightened. Behr glared at him, the guy's eyes as wide as saucers with shock. 'Fuck,' he said again, and hurried to the bar through a small crowd of onlookers who had noticed the confrontation.

Behr took the glass and beanbag out of Austin's hands and shoved them at McMurphy. Then he closed the space, backing Austin into a corner formed by the wrought-iron rails of the patio.

'What the hell is this about? What are you doing to me here, Kid?' Austin said, stunned by the violence.

'Don't talk to him. Talk to *me*,' Behr said, putting his face close enough to see Austin's big, dirty pores.

'OK. You want to know? You know already. I did some security . . .'

'At a pea-shake house?'

'Yeah.'

'And?'

'And some shit went down. So I quit and I never went back. And that's it.'

'That's not enough.'

'That's all you're getting.'

'And where was this?'

'I'm not saying.'

'The fuck you're not.'

'Said too much already.'

Behr shook his head and looked at this Austin. The guy was scared. Too scared to talk. There were a lot of ways to go about interrogating someone and developing information. *Army Field Manual*, 2–22, 3: Human Intelligence Collector Operations suggests that people tend to want to talk when under stress, and respond to kindness. That worked better for the police, who had a stressful setting at their disposal, and Behr wasn't about to hand out any kindness. There was the 'Mutt and Jeff', more currently known as 'good cop-bad cop'. But he worked alone. There was the 'we know all'. Again, it was tough to pull off solo. There was 'rapid-fire questioning', which could produce inconsistencies that he could then challenge, but this wasn't yielding much at the moment. It was too late for 'ego up', or flattering to create a bond. 'False flag', in which he would pretend he had the same interests as the person in question, just didn't apply. Methods got more complicated from there. The truth was, Behr had to manufacture his own stressful situation to cause the subject to be afraid *not* to talk, and he needed to do it in a hurry. *Do what the cops can't*, he thought.

'You're gonna give me what you know,' Behr said.

'Or what, you gonna grab my ear? You can't fucking touch me. Here or anywhere else. Come on, you know you can't do anything that'll make me tell you any-fucking-thing,' Austin stated, making his stand. The attitude pushed Behr right into the red zone. He felt McMurphy staring at him. When he was a cop he'd had to put a guy away clean and according to Hoyle. If a cop puts a guy away wrong, and the guy does a stretch of years, then the cop has a problem. Every bench press that guy does while he's away has that cop's name on it, saving it until he's out and comes looking. But he wasn't a cop.

Do what the cops can't.

'More than three grams,' Behr said.

'What?' Austin asked, his drunken eyes pinching in concentration.

'More than three grams,' Behr repeated.

A blank look was all that came back at him. Good, silence was a first step.

'One day – and you won't know when – you'll go to get in your car and the cops will roll up on you and take you down. And you know what? They're gonna find more than three grams of Charlie or rock in the dash, or the spare, or somewhere,' Behr said. 'It doesn't matter which. Because more than three grams of it makes it a Class C felony—'

'You're gonna fuckin' flake me?' Austin asked, his eyes focused in understanding now.

'Oh yeah. But guess what? It won't just be some lame Class C beat that nets you four years. Because when it goes down you'll happen to be parked within a thousand feet of a school, or park, or housing project—'

'Fuck—'

'That's Class B automatic. But how hard will it be for the prosecutor to make the leap to Class A? After all, they'll find a wad of five-dollar bills and vials and balloons and some other shit that makes it clear your intent is to deal. That's twenty to fifty, the presumptive sentence being thirty years,' Behr said. 'Thirty years in the state pen getting banged in the pants . . . well, that'll probably stop after about ten years when you're too old.' He grabbed a fistful of Austin's shirt. 'Maybe you think I won't do it. Do I sound like I won't do it?'

Austin's face turned to bread dough. The man looked positively sick. 'Fine. The fuck do I care. Get me a drink and I'll tell you.'

'Get him one, Kid,' Behr instructed, and McMurphy scampered off for the bar. Austin's gaze followed him.

'Fucking Kid. He told me you'd pay me for info. I knew it was bullshit, that's why I changed my mind—'

'Forget that. What happened?'

'I was working for a guy. Keeping order. Collecting the money. Guarding the payouts. It was the easiest job ever. Nobody stirred up dick. They just wanted to play. Tons of money was rolling in.'

'And then?'

'Then one day the house got taken down. Some thick-neck bastards came through the back door and whacked the dude's father.'

'Whacked him like killed him?'

'Whacked him with a pipe or a flashlight or something. They were all carrying weapons. Might've killed the old guy.'

'How many?'

'Three. Two were young, the other was older.'

'White, black, Latino?'

'White,' Austin said, seeming to relive some unpleasant moments in his mind. 'Soon as I saw it, I beat feet out of there, on account of what I knew. Chilled over Louisville for a couple of weeks with a cousin.'

'Did you?' Behr asked. 'What exactly did you know?'

Before Austin could answer, Kid McMurphy showed up again, empty-handed. 'Waitress is bringing it,' he said.

Then Austin spoke again. 'I'd heard that freelance shaking was over in this town. That a group of guys – a family – was making a play to incorporate it. I heard they were killing anybody got in their way.'

'Killing people?' Behr asked. He knew he was involved in a serious deal, but he wasn't in the mood to be fed an urban myth.

'That's what I heard – that they're like a murder machine. And people are believing it. Nobody's saying fuck-all or getting in their way.' Austin paused, as a waitress with three tall cola drinks on her tray stepped over with the pinch-toed walk of a second-rate stripper in her tall shoes.

'Thanks, Rose,' McMurphy said, took one glass and handed one to Austin. Rose looked scared, like she knew something heavy was going on. 'I didn't know what you drank, so I got you a double Beam and Coke, just like us,' McMurphy told Behr. Behr gestured to McMurphy that he should take the remaining glass and that was what Kid did.

'Who are these guys, this family?' Behr asked, when the waitress had drifted away.

'I don't know. Some brothers and a father or uncle.'

'Name?'

'The people who are whispering aren't whispering that.' Austin turned into the glare on Behr's face. 'So go ahead and fill my car with weight if you want, I'm telling you I don't know,' he said, and drank down half his drink.

'Who was your boss?'

'Name is Hector.'

'Hector who? He's Latin?'

'Yeah, Hector. He's a Honduran. Never caught his last name. I was only with him two months and we never exchanged business cards.'

'That's great,' Behr said. 'I want to talk to him. He still around?'

'Not if he's smart – and he was pretty smart. Tough little bastard too. I heard he kept shaking afterwards. Even managed to keep some players. Then I heard he stopped. Then I quit asking and quit listening. I think he split. Shut down the spot.'

'I'll ask him myself,' Behr said. Austin drained his drink, then he took the extra off McMurphy and started in on it.

'Would've been a different deal that day if I'd been packing,' Austin said, mostly to himself. 'Next time I work security, I go heavy—'

'Better yet, why don't you find a different field?' Behr said.

'I guess . . .' Austin breathed, the last of the defiance going out of his sagging shoulders.

'I'll just need that address,' Behr said. Austin gave it to him and Behr made to leave.

'Hey, man . . .' McMurphy said, 'could I grab a ride?'

Behr stopped. 'You just want to help, right?' he asked. Kid McMurphy nodded. 'Get yourself home, that'll help,' Behr said, and headed for the door.

THIRTY

BEHR FELT LIKE he was walking on a dirt cloud as he moved across the hardpan lot towards the house on Traub. It was a location that hadn't previously been mentioned in Ratay's stories, nor was it on the Caro list. Thick humid air ringed halos around the few working street lamps in the vicinity, diffusing their glow. Besides that, the house and those immediately around it were dark. When he reached the structure, he saw the windows remained intact. It wasn't vacant, as Austin had thought, or somehow the scavengers had steered clear of the place so far, the way hyenas avoided the carcass of an animal that had died of disease. Behr pulled out his Mini Maglite and turned it on as he reached the house. There was a marshal's sticker on the front door warning that seizure proceedings would be conducted within the next thirty days. He shined the flashlight into the windows and saw a front room that was empty save for a couch, a couple of chairs and a table. He knocked on the door and waited, but was greeted only by silence. Behr stepped down off the porch and continued around the house in a loop, peeping in the windows where they were low enough and where there weren't curtains pulled shut as was the case with the back bedroom.

Behr knocked on the back door and waited again, but once more got no answer. Finally, he arrived at the front and climbed back up on the porch. He knocked a last time, waited and tried the doorknob, which was locked solid. Then it was back to the car for his lock-pick kit. He chose the rear door for obvious reasons of cover, although the street and much of the neighbourhood beyond it seemed deserted. He paused when he saw that the lock was a Primus high-security double-cylinder deadbolt.

He was familiar with the lock, having tried them before to mixed results. They featured reinforced trim rings and a tapered housing to protect against wrenching the cylinder. The keys came with side milling that prevented bumping, and the series offered an integrated anti-pry shield that hindered picking. He went to work anyway and stayed at it for a good ten minutes, the MiniMag clenched in his teeth until his mouth ached. He paused only to rest his jaw and wipe the sweat from his face. The first lock – the latchbolt in the knob – had yielded, but he was having more trouble with the deadbolt above it, which looked newly installed. The door was seated so firmly that he wondered if a wedge of some kind had been employed, or if the door had otherwise been sealed shut from the inside. He considered his options for a moment, glancing at the nearby window. Nothing said 'call the cops' like the sound of breaking glass, even when the neighbours were uninterested, so Behr crossed that option off his list before returning to his car again, zipping up his kit as he went. This time he returned with a less sophisticated burglary tool – a short steel crowbar – and with it he went to town on the doorjamb. He chiselled away above the doorknob, wedging the sharp claw end of the crow between the door and frame, jacking it forward and back until the wood cracked under the assault. Paint and wood chips fell at his feet. Before long the door began to loosen in its mooring. He wiggled it, using the knob, and then went back to chipping. Bit by bit he cleared a space until he could see the smooth metal bolt that had been securing the door and giving him so much trouble. A power saw could cut through it in seconds, but that would make a window break seem subtle, so he began chipping away at the wood that held the metal housing that received the bolt. This was harder work, and the crowbar spun repeatedly in his hands causing blistering across his palms. But the wood succumbed to the crowbar's teeth, and finally the door was shaking freely in its frame, the bolt now wobbly with an inch or two of travel. Behr dropped the crowbar, stepped back and kicked the door. Big black foot scuffs from the soles of his trail shoes appeared on the surface, and he was sure the sound that resulted woke the neighbours all the way to Gary, but the door finally swung open.

Behr stood sweating for a moment in the newborn silence. He glanced around and saw no lights go on nearby. He snapped on a pair of latex gloves, picked up the crowbar and entered the darkened house. He'd been in so many one-floor bungalows of this type in and around the city he felt he could diagram it blind. He made his way down a narrow hallway past two closed doors. The air inside was hot and close, and there was a smell of decay in the air that told him a rat had died under the floorboards. He made his way into a sparsely furnished front room. He knew there would be a small kitchen off to one side or another and the bathroom opposite it. He tried the lights, but found the utilities had been cut off. He swept the corners of the room with the small beam of his light and saw a chair overturned. There was an unplugged flat-screen television, its viewing surface shattered, set off to the side of the room. He saw a few plastic balls with numbers on them that had rolled against a baseboard that told him the place had indeed once been a pea shake, as Austin had said. He kneeled to inspect what he was pretty sure was a bullet hole from a small-calibre weapon. As he got close to it, he took out his Leatherman tool and peeled a short knife blade from it in order to pry the bullet or fragment free. But then he saw the fresh knife marks around the original hole. Someone had beaten him to it. He leaned his face down close but couldn't find any blood. He stood, and from that moment stepped more lightly and made sure not to touch anything, because he knew he was at a crime scene.

He made a cursory sweep of the small empty kitchen and bathroom, and then, his heart hammering, made his way down the hallway towards the bedrooms. He gripped the doorknob of the first one gingerly and turned it, pushing the door open. That was when the smell hit him. There was no rat under the floorboards. It was a body. A smallish man was stretched out on a bare, blood-soaked mattress, his head nearly severed from a gaping slash along his throat. Behr stepped closer, using the inadequate stripe that his Maglite produced to inspect the body. The blood on the mattress was dry, and he could tell from the desiccated condition of the body that it had been there for many days, and that the smell, as bad as it was, had already peaked and had actually begun to diminish.

He moved to the body and carefully felt around in the pants pockets enough to know that any wallet or identifying documents had been taken. There was nothing under the bed save for some blood spots, where it had seeped through the mattress before drying down. He checked the small closet, which was barren save for a few T-shirts and a fleece-lined denim jacket.

Behr steeled himself and went back to the body. The head was thrown back, teeth bared and eyes clenched in an aspect that connoted great suffering. The throat had been chopped out by a beef knife, a machete or some other heavy-bladed instrument. Whether or not one blow had been sufficient to cause death, the killer hadn't stopped there. It looked to Behr as if half a dozen strikes had rained down on the man. He noted there were no defensive wounds on the hands or arms, which suggested that others had held the man down. The body had been through the swelling and the draining process and now lay on top of the dried, foul remnants of that natural progression.

Behr stepped back and then made his way out of the room towards the next bedroom, when he thought of Pomeroy's instructions and realized he needed a way to steer clear of what he had discovered. He couldn't call it in. It would lead to dozens of questions about his involvement and how he had come to be there, and even one question was going to be too many. He considered an anonymous call but couldn't do that from his cell phone because it would be traceable, and he didn't trust it from a pay phone either, even if he could find one that worked. He was at the door to the next bedroom when an idea came to him. But first he turned the knob and pushed. The door stopped with a slight, soft bump. Something was behind it. He pushed a bit harder and the object yielded, sliding across the smooth wood floor. He stepped into the room, which was set up as a makeshift office, with a desk and chair and ancient built-in cabinetry, one door of which was open. He trained his flashlight on the object at his feet.

'Oh no,' he said aloud.

Behr stood across the street a decent distance away, among a group of residents, neighbours, drawn by the sirens, who had gathered in the coming morning light to watch. A pair of patrol cars had been the second to arrive, with sirens and lights. Homicide had been next. Then Violent Crime. Then some brass, and a team from Coroner's. He watched them go in. The windows became illuminated by utility lights that were switched on inside, and that light was peppered by lightning storms of camera flashes. And then he saw something he couldn't remember witnessing more than two or three times in the entirety of his career: when the crime scene teams exited the house, almost to a man they were crying. He was too far away to see the tears, but there was no mistaking it. Eyes were wiped with the backs of hands, the shoulders of fellow officers were clapped, and arms were squeezed as the group tried to collect its strength and buoy one another in the face of what they were dealing with.

Before long the first gurney was carried out, bearing a zippered black body bag. Then, after a pause, the second stretcher came out. This one held a black body bag as well, but it was only half filled by the small figure inside it. A gasp rippled through the crowd and Behr felt dread and sorrow anew at the sight of it, just as he had inside the room. It was an image that would never leave him, seared as it was into the backs of his eyeballs. The body of a boy, two or three years old, dead of dehydration, curled at the base of the door. He was too small even to reach the doorknob.

The murdered man could have been the boy's father, or an uncle, or maybe there was no relationship, and Behr deduced that the boy had been left behind undiscovered after the killing. Or perhaps he had been discovered and left behind anyway. The bile had risen in the back of his throat when he'd seen the figure lying there, when he'd touched the boy's papery skin checking for a pulse that was long gone. He didn't know whether he'd been hours, days or a week too late, he just knew he hadn't found his way to the house in time, and that the thought of his failure would never leave him.

The stretchers were loaded into a coroner's van, which drove away. There was more flash photography inside the house, and the group on the street started to disperse. Behr turned his gaze from the house and found Neil Ratay, the black circles under his eyes behind his glowing cigarette tip visible in the coming dawn. He had been Behr's first call, and the first to arrive on the scene.

'What's happening?' Ratay had said when he reached the dark, quiet street.

'You're working the pea-shake stories. I need you to do something for me, and you'll get something for it,' Behr said. Then he had told him to call in the bodies to a police contact he could trust, to request the units and the teams, but to have it done by cell phone, to keep it off department radios and thus off the police scanners that would have brought every news organ in town into it. Behr told Ratay to claim he'd been tipped to the scene by a source he couldn't name, and that he'd found the door open. And then he let the reporter into the house for his look.

'I don't know what to tell you to prepare you for it—' Behr began.

'Don't,' Ratay said, and plunged in through the now unlocked front door with Behr's flashlight. He exited moments later, pale and unsteady, just before the first units arrived. He had lit his first cigarette with trembling hands and hadn't stopped smoking them since. They hadn't spoken a word to each other during all the police activity, mainly because Behr had fallen back away from him so they wouldn't be seen together but also because there was nothing to be said.

Now, preparing to leave, Behr approached.

'I guess "thanks" isn't the word, but—' Ratay started.

'Yeah,' Behr said, 'same to you.'

Then Behr saw a silver Crown Vic roll on to the set. A familiar figure got out. Captain Pomeroy crossed to an officer Behr didn't recognize, and they exchanged a few words. Pomeroy moved to the edge of the activity and took out his cell phone. Behr was wondering if he had even been seen. Then his phone rang.

'Yeah,' Behr answered.

'I tell you to keep shit quiet, and this is what you bring me?'

Pomeroy's voice came through the phone. Behr moved away from Ratay.

'*I* couldn't call it in,' Behr said. 'You said "no contact". It was the best I could do.'

'A goddamned reporter?' Pomeroy said.

'Yeah, one – and one the department's already in business with. One who you can trust. That was the trade-off so you wouldn't end up watching it on TV.'

'You know what it's gonna cost me to buy time on this?'

The truth was, after seeing what he had in that house, Behr didn't care all that much.

'What else do you have for me? You must have something else,' Pomeroy demanded.

'Not yet,' Behr said. He knew Pomeroy was looking for something solid, not some weak theories and rumours about a family.

'Are you jaking it on this, Behr?' Pomeroy barked.

'Does it look like I'm jaking it?' Behr barked back. They were almost to the point where the cell phones were unnecessary.

'Then find me these fucks *before* they act,' Pomeroy hissed, backing down the volume.

They stood there, Behr and Pomeroy, the gulf of the street between them, cell phones pressed to their ears. Before Behr could think of anything else to say, Pomeroy hung up, pocketed his phone and entered the house with angry strides.

'What the hell was that?' Ratay asked when Behr rejoined him.

'Nothing,' Behr said. He changed gears. 'So your contact asked you to hold the story?'

'He did. And I will. Not as long as they want me to, but for a minute or two anyway. There'll be a give-back too, of course.'

'Right.'

'Not to mention the give-back to you for putting me in this,' Ratay went on.

'File it,' Behr said, 'no sweat on that.'

'You want to tell me what you're working that got you here?' Ratay asked.

'I would, Neil, but I can't.'

'I figured,' the reporter said, and looked at him with eyes that seemed to bore right through him. Behr felt like the man knew the whole deal, and in a sense he did. He might not have had the specifics, but he certainly knew that these things generally concerned the same type of players – morally bankrupt animals – who were after similar ends: monetary gain, and some way to fill the empty pits of their souls.

They stood there for a moment, then Ratay spoke. 'Hey, Frank, not that it's any of my business . . .' Behr knew what was coming, '. . . but is everything all right with you and Susan? She seems like she's walking around under a rain cloud.'

'I don't know, man,' Behr said, feeling unable to hide the truth at the moment, 'we're in different places on the track. That's become clear lately.'

Ratay nodded his understanding.

'She's great,' Behr continued.

'She is, indeed.'

'I just . . . don't know if it's the right thing for everyone right now.'

Ratay sighed out a mouthful of cigarette smoke, dropped the butt and toed it into the ground. 'Well, don't be too quick to write it off, you've still got some life left in you.'

Behr gave a grim nod. 'Less every day,' he said. Should he go on and tell Ratay what he really thought? That it was a shit world, lousy with fear and not knowing and death, full of people in a constant state of panic and desolation, the more they learned the more the truth swam away, and that was why so many of them turned to God, even though He didn't do much back for them.

None of it would be new to Ratay, and Behr didn't imagine Ratay would want that for Susan, especially if he knew her current condition.

The reporter didn't argue with him, and instead seemed to be arguing with himself over his pack of Camels and whether he should light another. Then a man in a suit with a gold badge hanging around his neck stepped out of the house. Ratay put away the cigarettes. 'There's my guy. Time for the horse-trading.'

He crossed the street and Behr went to his car.

THIRTY-ONE

DEATH WAS ALL around him. He'd seen it in the dark of that house last night, and he'd seen it in the day, which he'd slept through, his dreams plagued by monstrous images that defied description. He still felt it upon him when he awoke, shaken and exhausted. It drove him to the place where killing was honed. Behr showered and dressed and put on his gun and, recognizing the urge to use it, grabbed his range bag and loaded it with the shells he'd recently bought. He went cross-town to Eagle Creek Park, to where the Indianapolis Metro Police shot.

The range was closed to the public during the week, and the parking lot was near empty. Before he even reached the range – a series of tables acting as bench rests beneath a slanted roof – he could hear it was quiet. Day shift was still on duty. Technically he didn't have privileges at the facility, but occasionally an ex-cop could get a break when things were slow. There were plenty of places to shoot around town, but Behr preferred this one. Perhaps it was just habit, perhaps because for a few minutes he could feel like a cop again.

Behr walked up and smelled the cordite and solvent in the air, odours that were long trapped in the dirt and the cinder-block walls that formed a corridor running towards the bulldozed earth backstop fifty yards down range. Sitting at a picnic table a short distance away from the firing line was the range officer, a guy he knew, Barry Gustus. In front of Gustus, resting on a newspaper, were a cup of coffee and a disassembled Glock .40 calibre with which he was tinkering.

'Hey, Catcher,' Behr said, crossing to him.

'Well if it isn't . . .' Gustus said, standing and shaking Behr's hand. Cops can be pretty creative when they're solving cases, but they spared their imaginations the workout when it came to nick-names. If a guy had body odour he was going to be called 'Stinko', 'Pig Pen' or, if there was a clever type around, 'Rosie'. Gustus had been on first response at an apartment-building fire a dozen years back. Flames and smoke were leaping out of a fourth-storey window and a father was holding a toddler, both nearly overcome by the smoke. Gustus ran beneath the window, the father took a desperate chance and dropped his child. Gustus caught that kid and instantly became 'Catcher'. He got his choice of posting after that and, gun guy that he was, he picked RO.

'Can I get out there and tear up some paper?' Behr asked.

'Sure, sure,' Gustus said. The look on his face made Behr wonder if the door Pomeroy had opened for him included the range and the captain had put out hushed word that he was OK, or if Gustus merely didn't mind.

'Care to join me?' Behr asked. It was a self-motivated offer. He never failed to learn something shooting next to Catcher. Whether it was stance, sight picture or breathing. The RO was an expert marksman who probably shot fifty thousand rounds a year. He was a master on a PPC course and moved through the stations with a powerful practised economy and lightning speed. His targets could have hardly looked better if he used a hole-punch on them. He was one of the most dangerous men in the city.

'I'm taking a break,' Gustus said. 'My lead level.'

'Where are you at?'

'Forty.'

'Damn,' Behr said. Forty micrograms per decilitre was disturbingly high, especially for a guy who shot outside most of the time. It was the downside of that much practice, breathing in lots of lead. Behr's lead level was probably a five. He could shoot a tight group at twenty-five feet. He was smooth enough changing mags if he ever played around with an automatic, and was almost as fast using speedloaders with his revolver. He could keep them all on the paper at fifty feet, but his pattern was nothing to write home about. Of course he'd never heard of a street shootout being decided at fifty feet. Gustus gave him a nod towards the range.

Behr put on his eye and ear protection and entered the shooting area. He set up in the first station, using the small staple gun in his bag to affix a body silhouette target to a slab of cardboard on a wood stand at twenty-five feet. He unpacked his target ammunition, glanced over at the wall and half smiled at the plastic-laminated pages he saw taped there. They hung in many ranges, locker rooms and briefing rooms he'd been in during his career. They were the 'Rules to a Gunfight' as set forth by the US Marine Corps:

> Always bring a gun to a gunfight.
> Bring more than one.
> Bring all of your friends who have guns.
> Anything worth shooting is worth shooting twice. Ammo
>   is cheap. Life is expensive.
> Bring ammo. The right ammo. Lots of it.

Only hits count. The only thing worse than a miss is a
  slow miss.
In ten years nobody will remember the details of calibre,
  stance or tactics. They will only remember who lived.

They went on and on, slightly comic in tone, but in a way that
didn't undercut the truth therein. A man could do worse than to
follow them. Behr loaded up with wadcutters and settled into his
shooting stance. It was muscle memory, instinct. The pressure
in the ball of his right foot, his left thumb snug against the gun
frame, steadying it. He began slowly, methodically firing in the
space between breaths. The gun bucked in his hand and he was
surrounded by the familiar acrid scent of gunpowder. He popped
open the cylinder and dropped the warm brass into his hand,
deposited it in a coffee can and reloaded.

He continued on, thinking without thinking, firing round after
round, creating a thick cluster of centre-mass hits on the target.
Despite the roar of the weapon, he operated in a place of noiseless
concentration. He didn't think anything could have replaced his
focus on the Aurelio murder, but now he realized that after a string
of bad deals he'd worked in his day the pea shake was among the
worst he'd seen. He changed targets and shot five boxes' worth of
the dirty-burning target ammo, the gun frame now searing hot
and streaked with powder residue. He considered what he had,
and what he had learned from Austin. A family. Was it possible
some family was acting in concert? He resolved to go deeper into
the backgrounds of the owners of the properties that had changed
hands. Maybe there was some connection, a thread that would
lead somewhere else.

Behr's anger rose up again, through the calm the shooting had
provided. Some more of the rules, from way down the list, found
their way into his head:

Do not attend a gunfight with a handgun whose caliber does not start with a '4'. *And its counterpart*: Nothing handheld is a reliable stopper.

Contrary to popular belief, and television and movie depictions, gunshot wounds rarely killed instantly. They didn't always render an adversary unable to pull his trigger and shoot back either. Plenty of law enforcement had died waiting for the bad guy to bleed out and getting fatally shot for their patience.

Behr began the rhythmic sequence of the Mozambique Drill. A double tap, centre mass – the kind of hits that deliver massive neurocirculatory damage and will kill eventually if not immediately – followed by a carefully placed headshot. Specifically right between the eyes. The final shot instantly shuts down the attacker's nervous system. No chance for return fire. The method was also known, for obvious reasons, as 'Body Armour Defeat'.

Behr performed the exercise, dropped his brass, reloaded and repeated. After three go-rounds, he noticed that cops had started arriving on the range. Behr turned and saw them sauntering in, range bags over their shoulders, salty with their youth and the power of belonging. There were half a dozen of them, with more cars rolling in. He wiped down his gun with a silicon chamois and set it aside to cool while he packed up the rest of his stuff.

Gustus appeared next to him and called out, 'Cease fire, guns down,' although Behr had already done so and no one else was shooting. A good RO always stuck to protocol. Gustus went downrange and dragged two racks of steel-plate targets into place at thirty-five feet.

'Man-on-man plate match,' Gustus said to Behr upon his return. Each rack consisted of five heavy steel discs, two painted white on each side of the middle one, which was painted red. It was a speed and accuracy contest with two shooters going head to head, the winner advancing tournament-style until there was a winner.

'I'm outta here,' Behr said.

'You can stay and play if you want,' Gustus offered. 'Most guys use autos, but it's a five-shot course so the revolver will do. You're allowed to reload if you have misses, but you usually can't win if you have to.'

Behr glanced at the cops putting on shooting glasses and ear protection. Several of them were stripping down to tank tops and taking off their duty rigs to replace them with quick-release holsters and paddle-style magazine holders. He didn't really recognize any of them until a new arrival caught his eye. As the officer peeled off his dark blade sunglasses, Behr saw it was Dominic, the prick from Aurelio's Academy. Dominic saw Behr too and they stared at each other for a long, charged moment.

'Sure, Catcher,' Behr said, already feeling like a fool, 'I'll give it a try.'

'All right,' Gustus said loudly when everything had been organized and the shooters had been divided into brackets. 'Fire as fast as you want, as much as you want. Just drop the red plate last and beat the guy next to you or you're eliminated. Fifty-buck kicker to the winner.' There were a few yelps of anticipation at the money prize.

Behr stood at the line, set to go. Standing a few positions down the line was his opponent, a large pale kid whose nametag read 'Weltz'.

'Load and make ready,' Gustus called out and Behr felt a surge of adrenalin race through him. Weltz racked the slide on his service auto and kept the muzzle pointed downrange. Behr made his preparations as well. In the ensuing pause he felt his heart pound and moisture leap to his palms. But this was just a taste of what happened to the heart and the senses if a weapon needed to be used in a tactical situation. The physical and psychological changes were many. Hearing can shut down. Time slows. The urge to spray and pray sets in, and fine motor skills disappear as ancient fight-or-flight reflexes rush to the surface. Near and peripheral vision can deteriorate and, worse, the eyes tend to fix on the target. This is a problem because the human eye can only focus on one plane at a time, which meant that if the target was sharp the front sight would be blurry, leaving the shooter little chance of hitting said target. *The only consolation was that the other guy was probably going through it all too*, Behr thought, *and you hope he hasn't trained as much or as well as you have.*

'Come on, Weltz, you got him,' Behr heard from over his shoulder. 'Watch out if you win, this guy's *sensitive*.' It was Dominic, making him feel nice and welcome.

'Commence fire,' shouted Gustus.

Behr raised the Bulldog and pulled the trigger. The first plate went down. When shooting for speed, rhythm was the key. Behr strived for tempo over rapidity, and the second plate went down. He heard staccato fire next to him as Weltz banged away. If all the shots were hits it would be over, so Behr assumed there were some misses thrown in. Behr broke his pattern as he skipped the middle red plate, but tried to regain the timing and took the next two in succession. He made a loop with his gun that felt exaggerated but was actually very small, as he moved for the centre red plate and fired, emptying his gun and dropping it. Silence fell as both of them were done. Behr looked over and saw all of Weltz's plates were down.

'Behr!' he heard Gustus yell from behind them. A groan went up among the cops. Behr dumped his brass and stepped back off the line.

'Fucking thing's firing low,' Weltz muttered of his weapon. 'Put two into the rail.'

Gustus pulled two cords attached to the target racks and the steel plates popped back up. The next pair of shooters took their places.

It continued that way for half an hour, everyone getting his turn, shooters moving on, others getting eliminated. No one talked to Behr as he kept winning. The second guy he flat-out beat. The third had a misfire and had to work his slide to chamber a new round, and by then it was over. Dominic was winning too. The kid was good. His tempo sounded like a Japanese drummer's. He hunched forward over his sights, using his weight to keep the muzzle stable, and his aim was sure. Behr had a feeling where it was going, and that was where it went. He and Dominic lined up against each other for the final.

'You want to borrow a real gun?' Dominic asked, sliding shells into the magazine of his Wilson Combat .45. The gun probably cost three grand, almost ten times what Behr's did.

'It's the Indian, not the arrow,' Behr said, arousing some catcalls of mockery, all the while trying not to think about how good he'd feel if he beat him.

Gustus called out the commands, and they made ready and began. By now his adrenalin had levelled and he was in a pocket of solid concentration. It was Behr's best round of the day. He was pretty sure he was ahead when he swung back for the red plate that would end it. Maybe he wanted to win too badly and was pushing too much, but he pulled the trigger while the gun was still on the way up, and the round hit the base of the last plate, perhaps two inches too low to knock it over. His five-shot was empty. He was dumping brass when he heard Dominic finish and looked over to see the cop with his left fist raised in the air.

'Good run, Behr,' Dominic said. 'Hey, Catcher, when do the

seniors shoot? He might feel more comfortable . . . Maybe he and Pomeroy can come down and do teams.'

The other cops laughed. Behr swallowed it, packed his gear, shook Gustus's hand and left.

'See you again,' Gustus said. 'Don't forget to get the lead out.'

Behr stood in the restroom, washing the gunpowder residue from his hands and looking at himself in the mirror. He considered whether the loser's eyes he stared into were the result of the shooting match or a whole lot more. Then he wondered why Dominic had gone and mentioned Pomeroy.

THIRTY-TWO

'**TIME TO OPEN** for business. This is not a drill.' That was what Dad had said. Their latest pieces of work had done what they were supposed to, and houses were shuttered or shutting down all over town. Now it was time for them to start earning as their test case had proved they could. Dean was to meet Knute near one of the first Latin houses they'd taken, where they were going to oversee a Spanish kid starting up and working a new shake. But Dean was running late. In fact he was doing something stupid and pathetic. The stupid part was that he was sitting in his car drinking; the pathetic part was where he was, in front of *her* building. Her old building, anyway, the last place he'd seen her. She was gone now. Gone somewhere, into the wind. He didn't know if he just wanted to see her old door, or was hoping she would swing by for something she forgot . . . Shit, he didn't know what he was doing. He just knew he missed her and needed to talk to her. He needed that bad. She just *understood*. He tasted the whiskey again. He'd told himself he wasn't going to finish the pint that afternoon, after lunch, when he'd opened this, his second of the day, but now he knew he was going to. He had fifteen, twenty more minutes to wait there before Knute would be good and pissed and everyone started calling him on his cell. He settled in and drank. Maybe he'd get lucky . . .

He was out there, that sonofagun. Setting out in his car. Just setting out there – not in the parking lot like he used to do, but across the street where he could still see real good. He was out there like some kind of stalker. Ezra Blanchard let his curtains fall shut and walked back and forth around his living room. It wasn't a trip that took long, cramped as it was, between the sofa, his car magazines and the hubcaps he'd been collecting for the last little while. He wasn't sure if he'd sell them or keep them. If he shined them up, maybe rechromed them, they'd look pretty sharp hanging up in three rows of six. He didn't bother picking up junk. He had wheels for an old Stingray Corvette, a Duster and an Olds 442 in the collection. But here he was, like a prisoner in his own place, because he had no interest in talking to that boy out across the way. He oughta call the cops, was what Ezra thought. No, he thought, not the cops. He oughta call his nephew Andre to come over and open a big, tall can of whup-ass on that white boy. But Andre was over in Iraq. No, he had another idea: *where'd he put that card . . . ?*

Behr was sitting at his kitchen table running a barrel mop soaked in Hoppe's No. 9 up and down the spout and through each of the cylinders of his gun. The smell of the solvent was both caustic and sweet, and it put him in mind of responsibility. Every time he shot, he cleaned his gun immediately. It was a habit, like breathing. A dirty gun was one you couldn't count on, one that could fail you. After he'd removed the fouling, he started running a patch puller through the barrel, until the patches came out bright and white. When he finished, he wiped down the frame and handle and, done with the target ammo, filled the gun with the Silvertip hollow points. Then his phone rang.

Behr drove fast cross-town. After some muttered introductions and 'sorry to bother you' stuff, Blanchard, the building manager, had told him that the boyfriend was back. 'The same asshole used to come 'round dating Flavia,' he said.

'The one who knocked you around?' Behr asked.

'The same.'

'Did you call that cop who came out last time? That lieutenant?' Behr asked him.

'Nah, I just felt like calling you, so that's what I did.'

'OK. Stay inside, I'll be there soon.'

Behr didn't know exactly why he felt so motivated to help the old man. Maybe it was the fact that the man had received that beat-down at the hands of the boyfriend. That just didn't sit right with Behr. He rolled up at the building a short time later, pulling right into the parking lot. After a moment, the door to Ezra's unit opened and he came out. Behr stood up out of his car, looking around for the guy.

'Hey, Mr Behr—'

'Hi, Ezra, where is he?'

'He's right over there.' Ezra pointed, and Behr turned to look just as a Dodge Magnum pulled out across the street, spraying some loose gravel. Somebody running always made him wonder, so Behr jumped into his car and gave chase.

'I'm being followed,' Dean said into his cell phone, feeling his heart going like a trip-hammer under his shirt.

'What do you mean *followed*?' Charlie asked.

'I mean someone's following me,' Dean said again, his voice

rising. He could hear the sounds of the bar in the background, some music, some voices. Things seemed quiet. 'Is Dad there?'

Charlie ignored the question. 'Are you with Knute?'

'Not yet.'

'What the fuck?'

'I was on my way . . .' Dean said, embarrassed, '. . . but I stopped by . . . her place—'

'For Christ sake, Deanie,' Charlie groaned. Then he half covered the phone, and Dean heard him speak to someone else. 'It's Dean. Instead of fucking heading to the fucking shake, he went to that skank's place and now he's being followed.'

'Negro please!' Dean could hear Kenny's voice bleeding through. 'Who's following him, a cop?'

Charlie's voice came through clean. 'Cop?'

'Don't know who the hell he is, but his head's practically poking through the roof of his car like the Flintstones. Is Dad there?' Dean asked again. 'He's behind me, like three cars, riding my ass. I don't know what to do.'

'Bring him here,' Charlie said. 'Bring him here.'

Behr entered the bar, his eyes adjusting to the darkness. He'd picked up the kid a block and a half away from Ezra's building, and it had been an easy tail, weaving in and out of sparse traffic, staying around the speed limit, as they headed out towards Speedway and this bar he'd heard of somewhere before. Behr's eye grazed the name of the place, the Tip-Over Tap Room, as he stopped his car. He thought he'd seen it on a napkin, or a matchbook, or some place. He didn't have time to think it through, as he saw the shaggy-haired kid go in the front door. Behr went right after him, hoping the interview would be as simple as the tail had been.

Behr grew concerned as he got inside and noticed the place was empty and that there was no music playing or any other sound.

He caught movement towards the rear of the place, and then there was a flash as a back door opened and the darkness was cut by a slice of streetlight. He saw the shaggy-headed silhouette of the kid he was chasing exit and the bar returned to darkness. He realized he'd been suckered just as he felt an energy at the edge of his peripheral vision, almost behind him. He turned as the blow whistled in, and he was only able to hunch his shoulders at the last moment. Pain came hot and fast, and the strike skipped up off his upper arm and clipped the back of his ducked head.

Was it the 10-gauge? The disconnected thought raced through Behr's mind as he went down. *Was he going out like Aurelio?* The ground came up fast to meet him, and he hit it and rolled and realized he was still conscious. Then he saw it wasn't a shotgun but a bat that he'd been hit with, and a blond-haired six-foot-plus young guy jacked with muscle was doing the swinging. The guy came around him, crouching low and winding up for another shot as if Behr's head was a Clincher softball. Behr covered up with his arms, sacrificing them, as the bat came in and bit into his elbow, but he managed to wrap his hand around it and use it to pull the guy down towards him. He raised his foot and drove it into an upkick with everything he had behind it. His foot connected low on the guy's jaw. It would have been a clean knockout, had the guy not had the good sense to yank the bat back and start pulling away. But it landed all the same, and Behr saw the guy's head turn and his knees sag.

Behr followed the kick up to his feet and found he was standing. The bat went back for another swing, somewhat unsteadily this time, and Behr flung himself forward, closing the distance, getting inside the range of the weapon. Behr stuffed the shot, wrapping the guy's right arm under his own left, and clipped him in the teeth with a forearm shiver. The guy stumbled back against a chair and would've gone down, but Behr still had the arm clamped under his. Behr chopped up with his left leg in a very ugly, sloppy sweep that nonetheless worked and cut the guy's ankles out from under him. The guy landed on the chair broadside, ribs first, and Behr heard the air go out of him and the clunk of the bat as it hit the floor and rolled away.

Behr leaned down to hit him again, when he felt himself doubled over, his neck caught in a powerful collar and elbow clinch.

Someone else, raced through Behr's brain, but before he could see who it was, or register anything else, a series of knee strikes danced up and pounded his body and face. Behr felt his lip split, but his teeth held, and he was able to turn and get a hold of his attacker's body. Behr sucked his elbows in, blunting any more knees, then managed to lock his hands in a seat-belt grip around his attacker's waist. Shooting his right leg straight out behind the man's feet, Behr fell to the ground and let gravity do its work. The second attacker hit the ground hard, and Behr scrambled immediately for top position. He was dealing with another muscled young guy, a few years shy of the one with the bat. This one had dark, spiky hair and Behr knew right away he had seen him before, training at Francovic's. He tried to keep his mind clear of such distractions as he went for knee on chest, but the younger man tucked to his side and pushed both hands against Behr's knee, shrimping away and sliding free in a perfectly executed elbow escape. The younger man rolled in a backward somersault and came to his feet, and in that moment's pause Behr saw a thing, beyond the prior recognition, that froze him. On a rope chain necklace around the guy's neck hung a Christ the Redeemer.

Aurelio's, echoed in Behr's head.

The younger man turned and flew for the back door. Behr moved to run him down and beat answers out of him, but before he could take a step the batter, who was back on his feet, without the bat now, grabbed him from behind, trying to catch him in a body lock.

Behr turned into it, fighting into an underhook-overhook clinch. They struggled around in a half-circle, each man grunting and looking for an advantage. Behr heard the rear door swing open as the other young man fled, and then the front door opened too. He heard feet, and voices barking guttural expletives, coming at him. Behr swung around and managed to drive the guy he was grappling with to the ground in time to see a fierce-looking man about his age coming at him from the back with a billy club in his hand. Then there was more yelling and the sound of boots on the floor. The cops had arrived.

'Break this shit up' were the first coherent words Behr processed. Three of them, in uniform, had come through the front door and flooded into the place. Behr felt powerful hands yank him back, while a pair of patrolmen went past him and interdicted the fierce-looking man's progress in his direction. The cops wrapped the man up, causing him to thrash and start screaming.

'Get the fuck off me!' the man yelled. 'Sonofabitch comes in here and beats on my kids, I'll gut him.' Behr saw the man's coal-black eyes flash with hate, and realized he'd stumbled into a family affair. The men he'd fought were this guy's sons, and perhaps the guy he'd been following was too. The blond man he'd thrown to the ground regained his feet and glared at Behr as the third cop, a round, stocky fellow sporting a handlebar moustache and lieutenant's bars, worked his way around to keep them apart.

'That's enough!' the lieutenant yelled. 'Back it the fuck up.'

The patrolmen pushed the one Behr had been fighting and the father into the darkness towards the back of the room, while the lieutenant dragged Behr towards the front.

'Hands on the bar,' he said. Behr knew better than to argue, so he put his hands on the oak and assumed the position.

'Gun, right lower,' Behr said, anticipating the lieutenant's finding it as he was frisked. The cop yanked Behr's pistol out of the holster.

'Gun up front!' the lieutenant shouted to the cops in the back, then to Behr, 'What's up, buddy?'

'I was—'

'I don't want to hear it. Let's see some ID,' he said. 'Slow.' Behr felt naked without his gun. He glanced towards the back of the room and saw that the father and son, both seated and squawking at the cops, weren't exactly getting the same treatment. Behr spat blood on the floor, pulled his driver's licence out of his wallet and let the lieutenant see his shield as he handed them over. 'The pistol permit and PI licence are all in there.'

'Uh-huh. OK,' the lieutenant said, comparing Behr to his driver's licence and glancing at the other documents. 'What happened?'

'What happened? I walked in and got hit by a bat. That guy and another guy jumped me,' Behr said.

'What bat?' the lieutenant asked. Behr pointed off into the darkness. 'What other guy?'

'He went out the back,' Behr said. The place was getting quieter now, the men in the rear reduced to violent-sounding mutterings.

'You're saying you were assaulted. Stay here.' The lieutenant crossed towards the back and spoke to the other cops, but Behr couldn't hear what was being said. After a moment the lieutenant was back. 'They say you started it. You want to press charges, buddy? 'Cause what do I have here, a bar fight?' the lieutenant said.

'Is that what they told you? It was no bar fight,' Behr said, turning from the bar, his eyes finding the lieutenant's nameplate. It read 'Bustamante'.

'Then what was it? Why don't you tell me what you're doing here?' Lieutenant Bustamante demanded. 'I know these guys, they may come on like hard-asses but they're real quiet business owners.' Behr said nothing. 'C'mon, you were on the job, give me something, otherwise I gotta bring you all in,' the lieutenant went on, in a more reasonable tone. 'You working private?'

Behr was tempted to pull him aside, to let him know the circumstances under which he'd come. He even thought about saying he was Pomeroy-sanctioned on the other matter. But something stopped him, and suddenly his eye found what it was: it was that nameplate. Bustamante. The name was familiar to him, and he remembered where he'd seen it: in the pea-shake property searches. A woman with the same last name had recently bought some houses. Coincidence? Or could she be his wife? It wasn't the most common name. Behr felt an uncomfortable sensation in his gut and suddenly needed to get his gun back and get out of there. He tried to measure his breathing before he spoke.

'You know what, why don't we forget about it?' Behr said.

'Yeah?' Bustamante asked, eyeing him.

'Yeah. Misunderstanding, spilt milk,' he said as evenly as he could. 'There won't be a next time, but maybe I come back one day, they'll be a little more friendly, we'll all have a drink.'

'There you go. Now you're thinking. Save me some paperwork and I appreciate it.' Behr put his hand out and Bustamante gingerly placed the gun on to his palm. Behr reholstered it just as gingerly. He peered into the darkness of the bar and felt those hate-black eyes staring back at him as he exited. The adrenalin was leaving him, and a dizzy head and a ringing in his ear took its place. He made his way to his car on unsteady feet and turned for one last look at the place. His eyes found the white light floating over the building. It wasn't the moon he was looking at, but the white illuminated sign over the door to the bar that featured a tilted-martini-glass-toasting-with-a-beer-mug logo. The Tip-Over Tap Room. Then it came to him. Schmidt, the Caro boy, had a pack of matches with the same logo in his room at the Valu-Stay. What was that? He'd picked up the matches some place? Someone had given them to him? Or had he been to the bar? It didn't mean much in itself, a simple book of matches. But Behr's head began to reel, as a long slow tremor of recognition snaked through him.

He was working one case, not two.

THIRTY-THREE

ERRY SCHLEGEL SAT on the weight bench in the back office of Rubber House. They were all crammed in – Knute, Charlie, Dean, Kenny and Larry Bustamante – and between the heat and the adrenalin of what had just passed, the room smelled like bulls.

'The guy's name is Frank Behr,' Bustamante told them. 'He was a cop. His kid died – shot himself with Behr's gun and the guy came apart, boozing and pissing people off until he got run. This was back eight, nine years ago. He's a goddamn hump and a loser now. People don't like him. He drinks down the bar from real cops, if they even let him in the door.'

The boys seemed to jump all over this description, to eat it up, and Terry saw how it boosted their confidence and he didn't like it. He didn't want them getting comfortable. Not now.

'You said "hump", but not a fuck-up or an idiot,' Terry said.

'No. Well, he might've been kind of a fuck-up—'

'Or maybe people are a little afraid of him 'cause he's got nothing to fucking lose.'

238

'Maybe.' Bustamante shrugged.

Now silence, concerned and edgy, fell over the room. It was what Terry wanted, because concern made people careful.

How the hell could Larry and Vicky even be related? he wondered of his brother-in-law, who was the furthest thing from careful. The dark, swarthy guy was all short and bulbous, while Vicky was blonde and still lanky and had been truly lithe when she was young. He'd never seen a brother and sister like them. Vicky said they had the same feet and the same space between the nose and lip, but the hell if Terry could see it.

'The question is, how did he end up here?' Terry asked the room.

'We told you.' Charlie spoke for the boys. 'Dean was at the girl's old place, the guy showed up and followed him here—'

The literal thinking was only going to get them so far. They needed to get philosophical. 'I know that. I mean how did he end up *here*? Why's he in it?' Terry said. Now Charlie shrugged.

'Maybe Larry can find something out?' Knute suggested.

'You sure that's a good idea?' Bustamante said, sounding as weak as a politician.

'Yeah, I'm sure it's a good fucking idea,' Terry barked.

'Maybe you should cool out for a minute. I mean if Dean hadn't given me a call, this thing could've turned into a real mess.'

'Fuckin'-A it would've,' Terry said. 'We'd be mopping out the front now, instead of sitting here.'

'No, I mean a real mess. The guy was packing—'

'Find something out, Larry. And you,' Terry turned to Dean, 'stay the hell away from the damn girl.'

'I don't even know where she is—'

'Stop looking!' Terry yelled. 'If you'd have been focused on business, we wouldn't have this problem. We gotta get these shakes open now, start some money flowing. You got your people in place?' Terry asked Knute.

He nodded. 'Most of 'em. The rest are getting in place.'

'Good. We've come too far, done too much work to let anything fuck us up.'

'So what do we do about this asshole Behr?' Kenny asked.

'Steer clear,' Terry said, 'for now. If he shows his face again, we do him up like Lyman Bostock.' There was a moment's quiet agreement. Even Kenny, the youngest, had heard the story, though it had happened more than a decade before he was born, of the professional baseball player from Gary who got blasted in the head by some psycho with a .410.

Terry stood. 'Call Pam back in. Let's reopen the place, keep up appearances. Besides, I need a drink.'

They stood and the meet broke. Bustamante exited first, followed by the boys. Knute hung back and looked to Terry, who spoke quietly. 'You're gonna have to get me back in touch with the guys from Chicago,' he said.

Knute just nodded.

THIRTY-FOUR

H E HAD SEEN the monster in that man's pig-iron-black eyes. He'd seen it and he couldn't un-see it, and the man was now in his path and Behr would have to deal with that. Behr pounded on Ezra's door, and when it swung open he nearly staggered inside. His car was parked cock-eyed, still running, in the lot out front.

'You all right, Mr Behr?' Ezra asked, after taking one look at him.

'I didn't catch the guy,' Behr said, and then sought a place to sit down. Ezra helped him to the plaid sofa, pushing away a pile of newspapers, and Behr told him what had happened.

'You need some Anacin?' Ezra asked.

Behr nodded and the older man went off into a kitchenette and returned with the pills and water, and a can of frozen orange juice concentrate, which Behr pressed against the base of his skull. He swallowed down the pills and used some water on his fingers to clear the blood from his mouth. Then he turned to Ezra. 'I won't be coming back here again. I've got to leave you out of this. But I need to know . . . that cop, the lieutenant who came by when you were assaulted. What'd he look like?'

'Well,' Ezra said, scratching his chin, 'he was a white guy. Medium height. Forties. Moustache.'

'Ezra, you just described three-quarters of the cops in America.'

'It wasn't a moustache like yours. It was longer, black, like one of them cowboy ones.'

'A handlebar?'

'Yeah, that's it.'

'Was he stocky?'

'A bit, yeah.'

'Was his name Bustamante?'

'Could've been.'

'Did another cop call him anything?'

'Just "Lieutenant".'

Things were colliding in Behr's head and he struggled to keep them straight. When Ezra called, he'd come to follow up on someone only tangentially related to Aurelio's world, and he'd followed it up, and he'd found a connection, albeit tenuous, he thought, to the pea-shake case, and he'd nearly had his head taken off for his trouble.

'You heard from Flavia Inez lately?' Behr asked. Ezra just shook his head. 'Let me ask you something else,' Behr said. 'When she left, how'd she get her stuff out of here? Who helped her?'

'A couple of guys.'

'Movers?'

'Not real movers. Some young guys.'

'Big kids? High school age?' Behr asked, getting an idea.

'Could've been. Since I got old, I can't tell age too good. But they weren't professionals.'

'How are you sure?'

'They didn't have the matching T-shirts, or a moving truck. Just one of them little jobs from U-Haul. They made two trips.'

Behr leaned back on the couch, processing, and switched the can of frozen juice from his head to his bruised and swollen elbow. He felt like he was back in high school algebra solving a formula and he'd just been given the value of X.

Behr pushed himself to his feet and turned to Ezra. 'If that guy comes back, you call me and not the cops. You can't reach me, you call the Statees. And you be sure to stay inside.'

'Damn straight,' Ezra said, his eyes serious and afraid as he nodded. 'I ain't gonna end up floating down by the railroad tracks.'

Behr just looked at Ezra and nodded, remembering the first time the man had spoken those words, and how they hadn't meant much to him then.

Night had come down at the end of a long day and Terry Cottrell had gotten himself cleaned up and ready to go out and meet some boys down at Brandy's Show Lounge. He was good and ready to see some fine women do their thing and hear what was happening out in the real world. He'd driven out and had pulled through the gate, stopped, wrapped the chain around the gatepost and just locked it all up when he saw a pair of headlights bouncing along the long dirt entranceway towards South County Municipal Landfill.

What the hell? he thought. *Gonna have to tell 'em there's no dumping after dark.* Cottrell squinted at the coming vehicle, trying to read its make in the black night.

There was no other traffic at this time of night, but as he reached the fence circling the dumping area Behr saw an old Camaro, its lights on, parked just outside of the fence. Terry Cottrell was behind it, in the midst of padlocking the gates for the night when he rolled up, almost bumper to bumper with the other car. When it came to information gathering, Behr found he did better staying friendly with people who knew things, doing favours when he could, and just asking. And when he found someone who knew something and asking didn't work, he'd start demanding. It wasn't something he'd had to do to a friend lately, but this was where he found himself and so be it. When he'd finished with the lock, Cottrell came around the front of his car and they stood across from each other in the bright glare of the headlights and Behr saw right away that he was not a welcome visitor.

'This time I talk, you listen and nod,' Behr said.

'You got me boxed in here,' Cottrell said, seeing his position between the car and the locked gate.

'Won't be long. Someone's been making a run on the pea-shake game city-wide. You knew it when I was here last and it's what you were trying to tell me with that Trafficante bullshit.'

A nod. Cottrell knew a guy who knew a dude, Marcus, who crushed beats down at a bar that was in the middle of all the shit. This was a good dude, too. Not hard, but smooth. Cottrell had met him a few times and could see Marcus had a talent for navigating social situations. There wasn't nobody he couldn't get on with, but even he was rattled and looking to scatter. Word was, he was waiting for the right time to get his gear out of the bar and drift away.

'It's a family.'

Another nod. Cottrell didn't know why he was confirming shit for him, but he couldn't seem to help himself. He just wanted Behr gone.

'From up Speedway. A bunch of brothers and a father, and maybe an uncle or some other partner.'

A third nod.

'The Schlegels.'

Cottrell didn't move. Now they were getting into some ground that was dangerous for *him*, and he wasn't about to give up this kind of information. But his eyes must have confirmed it, for Behr continued.

'They're killing anyone who gets in their way. No one's talking to the cops, because the Schlegels have the cops.'

This time Cottrell made sure his eyes remained still and cold. There was nothing more he should tell Behr, and nothing more Behr had the right to ask, but Behr couldn't seem to stop himself. 'Did they take out those PIs? You hear anything about that?' he asked.

'Man, if they told anyone about it, how the fuck would it be me?' Cottrell said. Since his silence wouldn't put Behr off, he hoped maybe some angry words would. In all the years he'd known Frank Behr, the guy had never come on all hard-core John Law like this, except that first time when Behr had busted him long ago. But it was like a flashback to that time now. Cottrell felt Behr there with his demand for truth, an immovable object in his path.

'Goddamn it, man, gimme something,' Behr breathed, sick with himself. He knew his actions were crossing someone off a very short list in Cottrell, and he regretted it, but Cottrell's claim rang like bullshit to him.

'Or what, you gonna put a beat-down on me?' Cottrell spat back. He turned to get to his car, but Behr stepped in his way.

'Is it just the cops? What else is there?' he demanded.

'Fuck you, coming down here asking, get out my grill—'

'No.'

Only the car engines sounded between them for a moment. It sounded like Cottrell's engine was missing every few seconds. They glared into each other's eyes.

'A'ight,' Cottrell finally said. 'I give you this, you keep it, or else a good dude gets his ass greenlit . . .' Cottrell flashed on Marcus, full of holes, dumped in a ditch somewhere.

Behr just nodded.

'Way I hear it is they got help from up north.'

'Chicago or Detroit?'

'Don't know, but peep's saying they brought in some outta-state boys.'

That was it. Behr had it, and had been right about pushing for it, but still he felt ashamed and put a hand on Cottrell's shoulder. Cottrell knocked it off.

'Next time we meet, we talk about the Colts or movies or whatever, and that's it,' Behr said.

'Hope it ain't soon,' Cottrell responded. Behr understood. The whole thing had rattled his friend, and Cottrell was not someone who rattled easy, and he sure as hell didn't like it. The night was still for a moment, the only movement the night bugs scrambling between the headlights. Finally Behr turned and moved back towards his car.

'You watch that dome of yours,' Cottrell said quietly. But Behr was already in his car and backing down the dirt track on his way out.

THIRTY-FIVE

MORNING HAD COME like an executioner's call. Dean, unable to
sleep, had spent a good part of the night sweating and
flopping about in a spinning bed. They'd drunk, the bunch
of them, as if it would change all the bad shit that was swirling
around them, until it was almost light. And maybe it had, for a
minute, but now he had a tub full of Jameson sloshing around
in his gut and his head felt like a thunderstorm. Putting a foot
on the floor hadn't helped at all, and despite the patty melt he'd
scarfed down at the kitchen table in order to soak up the whiskey,
he half felt like he was going to puke out the whole works. He
thought about that last hour they'd all spent the night before.
They'd doused their concerns for a moment and decided they felt
strong. Dad always made them feel that way, especially when he
leaned in and whispered that nothing had changed, they were still
on track, and Uncle Larry could keep shit locked down on his end.
They'd kicked everyone out of the bar at closing time and played
poker and kept on drinking. And when they'd gotten home they'd
made so much noise, the four of them, that Mom had come out of

247

the bedroom. At first she'd been pissed they'd woken her, but then Dad had started singing 'Dixie Chicken' and dancing her around the kitchen until she'd begun laughing. Finally, she'd pulled out the frying pan and had started to cook, and they told stories and ate until they all went to pass out. It was like old times when they were kids, but with whiskey, and for a while their troubles seemed far away.

Now Dean rose and staggered through the silent house to the kitchen, where he drank from the tap and belched and drank some more. The water momentarily diluted the poison inside him and he wiped a layer of clammy sweat from his face with a dishtowel. Then he turned and saw the greasy frying pan, and the plates scattered across the table, dirty with chunks of meat and sodden bread and smeared with ketchup. He went to the front door, for some fresh air and the morning paper.

'BODIES FOUND IN NEAR NORTHSIDE HOUSE ID'D AS FATHER AND SON' screamed the *Star*'s headline. It was the address of the last pea shake they'd taken down. Dean's stomach elevator-dropped. He was awash in dread as he read the account of the discovery of the dead boy. *A child.* It rang in Dean's head. His hands began to shake and his blood turned to ice. A low moan escaped his belly as the enormity of what they'd done settled on him. *He'd killed a kid.* Then, from an even deeper place, came a spasm, and a roiling wave of vomit splattered down on the front step from where he'd just picked up the paper.

THIRTY-SIX

HE STOOD ALONG *the riverbank and listened to the black water rush by below his feet. The better part of a bottle of Maker's Mark rolled to its own current within him. His life was over – at least life as he knew it – killed by a pain he could not even estimate. He reached to his belt and felt the gun there, hard and unyielding. Its existence mocked him. He gripped its cold handle and lightly touched the trigger, where that precious small finger had somehow found its way. With a brusque fury he yanked the gun free and hurled it into the night with a force that tore things deep in his shoulder. He couldn't hear the splash for the howl that erupted from within him.*

Darkness lifted like smoke from the water as Behr came back to the present. He had trudged along the muddy bank of the White River for several miles, scanning the shallows with his light, which he now clicked off as dawn had arrived. He hadn't been this close to the White in years, since that night when it was finally all over for his boy and he'd driven out to fling the 9mm Tim had died by into its waters. Behr had never wanted to see that weapon again, same as the face that stared back at him when he looked in the mirror. He did his best to shake off the memory and continued on.

Wherever there is money, there is violence. It was a truth. In business the violence is in the boardroom, in illegal business the violence is in the street. Despite the fact that he was hard tired and the left side of his head felt like it had a railroad spike lodged in it, Behr knew he had a long night ahead of him. After leaving Cottrell, he went home and worked quickly. He needed a piece of information and some supplies. The information didn't take him long to obtain now that he knew what he was looking for.

He found it in the state marriage licence database, and was able to back it up with an old announcement in a local news archive, and then tax and school records. Bustamante, Victoria and Bustamante, Lawrence, the police lieutenant, were not married, they were brother and sister. Twenty-three years earlier Victoria had married Terrence Schlegel in a ceremony at Garden of Gethsemane Church in Speedway. They had three sons, Charles, Dean and Kenneth, twenty-two, twenty and eighteen years of age, who had attended area schools. Terry Schlegel, the father, was listed by the Alcoholic Beverage Commission as the permittee of the Tip-Over Tap Room. Behr selected 'Print' and jotted further notes while the machine whirred to life. Then he'd begun putting together the supplies he needed – a map, flashlight, boots and a Thermos bottle full of coffee. The threat that the man he now knew was Dean Schlegel had made to Ezra was not idle, or abstract, Behr believed. He marked the map with a highlighter, starting at the southernmost likely point in the area, where railroad tracks touched or intersected the White River. He steeled himself and drove out to the first spot, an area near West Troy Avenue that was fairly industrial in character, and then he started in.

The night air had been chill next to the river, and his boots and pants quickly became soaked up to the knees, yet he'd warmed as he alternately walked the tracks and the bank. He was aware of how easily he could miss what he was looking for. He could walk right by it. He could be looking in all the wrong places. His instincts and his source could be wrong altogether. Still, he carried on until he felt satisfied that the first spot held nothing. He hiked back to his car and drove on to the next location, a place where the tracks ran next to Waterway. He covered both sides of the river and found nothing but loose refuse, a cache of beer and soda bottles, and rusted car parts. Next he parked on South West Street between Raymond and Morris, where he slid down a steep gravel and dirt pitch next to a railroad bridge that crossed over the water.

The mud along the bank sucked at his hopes as it did his feet, but he kept on. He kept on although all he found was an array of trash and detritus similar to that littering the other spots. Then, when he was nearly through with the area, he stumbled across the carcass of a large dead dog. The hindquarters of the animal lay in the water, a weak current lapping against it until the dark fur had grown matted and wet. The dog's one visible eye had gone green and opaque in death and was turning gelatinous. Behr looked it over, checking for tracks that would indicate from which direction it had come. He couldn't spot any sign, but finding the body buoyed him to continue.

He decided, though it seemed a bit unlikely due to its proximity to the city, to move on and try a spot in the shadows of the White River Parkway Drive, near the Chevy plant, continuing on his south-to-north route. When he parked he saw that despite being only several minutes' drive from downtown, there was a certain abandoned quality to the area, perhaps due to the hour, which made a dump possible. He had gone over a quarter mile from the tracks and had neared a sloppy, marshy area along the bank when he stopped. He saw the cluster of dark green plastic contractor bags in the distance ahead of him. He wouldn't have thought much of it except for the way they were all stacked together. They couldn't have landed that way if they'd been thrown from a passing train. The location represented a lot of effort for some illegal dumping. The bags were all neatly cinched with large plastic twist ties. Behr walked slowly across the expanse towards the bags, dread rising within him. The water here was dank and fetid. He became acutely aware of the slurping sound the mud made under his feet.

He circled to the far side of the pile, carefully avoiding some footprints in the soft, wet ground, then paused and looked around. He peeled a blade free from his Leatherman tool, reached for the nearest bag and sliced into the top. A thick wave of black flies rose up into his face as the bag gaped open and the smell hit him. He waved away the insects and saw the white of sawn-off bone, encased by pale, deteriorating flesh. The bag contained a pair of lower legs, the feet still shod in dress socks and black wingtips. He was pretty sure he'd found Bigby and Schmidt.

'Get Pomeroy on the line,' Behr said. He leaned against the quarter panel of his car talking to Karl Potempa at the Caro Group on his cell phone. He'd dialled as soon as his hands had stopped trembling.

'Who would that be?' Potempa intoned in his smooth voice, for which Behr wasn't in the mood.

'Don't fuck with me, get Captain Pomeroy.'

There was a brief hold during which Behr watched the sickly slate green of the White River burble by.

'Yeah?' Pomeroy's voice came on, trying to hide his concern under a mask of irritation.

'We're all on,' Potempa said, 'and the line is secure.'

'Off West Washington and White River, on the southwest bank of the river.'

'That spit of land below Chevy?' Potempa asked. Behr could hear a pen scratching against paper.

'That's right. Where it gets marshy. Against the hill below the track bed, that's where you'll find your A team. There are four trash bags—'

'Oh crap—' Potempa croaked, his voice gone rough.

'Jesus Christ—' Pomeroy added.

'Yeah, all of it.'

'What's their . . . condition?' Potempa wondered, grasping for control.

'Their condition is all damn done. Chopped up and bagged. Feet, hands, heads. I didn't dig around much, I didn't want to disturb the scene, but it looks like they were bled and quartered somewhere else. Thanks for this, by the way,' Behr said.

'Have you developed any information on whom—' Pomeroy started in.

'Whoa,' Behr said. 'You asked me to find 'em. They're found. An ex-Treasury and a fifteen-year Philly PD, like they just ran into Bill the Butcher. You wanna know "who", that's a different deal and I pass.'

There was a long beat of silence, then an audible sigh. 'All right. West Wash and White River.'

'Yeah,' Behr said, 'bring your galoshes,' and he hung up on them.

Behr retired to a vantage point near the Chevy plant grounds where the tracks split and he was able to park and watch the personnel arrive, sirens wailing in the distance. Uniforms and plainclothes, Violent Crime, Crime Scene and Coroner, they all descended on the site. Pomeroy, other brass and some blue suits that must've been Caro boys arrived too. They all executed their tasks with the diligence and instinct of worker ants.

Then a navy blue Cadillac STS rolled up and Potempa picked his way across the mud over to the hub of the activity, where he shook hands with Pomeroy before taking a look. When he caught a glimpse inside the bags he sagged back and Pomeroy caught him by the elbow to keep him upright.

When it was finally close to done, when the body parts had been packed up and Potempa had been seen back to his car by a uniform and had driven away, Pomeroy broke off from the rest and made his way along the tracks towards where Behr waited. The captain scrambled up the loose gravel lining the railway bed and was breathing quickly by the time he made it to Behr. Behr could see by his shoes that Pomeroy hadn't realized he was serious about the galoshes.

'There was a castable footprint down there. I'm assuming your crew saw it.'

Pomeroy breathed and nodded. 'Listen,' he started, breathed again, swallowed, and then continued, 'you can't be done with this.'

What he'd found had Behr thinking it was time for him to leave it alone. 'You or the Caro boys should do it yourselves.'

'Just tell me what you have.'

Behr broke it all down for him, winding his way through what had previously seemed random. When Behr got to the part about the Schlegels and the connection to Lieutenant Bustamante he expected disgust, or at least surprise, from Pomeroy. Instead all he got was a dull nod. 'So you might want to have Internal Affairs grab a look at him.'

'They already are,' Pomeroy said.

'You knew?'

Pomeroy didn't speak to the question, but instead asked one. 'You have a next move?'

'This isn't just local shit. Pros from Detroit or Chicago or Cleveland or somewhere are likely involved. There'll be nothing. No way to find 'em. And if I did, what the hell would I do then? You want me to build a case or try and take 'em down? Either way, it's not what I do,' Behr said. He shut his mouth, a little embarrassed at how easy it had all come out.

'It may be pros. *May* be. If it is, you're right. You won't find 'em. But they didn't come down here on their own, and you know it. I want who hired them.'

Behr didn't move. 'I think we know—'

'The linkage. Get me the local linkage,' Pomeroy demanded.

'You want the linkage,' Behr repeated. He was close enough to Pomeroy to see small patches of rosacea on his cheeks below the man's unwavering eyes.

'Get me the linkage.'

THIRTY-SEVEN

BEHR SAT OUTSIDE a Circle K store lacing up a pair of dry shoes he had in the trunk, downing a quart bottle of Gatorade and feeling *handled* when his phone rang. He'd heard old detectives, lifers, espouse a theory that there were no coincidences. That everything on a case was connected and that there wasn't such a thing as separate cases in the first place, that everything, all the cases an investigator looked at his whole career long, was interrelated in one long indecipherable chain that could only be understood at the very end. Behr didn't go in much for the mystical bullshit, but it was easy enough at the moment to see what they meant. Aurelio had been killed, and he'd walked into it, and Dominic had seen him there, and his name had rung a bell so he'd reported it to Pomeroy, who'd seen his opportunity. Maybe Pomeroy had smelled the connection, and had gone outside of the department because he suspected what Behr had now learned about Bustamante – he had a dirty cop tipping and steering and otherwise protecting the Schlegels from the inside. Maybe Pomeroy hadn't had the Schlegels or even Bustamante at all. There was still a lot that wasn't clear to him, especially whether or not he was willing to stick, or whether he should drop it and walk away and live his life, whatever that might amount to.

Behr reached slowly for his still-ringing phone. 'Yeah?' he said quietly, without even bothering to check the caller ID.

'Sorry it took so long, Frank,' a voice said.

'Tommy?' It was Tommy Connaughton. 'You got something?' Behr asked.

'I finally got into that Santos account.'

'OK.'

'But the cheques weren't presented at a bank. They were cashed at Check Express, a Western Union-type place.'

'Shit.'

'So I hacked *them*, no charge,' Connaughton said, a smile of pride in his voice.

'Good man. And?'

'Flavia Inez. Or Inez Flavia. I don't know which – it was recorded differently on each transaction. Someone there is worse with the Spanish than me.'

'She's the girlfriend,' Behr said, certain of what he'd suspected at first but had too quickly moved off.

'What?'

'Nothing, go on.'

'Anyway, those two cheques – one for four thousand, the other for seventy-five hundred – she cashed 'em.'

'Thanks, Tommy, send me a bill,' Behr said, hanging up and swinging his feet inside the car. He turned the ignition and started to drive.

It was quarter to eight by the time Behr reached Dannels's house. It wasn't his final destination, but he needed another piece and hoped he wasn't too late. He jumped out of his car, in time to see

Dannels backing a well-kept Bravada out of the driveway, and ran around to the driver's window.

'Oi, mate, you look like an all-night trucker,' Dannels said, his hair still wet from a shower, a conservative striped tie knotted around his thick neck.

'Hey, man, I know you're on your way to work, but did Aurelio come into any money recently?' It was a question Behr should've asked the first time if he'd been thinking straight, but he hadn't been.

Dannels's eyes lit. 'He hadn't come into any. He'd won some.'

'Won it how, fighting?' Behr asked, knowing the answer.

'Nah, he dumped his fight purses into the school. That was his business. This was his fun. He loved the gambling. Lotto and pea shake,' Dannels said. 'Must be a cultural thing. I ran the probabilities for him many times, the odds of winning long term at lottery-style betting – it's piss-poor. But he kept spending thirty, forty, fifty bucks a day on that crap. Then he hit a couple of shakes a few months back, five or ten thousand, I don't remember how much. He was so fucking happy, mate. Acting quite vindicated about his gambling prowess with me.' Dannels smiled despite himself. It was what Behr knew, that the wins jibed with the deposits in the chequebook. And there was something beyond that too. He knew that Aurelio hadn't met Flavia Inez by accident.

THIRTY-EIGHT

THE LIVING ROOM smelled lightly of sandalwood incense. Behr had been sitting on the sofa for a long time. Perhaps three hours had gone by. He'd reviewed his notes a dozen times and had dozed. He had already searched the place top to bottom and sideways. He hadn't found any financial records or journals, calendars, organizers or diaries. Another thing he hadn't found were any haircutting implements. Besides her personal brush, there wasn't a single pair of scissors, a clipper, a comb or cape in the place. But he had discovered $3,800 in cash secreted in an empty jar of cold cream under the bathroom sink, and because of that he knew she'd be back. Eventually. When he had arrived a woman had been steering a baby in a stroller, with another slightly older child in tow, out of the building. The look of gratitude on her face as Behr held the door for her made it plain she wouldn't be asking if he belonged. When he'd reached Flavia's door, after knocking repeatedly and pressing an ear against the door, he'd made fast work of the old and basic Kwikset lock. She hadn't bothered with the deadbolt. When he finished his search he had taken his seat.

His phone buzzed once, and he checked it and saw the incoming call was from Susan. The phone buzzed again when her voicemail hit, but he didn't listen to it. Instead he gazed down at the coffee table, at the pile of cash there next to a scattered handful of Trojan Twists. His stomach ground on itself in hunger, and he considered whether he should help himself to some empanadas he'd found in the kitchen or do something ridiculous like order a pizza, when he heard keys jingling outside the door.

Susan Durant pulled over outside the Broad Ripple location of Women's Choice Clinic and turned off the engine. She sat there staring straight ahead for a long moment, and Lynn, sitting in the passenger seat because someone had to be there to see her home after the procedure, did the same. She had been crying too much, feeling nauseous and with headaches all day. She knew it was probably the hormones, but the realities of the situation weren't helping any. In fact the only time she'd felt halfway decent over the past few weeks was the moment she was drinking her morning cup of coffee – she'd read that one cup a day was OK – or eating pizza or pasta. Literally the moment she was eating it. While she was chewing the crispy crust or shovelling in the noodles and sauce she got a few seconds' relief from the hollowed-out panicky feeling in her stomach. But as soon as she put down the fork and wiped her mouth, the queasy feeling would rush back over her and she'd long to be in her bed in a dark room. It seemed to be getting worse. She'd even thrown up in her mouth at work the other day, for God's sake, and, not wanting anyone to know, had had to swallow the vile stuff down.

'Suze?' Lynn said.

'It wasn't supposed to be like this, Lynn,' she said, not looking at her friend. 'You know what I mean?'

'Yeah, I know.' Lynn nodded. 'It never is. That's what my parents said when I came out. Then I figured out it is what it is, and you've gotta deal with it.'

Susan nodded slowly and thought about Frank, off somewhere chasing down whoever killed his friend, and who knows what else. He was probably only across town, but he felt a world further away than that.

'Well?' Lynn said, patient, her words a gentle prompt. Susan reached for the key in the ignition.

The yellow and white striped tent was doing little to cut the sun's glare, as pit bulls of all sizes, coat colours and quality were being unloaded from trucks and cages. It was the end of the summer Bully B-B-Q. Terry Schlegel rubbed his face and drank his third Diet Pepsi of the morning and thought of the story on the cover of the newspaper. He'd been pushing hard, and he knew taking the little Latino out from spite might've been over the line, but as for some kid getting caught up in it, that wasn't something he'd planned. A group of six or seven bull pups growled, barked and yelped as they tumbled over one another playing grab-ass in some owner's pen. Terry just wasn't in the mood for this. The hangover was gripping him hard, and the pair of corn dogs he'd downed and the sodas weren't helping. The splattering sounds that Dean had produced that morning played in his mind. It had woken him, and the noise of the spraying hose as Dean cleaned off the cement steps hadn't allowed him to go back to sleep. The memory, and the smell of slow-cooking smoked pork rising from a large steel-barrel barbecue pit, were enough to turn his stomach. Then he saw Charlie's Durango pull up and glanced over to see him and Kenny pile out of the SUV. They circled around back and unloaded their pair of tiger-stripe bullies. He felt a surge of pride at the sight of his boys, tall and strong, wrangling those beasts they pretended were dogs. He watched several passers-by greet them. Black dudes,

Latin guys, white girls. His boys were *faces* in this part of town, they had a *name* and were treated with respect, and it made Terry feel good. He kept watching, waiting for Deanie to join them.

There was Charlie, the strong one, and smart, the most like him. Oftentimes Terry wondered what was going on behind the boy's eyes, so cryptic already despite his only being twenty-two years old. Then there was Kenny. The kids considered him the crazy one. And it was true: consequences didn't seem to occur, much less stick, to the boy. Where'd the attitude come from? Maybe it was shades of the young Vicky. The boy was a real wild card. Terry wanted to look upon them all, his three sons, together in the bright sun. But he kept on waiting until finally Charlie and Kenny closed up the car and headed into the day's doings.

Sleeping it off, Terry supposed of Dean. Dean. He was just muddled up right now. He thought too much and got lost because of it. That was what had got him into trouble with the Latin chick. It was a long shot turning out one winner kid these days. When it came to three, the odds just plain sucked. At least one had to be a numbnut, so he was ahead of the game, he figured. He didn't know whether Charlie and Kenny had seen him or not, or whether they were focused on registering the dogs for whatever competitions were being held that day, but one way or another they didn't come over to him.

Just as well, he thought. He wasn't there to see his sons, or the dog show, but to meet. He had a sit scheduled with Campbell Doray. It was a little soon. He'd hoped to get a dozen or more locations up and running and turning a profit, and they'd only done that at a fraction of the places. But they'd sure as hell put a major pinch in the shake business across town, that was for shit sure, and any businessman could see the opportunity to fill that void. So while they hadn't done as much as he'd hoped as far as revenue yet, with all the recent attention it seemed like a good time to get out, to monetize their efforts and to move on. He assumed Doray would be happy to complete the deal now.

But he's late, Terry thought, *more than half an hour*. That was when he saw Larry Bustamante, dressed in civilian clothes, trundling towards him across the parking lot.

Fuck me, Terry thought, *this isn't good*. He could see by the way Bustamante's shirt was fitting, tight around his belly but smooth, with no telltale bulge at the hip, that his brother-in-law wasn't wearing his gun. He didn't have one in an ankle holster either, because the big slob was wearing khaki cargo shorts and those rubber sandals over white tube socks. After a moment, Bustamante spotted him in the bleachers and headed over.

'Vicky tell you I was here?' Terry asked.

Bustamante nodded. 'Who're you meeting?'

Terry couldn't see the harm in telling him. 'Camp Doray.'

'Yeah?' Bustamante asked. He sounded sceptical, like he knew something. 'He still wants to do it, even after all the press and shit?'

Despite the stifling weather, Terry felt gooseflesh rise on his arms at Bustamante's words. It confirmed what he suspected: *Doray wasn't coming*. Terry felt his face clench into a grim mask. *Things had gotten too hot*.

'Yeah, yeah, he's not supposed to get here for a while.' The day's temperature, the pork smell and exhaust and smoke in the air, and the sun-warmed odour of dog shit wafting over him conspired to make Terry queasy. He swallowed down on it hard and forced himself to meet Bustamante's eyes.

'And you? What do you want?' Terry asked. Bustamante fidgeted and looked around but didn't speak. 'Out with it. What's up? I know it's something. It's all over your face.'

'They found the . . . package down by the river.'

Fuck! Terry was sure his heart ceased pumping and his blood stopped flowing for three seconds. *Already? How'd they find it? Who found it for 'em?* He wanted to shout the questions into Bustamante's stupid, fat face. But he sipped air and spoke in what he hoped was a calm voice. 'Well . . . we figured they might, eventually. How come I didn't see it on the news?'

'Just happened. And they're keeping it clamped down. When I heard, I knew you'd want to know,' Bustamante said, and settled into loud nasal breathing.

'Anything else, Lar?'

'I think I . . . I need a lawyer, Terry.'

THIRTY-NINE

'ARE THESE FROM the box at Aurelio Santos's house?' It was Behr's first question to Flavia when she'd entered, closed the door behind her and turned to see him sitting there. He watched her struggle with the impulse to run, think better of it and then walk to a chair across from him, where she sat. There was a slight tremor to her hand as she brushed a lock of hair back behind her ear, but she was doing a fairly impressive job of controlling her nerves considering someone had broken into her apartment. She looked at the Trojan Twist condoms that rested on the coffee table like she'd never seen them, or any other, before in her life.

'No—' she began.

'Don't say "no",' Behr said, 'I don't want to hear it.'

She fell silent and it allowed him to take her in for a moment, her tanned legs, shining under a layer of moisturizer or perhaps their own natural shimmer, spilled out from beneath a brief skirt. She wore a tight tank top that highlighted her toned arms and her breasts. She'd lost a bit of weight since the last time he'd seen her, and it suited her, though he remembered the prior fullness had suited her too. It looked like she'd been missing some sleep because she had slight dark circles under her eyes, which made her appear vulnerable and oddly young. He saw her glance at her $3,800 sitting there in a folded pile next to the condoms.

'Whose money—' she started to ask.

'Come on,' Behr cut her off. 'He put you here, Aurelio did, in this apartment, didn't he?' When she didn't respond he continued. 'Juan Aybar and Max Sanchez moved you in when you split from your old place.'

Something about the details got to her. She looked up at him. He met her gaze and she nodded once.

'Yes, Maxie.' She smiled briefly. 'They were so nice.'

'Come on, time to tell,' he urged.

'I used to see Auri at El Coquí,' she began.

'The restaurant?' Behr had heard of the place, which specialized in Latin-prepared seafood.

'Yes. And I recognized him from the shake house.'

'You're a shake girl,' Behr said, appreciating how much business she must have rung up as hostess at the betting parlours.

'Yes. I served drinks, made conversation, drew the numbers—'

'You got the players to spend more.'

'OK, yes.' She sighed. 'I was working and making nice money for a year, year and a half, but then things changed. There was some kind of fight over the business, and some new owners took over. We were closed for a few days, but when they reopened they kept me on. Things seemed cool, but then I made a big mistake.'

'You stole?'

She shrugged. 'I always took a little, they made so much they never noticed. But it wasn't that. I started seeing one of the bosses.' Behr looked at her, but checked his questions because she was starting to roll. 'He seemed so nice at first. He was the quiet one.

266

He was sweet to me, and handsome. Then things turned to shit and I wanted to leave it, but I couldn't go.'

'Couldn't leave the guy or the shake house?'

'Neither.'

'This was the same guy who put the beat-down on old Ezra,' Behr said. She didn't answer. 'Which one of the Schlegels was it?' he asked. He saw blank fear whiten her face.

'Dean,' she said, in a voice that sounded tiny and far away. 'They put him in charge of the house, and I didn't see the others in the family much for a while, so it wasn't so bad. I had to keep dating Dean a little to keep everything quiet. After another few months I would've had enough to disappear. But then this new asshole with a briefcase, Gary, started coming and checking the books all the time. He was some kind of an accountant, and he wanted to check on how the location was doing. I knew he knew when he started looking at me.'

'Looking at you?'

'He would come out of the back office and just look at me. Not like he wanted to fuck me, but like he knew. It made me cold, like he could count everything I had taken.'

'And then Aurelio started coming in?'

'Yeah, he started coming in. He started asking me out. I really liked him . . .' She paused and looked into Behr's eyes. 'I did, I really did.'

'Uh-huh,' he said, 'go on.'

'Then I found out he was the fighter. Kenny, the youngest brother, used to stay ten feet away from him. He treated Auri like a god, but he was afraid of him. I saw it right away. Even Charlie kept his distance. I figured they couldn't fuck with Auri, he was so tough, so we started dating.'

Behr nodded, starting to understand the exit plan she'd developed for herself.

'He didn't know or he never would have done it,' she said quietly.

'Done what?'

'I rigged him for a win. A big one. When he hit he was so excited. We went out to celebrate, and that's when I told him about the Schlegels and my problem.'

'How'd he react?'

'He was mad. So mad. At first. He wanted to go bust them up. Especially Dean. But I calmed him down . . . and he gave me the money. The way it worked out, I didn't have to skim any more – paying Aurelio on a win was like paying myself, and no one would know it . . . not even him.'

'So you did it again?' Behr said, now asking questions the way an investigator should: basically knowing the answer already.

'Yes.'

'He was in love with you.'

'I think so. He said he was.'

'And you?'

'It was still early.'

'So you were just playing him.'

'No. He was special. We had good times together.'

Behr stared at her, trying his best to read what was going on behind her eyes. They might as well have been the Dead Sea Scrolls for all he could make of them. 'Then what? He moved you here so they couldn't find you?'

'Yes.'

'And what, the Schlegels figured it out, caught up with him and killed him?'

'I don't know,' she said.

'What do you mean you don't know?' Behr shouted, jumping up from the couch and causing her to cower back.

'I don't, I swear it. I wasn't there!' she said.

'What did you think when you found out what happened to him?'

'I was afraid. I thought . . . I knew.' She put her face in her hands. Her shoulders shook. If she was crying, Behr couldn't hear it.

'You're going to be a witness,' Behr stated.

'I can't be a witness,' she said into her palms.

'You can. You'll see.'

'No,' she said, pointing her chin up at him in defiance, her eyes dry.

'Don't go anywhere. I have to go take care of some things. I'll be briefing the police. But I'll be back and I don't want to have to go looking for you. But you know I will, and you know I'll find you.'

She nodded. 'Can't you . . . let me out of it? I'd do anything to stay out of it.'

Behr looked at her. 'Is that right?'

'Yes. I know . . . how to do things . . . Give me a chance.'

Behr took her in, sitting there. He found himself feeling for her. She'd gotten herself all jammed up. She had only herself to blame, but she couldn't have known the kind of animals she was dealing with.

'Like I said, stick around.' This time he said it with less conviction.

She nodded, sadly, and then quietly began to weep. She tried to hold it back, but the tears welled up in those black eyes of hers and spilled down her cheeks. 'If it wasn't for me, Auri wouldn't have gotten hurt.'

Behr felt his throat thicken. They'd both lost Aurelio, they were bonded in that, and he knew how she felt. He had an impulse to reach out for her, to give her some comfort and tell her it would be all right.

He was about to, when he suddenly felt like he was watching

the moment from above the room, and in that instant he saw it for what it was. She was gaming him. She'd laid out the sexual suggestion, and when that hadn't worked, had come over the top with the tears. And dupe that he was, he'd almost gone for it.

'Stick around,' Behr said, his voice cold. 'I'm not your mark.'

She looked up at him, pushed a strand of hair back and wiped a cheek. The tears were done.

'I see that,' she said. Her voice was low and quiet, but colder than his nonetheless.

FORTY

CHARLIE SCHLEGEL DIDN'T give two loose shits about the Bully B-B-Q or whether their dogs took any honours. No, he was here for business, not for fun this time. He and Kenny stood by a table gnawing on the half-dozen corn dogs they'd bought, dropping pieces for their brindles, Mr Blond and Clarence. As always, Kenny couldn't let it go at that. He got down on his knees and started feeding Clarence a corn dog out of his mouth.

'Come on, boy,' Kenny said, 'grrr.' The dog took the meat, lapping saliva all over Kenny's face. But Kenny kept the stick clenched between his teeth, and the dog clamped down on the other end. Then Kenny and Clarence commenced a vicious tug-of-war. 'Let's go, Clarence,' Kenny urged between gritted teeth. The dog's muscles rippled under his shining coat as he hunched his shoulders and pulled.

'Get up, you dipshit,' Charlie said. He didn't listen and Charlie gave Kenny a kick to the ribs. 'Come on, knock it off.' Kenny transferred the stick from his mouth to his hand, then pushed Clarence's nose back until he let up on the stick.

'What, man?' Kenny said.

'The point's gonna hurt his mouth,' Charlie answered.

'Nah. His mouth is like leather.'

'Nah. His mouth is soft.'

'Whatever,' Kenny said, dusting himself off.

'There they are.' Charlie pointed. Coming across the tented area, a measly blue bull pup on a thick leash, were Peanut and Nixie.

Charlie handed the leashes to Kenny and walked towards them, Kenny following. When the two groups came together, the dogs greeted one another with friendly curiosity, sniffing and circling. The men weren't so civil.

'What is that thing, a squirrel on a leash?' Kenny asked, for the moment able to keep the smirk off his face.

'Man, shut the fuck up. That's a pedigree dog,' Peanut said, taking the bait. Nixie's narrowed eyes just went deader than they'd been in the first place.

Kenny shook his head. 'If you bought that, you got took. Hope you used food stamps.'

'What about your mangy-ass mutts?'

'No, these beauties are pure class,' Kenny said. And now the smirk followed. Nixie stepped forward and squared with Kenny, who stuck his chest out and went eye to eye. He also let the leashes drop from his hand and Clarence and Mr Blond took the opportunity to light out across the tent.

Charlie shoved Kenny in the shoulder, breaking the stare-down. 'Get the fucking dogs, would you?' Kenny shook his head and walked off after them.

'You pricks finally ready to do this?' Charlie asked. Peanut nodded and slid a wad of money up from his pants pocket so it was just visible.

A lot of barking and an angry 'Tend your damn dogs!' reached Charlie from the owners' pens. In another few minutes he'd be dealing with a chewed-up dog thanks to Mr Blond or Clarence, or Kenny beating the shit out of some owner or enthusiast.

'Good,' Charlie said. 'Let's put the dogs up and figure a place to meet.'

Knute Bohgen hated being right. And that was the thing of it – he usually was. He thought Terry's pea-shake play sounded nuts when he'd first heard it, but then he thought maybe shit had changed while he was inside and out of step, and had gotten swept up in the ambition, so he went with it. Now they had a nice mess on their laps. Knute lived in the back unit of a two-family house, but he was currently in the front kitchen fixing a peanut butter sandwich. The couple that usually lived in the unit had gone away for the rest of the summer after the Brickyard 400, so Knute had let himself in and had the run of the place. He preferred it to his own, which was an under-furnished rathole, and wondered what he was going to do when the couple got back. He crossed to a recliner that was in front of a 36" flat-screen. He supposed he could get some of his own stuff, but he wasn't particularly flush at the moment – especially after last night. That little pecker Kenny had busted him out in the poker game. Knute thought he'd caught the kid with his hand in the cookie jar raising from the small blind, and went all-in pre-flop with a wired pair of fours, but Kenny called and showed a pair of Kokomos that stood up when no one improved. The rest of them had howled when he lost his three hundred. He would have paid double that to skip the ribbing. He shouldn't have even been playing, drunk and distracted as he was with today's task – booking the Chicago guys as soon as Terry got his ass here.

Knute stopped chewing a few minutes later when he heard tyres on gravel outside. Then came a car horn and he exited out the front door. Terry was there by the side door behind the wheel of his Charger, a scowl knotted on his face.

'Gimme some of that,' Terry said absently as Knute climbed into the passenger seat. Knute tore the remaining half of the peanut butter sandwich in two and handed a piece over.

'I thought you live in back,' Terry said.

'I do.'

'Chalky,' Terry remarked of the sandwich.

'It's all they had,' Knute responded. Terry gave him a quizzical glance but didn't say anything. 'Did you meet Camp?' he wondered, though based on the grimace Terry was sporting, he had a pretty good idea of the answer.

'We've got issues there.'

'You ready to do this thing then?' Knute asked.

Terry nodded. Knute pulled out a pre-paid cell and dialled a number he had memorized. It rang several times. Knute felt Terry's eyes scanning his face, but he kept his gaze forward. Finally, the ringing stopped.

'Who's this?' a dry, granular voice enquired.

'Knute from down south,' Knute said. He could hear the noise of plates and glasses clinking in the background, and the sound of a televised baseball game. 'This Bobby B.?'

'You got me. Indy Newt?'

'Right. What're you doing?'

'Watching the Cubbies. They were in first place, looking like they were gonna get something done post-season, but now . . . The fuck're you doing?'

'Hold on,' Knute said, extending the phone, which Terry took.

'Hey, man,' Terry said, 'we have a complication from that other piece of work.'

'This T?' Brodax asked.

'Yes, it is.' A moment's angry silence passed.

'What kind of fucking problem?' Brodax demanded, his voice

charged and not so low that Knute couldn't hear it bleed out of the phone.

'A clean-up problem.'

Silence reigned on the line.

'Some asshole's been poking around,' Terry went on.

'Law enforcement?' Brodax asked.

'He has that smell.' There was a breath; Terry wasn't happy about what came next. 'He turned up – someone turned up – that . . . package down by the river.'

'And now you want me to make another package,' Brodax volunteered.

'Something like that,' Terry said.

She'd finally managed to stop the darned waterworks. In the end, she hadn't been able to go inside the clinic and do what she'd planned. She got herself together and drove Lynn home, and the smile her friend had given when she'd climbed out of the car made her sure she'd done the right thing. For the moment anyway. But Susan needed to see Frank. Not just to talk to him, but to look into his eyes. They'd been apart too much lately, he on his cases, she with her situation, and whether this break was for good or not, they needed to hash things out. She'd suddenly understood with clarity what was at issue between them. She'd gotten a tiny taste of it outside of that clinic, and it was enough to make her shudder. It should've been pretty obvious considering what he'd had and lost in his life. Deep down she'd known it from the moment she'd told him the news and things had started crumbling between them, but she'd been unable to do anything but take it personally. She had her own baggage, she supposed. Hey, it was only fair. But now a phone call wasn't going to do it, so she headed to his place. If she was going to have his kid, to raise it with him or without him, there was a lot to talk about.

She called on her way, just to see if he was home, and had gotten his voicemail. It didn't dissuade her though. She figured she'd find him there, not answering his phone, or would just wait until he arrived. She hoped it wouldn't be long, but she had her key, so if he truly wasn't home she'd rest until he showed up.

When she reached his place, she glanced towards the parking area in the back and didn't see his car. She parked on the street, grabbed her bag and headed for the door. Her key was in the lock when she felt a creeping sensation and stopped. Her neck felt frozen, unable to turn her head so she could look to confirm what she knew in her bones: someone was watching her. *They're here for Frank*. It echoed in her head. Her car seemed miles away back down on the street, a distance that was suddenly too great to traverse. She squeezed the doorknob, wondering what awaited her on the other side. Still, it was the only choice now. She forced herself to turn the lock and open the door. She swung the door open, entered, closed it behind her and turned the lock.

The place felt empty. But her heart was pounding now and she didn't know if she could trust herself.

'Frank?' she called out. There was no answer. Total stillness. Only the low hum of the refrigerator broke the silence. *Should she call the police?* She tried to imagine what she'd say – that she felt like someone was watching her sort-of-boyfriend's house, send a SWAT team? Maybe she was just panicking. Maybe she was just hormonal. She went down on her knees and peered out the bottom of the front window between the blinds. She could see the fenders of several cars on the street, but nothing else. She sat back against the wall and looked at the locked gun cabinet. She could smash the glass and try to load a shotgun, but it had been fifteen years since she'd fired one – shooting a few clays with her dad – and she didn't know if she could even break the glass, much less find the right ammunition and load a gun. Frank had offered to teach her many times, but she'd always said no. The idea of handling guns was unpleasant and ugly to her, but she wished she had taken him up on it now. There was one thing she needed to do, she realized, before she did anything else: she had to check the place to make sure she was alone.

Convenience stores. It was a silly thing, but they were what Knute loved. And he loved everything about them. The fluorescent lighting, the bad music, the linoleum floors, all the choices – that was freedom to him now. Pepsi, Mountain Dew, slushies, Little Debbie Marshmallow Pies, Twizzlers, BBQ-flavoured Fritos, jerky snacks, fifteen brands of beer and porno mags – all the shit he couldn't get when he was inside, at least not without a major effort and expense, and definitely not on his own timetable. He had to take a hell of a squirt right now courtesy of the Big Gulp he was sucking on. Dr Pepper, ah the good doctor. Together with a bag of Funyuns it was a gourmet junk-food pairing. When they thought about the possibility of going back and doing another stretch, most guys who've been inside can't face the prospect of no women. That was a tough one for sure, but it would be harder still living without the ability to visit a Kwik Mart or 7-Eleven whenever he damn well pleased.

It wasn't really a question anyway. 'Not going back' is what all the cons say in the movies, Knute thought. But 'can't go back' is the truth. He died some in prison in Michigan City, his body just didn't catch on. But if he went back, it surely would. And if he kept on following blindly behind Terry and those dumb-ass dreams of grandeur, that was exactly where he was headed. Back. Cold fucking cement, surrounding him like a coffin. A narrow, opaque slice of window that only hinted at the light of the day. Icy-blooded evil bastards around him on every side. Terry was a bad ass – as bad a man as he'd seen who hadn't been locked down – but Camp Doray not showing had rattled him. Terry tried not to show it, but Knute knew him too well. Now the man was ready to admit what Knute had already figured: it was time to cut losses. He was glad, real glad, when Terry had gotten him to bring the Chicago guys back in the mix. They were expensive, but worth it – especially for this Behr motherfucker. What Knute had learned about him – how he'd managed to run shit down and end up at their door, how he'd scrapped with Kenny and Charlie at the same time and was still walking – well, that told Knute he was serious business. And that was what those Chicago guys were for. Knute knew plenty about hurting and killing, and about the removing when it was all done, but even he had learned volumes watching those guys work.

Now, as long as Terry was footing the bill, Knute was happy for them to come back and make their troubles go away. He half wished they wouldn't stop with Frank Behr but that they'd go on and button up Fat Larry too. Hell, maybe Knute would take care of that himself. Either way he was happy to sit on Behr for the time being, to clock his comings and goings and hand him over when Chicago came to town. Then a car rolled up and a tall blonde with a bouncy ponytail bopped out and caught his attention. He turned down the Scorpions disc that was playing in the car and hit bottom on the Big Gulp as he watched her climb the steps to Behr's unit. He'd already decided that Behr wasn't home by taking a good look around and had settled in to wait, but this was an added bonus. It meant Behr might be coming home soon, maybe for a little afternoon delight – that sure wouldn't be delightful for long.

He watched the tall bitch key her way inside, and all went still again for a few minutes. Then the piss pressure hit him low and hard. He thought about letting it go into the Big Gulp cup but wasn't in the mood to get sprinkled with the end drops, so he eased himself out of the car. He'd just unbuckled and begun when he was pretty sure he heard a door open and close. He was mid-stream when he crouched down a bit and thought he caught the bitch's ponytail dunking over a fence in the back and then disappearing. He tried to force out the rest of it and buckled up as he went for the car door, but he had a feeling he was going to be too late. And he was. When he got around the corner he couldn't find the blonde bitch anywhere.

She heard him before she saw him, his car anyway. The screeching sound of brakes came to her inside the quiet lobby and she looked out to see his car parked roughly by the kerb in a cloud of tyre smoke. Thick, greasy rubber marks tailed off behind the vehicle. When Frank jumped out, dirty and wild-eyed, and crabbed low – as low as he could get, considering his size – his hand against his lower back, gaze cutting about the parking lot in all directions, she felt a warm wave of safety wash over her. She understood many things about her life in that moment. He hit the door, his eyes still intent and vigilant as they swept the bank, and then he saw her. She rushed to him from her position near the bank guard, where she had been waiting restlessly for five or six minutes. They embraced and he leaned back and touched her face: that was when she felt her tears start to come.

She had dropped down beneath the window in his place, her back against the wall, and had just decided to hell with it, she was calling the cops and would deal with the embarrassment later, when her cell phone rang. She'd dug it out and gasped, 'Hello,' and heard Frank's voice.

'I'm ten minutes away,' he'd said, after she'd told him where she was. 'You need to get out of there. Go out the back and meet me at the National City Bank, there's a security guard there.' She'd never heard the kind of urgency he had in his voice.

'Should I call the police?' she'd asked. There was a pause while he weighed it.

'Call 'em, but don't wait for 'em. I'll explain it later. Can you make it?'

'I think so,' she said, thinking of the child she was carrying and suddenly feeling strong. She used the landline and spoke to a 911 dispatcher and said she was being followed.

'Stay on with me until you go for it,' Frank told her. She poked her head up and glanced out the bottom of the window. She thought she saw some movement at the front of a nearby car but didn't want to raise herself up for a proper look. She saw a flash of denim, a man's lower body clad in a pair of jeans. Her heart thundered when she thought he was heading for the building, but he stopped and relaxed into his stance and she saw he was relieving himself behind his car.

'I'm going,' she said, and headed for the rear door.

She'd made it. She ran the whole way, six long blocks, after climbing a low fence at the back of the building. She didn't look back a single time to see if she'd been spotted or if she was being followed. She didn't think she could possibly have run any faster no matter what was behind her. It was like a tight race in the pool: looking was only going to slow down your touch.

The worry he saw on her face made him feel sick for a moment and then a hot bolt of anger shot through him. He knew he wasn't walking away from anything now.

'Suze,' he said, 'are you all right?'

She nodded, mute, tears spilling down her cheeks. Behr pulled her close again and met eyes with the guard across the lobby, a middle-aged black man, who turned away.

'Is everything OK . . . with this?' he asked, touching her belly. She nodded again, placing her hand over his.

'What's going on, Frank? What's happening?' she asked.

'The guy – was he around my age, big?' he asked.

'No.'

'Young, early twenties, muscled up—'

'No. He was on the small side. Late thirties. I couldn't see too well, but I think he had some kind of scar on the side of his face.'

Behr gritted his teeth. He had an idea who she was talking about.

'Why didn't you want me to wait for the police?' she asked.

'Too long to tell right now.' That was when Neil Ratay pulled up outside. Behr had called him as soon as Susan had hung up with him. From the looks of things Ratay must have run to his car and lead-footed it over.

'Frank?' Susan asked, as he led her out of the bank towards Ratay's car.

'I need to put you somewhere safe and I can't watch you right now. I figured you'd be happy to spend time with him.' Behr's eyes searched the parking lot while they crossed to the reporter, who had gotten out of his car and waited for them.

'Neil,' Behr said.

'Frank,' the reporter answered. His eyes held questions but he didn't ask them.

'Thanks for coming,' Behr said.

By now Susan had calmed a bit. 'Hi Neil, sorry about this,' she began, but he waved her words away with a cigarette he'd just lit.

'So I'll work from home today, no big thing,' he said.

Behr gave him a nod. 'There shouldn't be much danger. It's just a precaution because she walked into it. Even if they know who she is, he didn't follow her here. Just stay off the street for a while.' Behr's mouth shut. He looked at Susan. He couldn't speak what he wanted to, not with the thoughts swirling in his head – thoughts of causes, violence, results and revenge, of *linkage*.

'How long?' Neil wondered.

'Not long,' Behr said. He put his hand on Susan's back and steered her towards Ratay's car.

'What about you?' Susan asked, her voice steady now.

'I'll be fine,' he said.

'Frank—' she started.

'Neil, would you mind?' Behr said, gesturing at the cigarette and then to Susan as Ratay moved to get in his car.

'Sure,' he answered. Ratay paused for a moment. 'Oh . . .' A half-smile of knowing came to his lips as he flicked away the cigarette.

FORTY-ONE

I T WAS FINALLY payday. 'Bout fucking time. After all the work: lugging the equipment, installing the lamps, tending the plants, making the connections. Yeah, it was about fucking time. Charlie Schlegel stood in an alley off Lambert Street with Kenny, waiting for Peanut and Nixie to show. He had the shit in the back of his Durango and they were leaning against it when Peanut's Neon came around the corner. He pulled up close, and he and Nixie got out of the car.

''Supps?' were exchanged and Peanut handed over a thick envelope of money before Charlie passed an old nylon gym bag containing the weed and oxy. It should've been that easy.

'Count it, bro,' Kenny said, evoking noises of displeasure from Peanut and Nixie.

'Man, it's all there,' Peanut said.

'I know it is, 'cause if it's not, I'm gonna take a reciprocating saw to that piece-of-shit ride you're so proud of,' Charlie said, jutting a thumb over Peanut's shoulder towards the Neon. Kenny smiled; the other two did not.

'Lemme know when you need more,' Charlie said.

'Uh-huh,' Peanut answered, turning back for his car.

'Yeah,' Kenny said, 'don't smoke it all in one place. We know how you folks get.'

Peanut stopped and turned.

'Yo, what fucking "folks"?'

'Dirty African folks,' Kenny said, smiling and squaring with Peanut. Charlie tucked the money into his pocket and smirked.

Peanut shook his head, looked down, then swung his right hand, open-palmed, and bitch-slapped Kenny hard across the face. Everything froze for a moment, as if none of them could believe it had happened. Then Kenny, eyes full of rage, lunged forward, dropped his level and laced an arm under Peanut's and around his back. Kenny pivoted and flipped him to the concrete. Peanut landed on his shoulder and the side of his face with a slapping sound that forced the air out of him. Kenny dropped a knee on Peanut's chest and began punching.

Charlie shook off the momentary surprise and stepped forward towards the action and right into the point of Nixie Buncher's Piranha automatic knife. Charlie staggered back, swatting ineffectively at the blade, which landed two more times. Liver-stuck, Charlie sat back and landed heavily on the sidewalk. Kenny looked up and met eyes with Nixie. The knife, slippery with blood, hit the pavement with a clink. Kenny jumped to his feet and went to his brother, who was slowly reclining back on to the ground. A groan of air escaped him.

'Chick,' Kenny said, coming close and seeing the massive amount of blood spilling out through his brother's hands. 'You motherfucker!' Kenny screamed, yanking the Smith & Wesson out of Charlie's belt. Nixie had already started sprinting and was halfway down the block by the time Kenny was done fighting with the safety. Peanut had struggled to his feet as well and was making a run for it, weaving unsteadily away, when Kenny fired half a dozen times and lit him up. Hit all over the back and legs, Peanut tumbled forward on to the ground, his cheek pressed against a crack in the cement. Kenny stood and put two more rounds into Peanut's upper back, ending him.

'Cocksucker,' Kenny said, kneeling back down, cradling Charlie's head. His brother sputtered but couldn't seem to talk. 'Goddamn it, Charlie, what good is a piece if you don't pull it, asshole?' Kenny groaned. Charlie's breath came heavy in his chest and sounded like a kettle on its way to a boil. Kenny scrambled Charlie's cell phone out of his pocket and dialled 911.

'Yo, send an ambulance!' Kenny yelled the location off Lambert. 'There's a white guy stabbed down here. Forget the spook who's been shot, he's done. Just treat the other guy.' He snapped the phone shut and wiped greasy sweat from Charlie's face.

'Don't fucking die, bro,' he said quietly. 'C'mon, Charlie boy.' He waited there for another minute, until he heard sirens in the distance. He wiped off the gun with his shirt, and then placed it in his brother's hand. He felt a slow, heavy drumbeat kicking in the base of his skull and heard the echo-effect lyrics in his head:

You're nobody, till somebody kills you . . . I don't wanna die.

He tried to shake the stupid shit off, took the envelope of cash out of Charlie's pocket, left the bag of weed, climbed into the Durango and drove away as slowly as he could make himself go.

The heat had finally broken. The day had started much cooler than any had in months, and it had stayed that way. Vicky Schlegel went through the empty house turning off the air conditioners. Why keep the house cool when no one was home? Everything was costing a fortune now: electricity, food, gas, booze. Well, maybe not booze. They had plenty of that. Terry brought home cases' worth from the bar. And he and the boys had been coming home with a real snoot-full lately too. They were under a lot of pressure, she supposed, and needed to blow off steam. They were all handling it well enough, it seemed, except for Deanie. He was the one she was worried about. He'd sicked up all over the place that morning and made a big racket over something he'd seen in the paper. The rest of them had tried to calm him down, but nobody would tell her what it was about. She'd make Terry tell her later, but for now she didn't know. And then they'd all gone out. She went to take a shower, and when she was done the cars were all gone.

It was when she'd finally shut the last window unit off that she heard it, the low hum of a running vehicle coming from the garage. The odd thing was, they never used the garage – there was too much crap in there to park inside, and any work on the cars took place down at Rubber House where there were countless Latino mechanics to do dirty work like oil changes. The sound of the engine grew louder as she reached the door and opened it. A cloud of exhaust and horror hit her and she staggered and pressed the button raising the door to the outside. Household junk had been pushed to one side to accommodate Dean's Magnum. Fresh air flooded in as she crossed to the driver's side of the car where a figure was pressed against the window. Even with his face distorted like a horror movie monster because of the plastic bag stretched over his head, she could see it was Dean, her boy, his face bright red and lifeless.

'This is it,' Behr said into the phone as he raced towards the Speedway address. 'I got you what you wanted.'

'Linkage,' Pomeroy said.

'That's right, by witness statement. A shake girl.'

'Schlegel?'

'Yeah.'

'Where's the girl?' Pomeroy asked, and Behr gave him the location.

'They don't know where she is—' he added.

'I'm gonna pick her up anyway,' Pomeroy said.

'Good idea.'

'And you?'

'On my way to the home address—'

'Behr—'

'I've got something to settle.' Behr turned off Crawfordsville Road and on to the Schlegels' street and started scanning house numbers.

'Your friend? Let's not get stupid here—'

'It's more personal than that now.'

'Behr!'

But Behr hung up on him and tossed the phone on to the passenger seat. He saw the rambling house he was looking for at the end of the block. It was fairly well kept, with a slightly yellowed yard and a chain-link dog run jutting out from around the back. The garage door was open and a thin blonde-haired woman was pounding on the driver's side door of a Dodge Magnum and screaming. Behr rolled into the short driveway, jammed his car into park and paused. The woman didn't seem to notice him as she began to yank on the door handle, but the door appeared to be locked. Her head whipsawed around the garage, and she moved to a workbench. She ran her hands over a pegboard, selecting and discarding car keys. Now Behr got out of his car and watched as she scrabbled around the loose tools on the bench and came up with a wooden mallet. She went to the Dodge, which Behr could hear was running, and began pounding on the driver's side window. He noticed a shop-vac hose taped over the tailpipe and running into the cracked rear passenger-side window. The heavy odour of exhaust was in the air. Behr crossed the driveway towards her as the driver's side window shattered, the safety glass pebbling into a thousand pieces. Mad piano, baroque guitars, machine gun drums and a distinctive voice playing on the car radio spilled out of the gaping hole. Behr recognized the song. It was Meat Loaf's 'Bat Out Of Hell'. A bereft wail escaped the woman as she reached inside, opened the car door and a body slumped out.

The kid was dead, that much was clear enough. After a moment, Behr recognized him as the one he'd followed from Flavia Inez's old building. It took him a moment because the young man had a plastic bag over his head that the woman tore away to reveal his face, cherry red thanks to the carbon monoxide poisoning. It seemed he'd wanted to be doubly sure. The woman had slumped to her knees by the time Behr approached and she looked up at him with dazed and distant eyes. She began backing away across the cement floor of the garage. Behr extended what he hoped was a calming hand.

'Ma'am,' he said. It seemed to ignite her. She leapt to her feet and bolted inside the house. Behr took a look back over his shoulder. No units were responding as yet, and if sirens were sounding in the distance the operatic rock music blasting out of the car stereo was drowning them out.

Shit, Behr sighed, and headed inside the house after her. He didn't have much choice, and went quickly because he didn't know what he'd find waiting for him in there and didn't want to give her time. He moved down a hallway, the house silent around him. He came upon her in the kitchen. Her eyes flashed with hatred. Her feet, shod in sneakers, squeaked on the linoleum floor as she came at him, slashing, with a boning knife.

Rush in. Close the distance. Get inside striking range.

The staccato thoughts of what he was supposed to do when facing a knife screamed across Behr's cortex. But instead, he found himself leaping backwards, instinctively trying to clear the weapon in the other direction. It was a mistake. She cut him on the outside of the left forearm, and he felt the cold burn immediately. The floor would soon be slick with blood, difficult to keep his balance on, his hand perhaps not functional if she'd nicked a tendon. The pain woke him up to the fact that this was real, and as she stumbled forward for another strike Behr set his feet and drilled her in the face with a straight right. The shot caught her flush on the cheekbone and sounded a loud crack. Her feet ripped up and out from under her and she landed flat on her ass and her head went back and hit the kitchen floor. Behr felt something for the blonde laid out there, what looked to be her son dead in the garage, but he stuffed it down deep and kicked the knife away. He checked his arm. Blood was seeping from a three-inch slash, but the wound wasn't deep. He grabbed a dishtowel and wrapped the arm before checking the rest of the house. The rooms were all empty. He discovered the woman's purse on her unmade bed, rifled it, found her cell phone, which he snapped in his hands. He took the battery for good measure and returned to the kitchen, where the woman was stirring slightly and moaning on the floor. He considered waiting for her to come out of it and questioning her but didn't want to invest the time or get entangled with the responding officers. On his way from the house he ripped out the telephone landline where it fed in by the side of the open garage door that held the car and the dead kid and then he was back in his car. He placed a call to Pomeroy's cell phone, but it rang through to voicemail. He left a message of what the police would find at the Schlegel residence, and though he knew he should stop, pull over, turn off his car and call it a day, he signed off by saying: 'I'm heading for the husband's work addy.'

Where the fuck is everybody? Terry Schlegel wondered, closing his phone. He'd called them all in succession. Charlie, Kenny, Dean and

Vicky. It was like some kind of cell phone outage, Terry thought, as he dialled into the AMSEC safe that was set in the floor of his office at the garage. The only one whose location he had locked down at the moment was Knute, who would be coming by in a few hours once he'd met up with the Chicago guys. Fifty-seven thousand in cash was what he had in the safe. He'd have seven left in his pocket when it was done. It seemed like a good time to carry extra cash, as he'd be needing it to make himself scarce for a while. He filled a small tool bag with the rubber-banded bills. Beneath the money was the stainless Smith & Wesson .40 calibre Charlie had given him a while back. Some might have thought it a strange gift, but that was the kind of family they were – they did things their own way, they had their own kind of closeness – and if people didn't understand it, they could go fuck themselves. Terry checked the clip on the Smith, racked the slide and tucked it in his belt. He was closing the safe when there was a knock at the door.

'Yeah?' Terry called out.

'Boss?' It was Raul, his shop foreman.

'Come on,' Terry yelled, standing up. The door opened. Raul was standing there, and beyond him was a flash of blonde hair and skinny legs in tight faded jeans.

'You got a visitor,' Raul said, his tone and his expression blank.

That's 'cause he's smart, Terry thought. *He knows better than to come smirking around my office*. The foreman cleared and revealed Kathy, that little girl from the bar who went to high school with Kenny. She'd boned how many of his sons? He didn't care, and neither did they. He'd brought her to the garage that night not long ago. He was usually pretty good with the discipline but the blonde hair, the little slip of a body, the jut of her chin that spoke of her tough attitude – it all put him in mind of Vicky when she was young. This Kathy, with the hundreds of little scars along her arms, like she was trying to erase herself but not all at once, was like a time machine. They'd shared a bottle he had in his desk after he'd shown her a GTO that was getting a full makeover. He'd stuck his dick in her mouth that night and she'd bounced her face on it like some kind of lobotomized mental patient. He'd been fairly sick about it for a week, and then he'd forgotten it. He didn't expect her back, but here she was.

'Thanks, Raul,' Terry said. 'I want you guys closing up early today. I've got something I've gotta do and I may need the space.'

'Sure, boss,' Raul said. The foreman and the rest of the guys all knew that they'd be paid in full despite the short hours. Raul turned to spread the good news to the others and left Terry with the girl.

'Kathy,' Terry smiled, 'what can I help you with?'

'Hi, Mr . . . I mean, Terry,' she said, and smiled.

As he drove, Behr felt like a locomotive hurtling towards a tunnel.

He couldn't stop.

It seemed clear enough.

He should stop, just pull over and turn off the car, and wait for the police . . . He probably had enough to jam the Schlegels up all the way . . .

But something had tripped in him and it pushed him on. He couldn't let it set. He'd been training his whole life, he realized, for some fight, hoping like hell he'd be strong enough and ready when it came. It wasn't the one in the bar, or the one in Francovic's place, or any other scrap he'd been in – that was clear to him now. He thought of Susan, of the baby she carried, and the fact that they – the Schlegels and their scumbag friends – knew who she was, and that she was in this thing, and suddenly he knew what he was fighting for.

He drove into the parking lot of Rubber House, the body and tyre shop that Schlegel owned, and saw that he had gotten there before the police. The place looked closed; only a Dodge Charger was parked around the side. His immediate concern, as he nosed into a spot right near the door, was that he was too late and had missed Schlegel and wouldn't be able to find him. He crossed to the door of the building, looking and listening but not seeing any sign of activity. The front door was unlocked when he tried it, and he bit back on the saliva in his mouth and opened it.

Inside, the waiting room was shadowy. Behr felt his pupils draw wide and pull for light as they adjusted to the half-darkness. He continued past the counter into the first work area where the repair bays were dimly lit and quiet. He was aware of the noise of his shoes and the heavy thud of his steps as he made his way across the cement floor. He stopped and tried to calm his breathing, and thought he heard voices coming from the back. He moved towards them, hoping not to disturb the speakers and to hear what they were saying. Then the low grinding noise of a bay door rolling up somewhere deep in the building washed the voices away. He continued towards the noise, picking up his pace now, using the sound as cover for his movement. He rounded the corner towards a back loading dock where afternoon light spilled in through the gap and bathed the garage in yellow. There was a moment's pause as the door finished its journey, and then a male figure emerged from an office and headed for the open door. Following a step behind was a teenage girl. She saw Behr first, and stopped.

'Ter,' she said, and the man stopped too. Even in silhouette Behr recognized him from the Tip-Over Tap Room. Then the man turned and stepped away from the backlight towards him, and Behr saw those dark malevolent eyes, flat as flint. It was him.

'Schlegel,' Behr called out, part statement, part warning, part war cry.

A stainless and black automatic was clutched in Schlegel's hand as it rose from his belt. Behr felt the air go out of him as he bent his knees, lunged forward and to the right and reached for the small of his back. He had an angle as his gun jumped into his hand. It wasn't at all like the time he'd pulled it at Francovic's gym, deliberate and slow. This was instinct, survival. The taste of metal came to the back of his throat. A familiar cold darkness squeezed his chest that he was unable to breathe through.

Schlegel pulled the trigger and his gun bucked while Behr was still raising his weapon. Behr felt an overwhelming impulse to fire back as fast as he could and for as long as he could until he'd gone empty. Giving in to it would mean his death. He saw Schlegel's gun jerk again. More rounds were coming his way and, worse, he realized his eyes were locked on his opponent. With an effort as physical and demanding as any he'd ever put forth, Behr held fire as he levelled his weapon, hunched down over the sights and focused only on the front blade. It grew sharp in his vision – Schlegel's body a mere blur ten yards away – and he fired twice. Behr raised his weapon to put a third round into his target's head, to finish the Mozambique, but there was nothing in his sight picture – Schlegel was down.

A cold wave of adrenalin hit Behr like a six-foot breaker. He started to shake as noise and colour rushed back in around him. He felt his chest heaving and became aware of a high-pitched screech and looked to the girl who was crouched down in a tiny ball not far from Schlegel. She was screaming. Behr took a step forward and extended his left hand towards her.

'Stay . . . stay right there,' he said, not hearing the words clearly, as his ears were ringing from firing in the enclosed space without ear protection. The girl broke off her scream and looked up at him. Then she rose and bolted for the open loading-dock door. 'Hey,' Behr said feebly, but he didn't consider going after her. She stumbled and fell as she jumped the three feet from the dock to the parking lot, but got up and darted away with the speed, if not the grace, of a cat.

Behr moved towards the fallen man, cautious, his gun raised ahead of him, and saw that Schlegel was hit twice, about two inches apart, in the chest, just left of centre mass. The slow, heavy rounds of the big-bore revolver had done their work. A coarse, bronchial grating noise accompanied Schlegel's breaths, followed by the telltale bubbling of a sucking chest wound. Blood and urine pooled beneath his body. The silver automatic rested five feet from his hand, and it was clear he'd never touch it again.

Behr dropped to a knee right next to Schlegel. 'Aurelio Santos. Was it you?' he asked.

After a moment, Schlegel issued a weak nod. 'It was all of us . . .'

'You, your sons and that partner?'

Another weak nod came from Schlegel. 'And the Chicago guys,' he added.

'Who?' Behr demanded, a cold chill running through him.

'Bobby B. . . . some guy Tino . . . a quiet one.'

'Pros?'

A third, almost imperceptible nod came from Schlegel. 'Had to. Couldn't handle the guy.'

'You wanted to know where he'd put the girl?' Behr asked, but Schlegel's eyes got glassy. Behr slapped him a little, trying to bring him around.

'Who pulled the trigger? Was it you?' A feeble hand came up and waved at Behr. He couldn't tell if it was Schlegel saying no or a pointless attempt to shoo him away. No more details came forth. Behr realized he was as close as he'd ever likely be to knowing exactly how it went down that night – and that he was headed to Chicago.

Then he asked the pointless question, the one cops, detectives and investigators rarely profited from. The one for which he both already had the answer and also never would. Not a satisfactory one anyway. 'Why?'

'We shouldn't have never even been there,' Schlegel rasped. 'The fucking skank. My son . . .' A wheeze was followed by a gurgle, and then all sound stopped.

Terry Schlegel had ceased being. Behr sat down on the cement floor next to the body to wait.

FORTY-TWO

BEHR DROVE SOUTH on I-65 towards Seymour as he slowly came out of the haze in which he'd spent the last several hours. The cops had gotten there within moments. A pair of uniformed Speedway officers and then a second pair of Northwest District boys stormed the place before the brass arrived. Behr had his weapon holstered and sitting on the ground next to him and had his wallet held open so they could see his tin when they walked in. It was the last conscious thing he'd done before he was overcome by shock at what had happened, and why tiny hurtling bits of metal had stopped another man, but had passed him by and left him alive. Nobody did much talking until Pomeroy walked in. Behr was vaguely aware that they'd locked down the building and the surrounding block. Paramedics and medical examiners and crime scene photographers dealt with Schlegel's body. Numbered evidence cards were set up next to the shell casings he had fired. Investigators were locating the rounds in the wall high and to the right behind Behr, though they had found only three of the four so far. Four rounds. Schlegel had fired first and at twice the rate of Behr and for whatever reason he had missed. Behr knew the model of gun. It had a notoriously long trigger pull. Maybe it had caused Schlegel to yank his shots. That could happen without sufficient practice. And even with practice, it wasn't easy. They handed Behr a bottle of water and helped him up.

Pomeroy oversaw his questioning, during which Behr gave a dry recitation of what had led him to the garage – leaving out his contact with Pomeroy and the Caro Group – and what had occurred in it. They told him he'd have to come down to the shop and run through it again soon and that he could bring counsel. When the cops recording him and taking notes were done and had drifted away, Pomeroy told him that they'd collected Flavia Inez and that she was giving a statement. They'd also picked up Victoria Schlegel, who was currently under suicide watch at Carter Hospital in a hysterical condition. Charles Schlegel had been discovered stabbed to death, after a 911 call, in an apparently unrelated incident, though Behr didn't believe in 'unrelated' any more. Kenneth Schlegel and Knute Bohgen were currently unaccounted for and would be sought for questioning. It was going to take a while but a slew of charges ranging from criminal conspiracy to promoting gambling, to extortion, to murder would eventually be mounted against them.

'They've gone to ground,' Pomeroy said. 'I wouldn't worry about them right now.'

Behr nodded blankly.

'I'll get this back to you as soon as I can,' Pomeroy said, raising a plastic bag that contained Behr's gun and holster. Behr nodded once more.

'Some special family you turned up,' Pomeroy said, shaking his head.

The work continued around them, though it had slowed as it

entered the wrap-up phase. Equipment was being packed. Silence had fallen between them when Behr asked, 'Can I go?'

Pomeroy eyed him for a moment before agreeing.

What the hell did he know of family, Behr wondered, *other than that he'd just helped destroy one?* He was headed south towards the remaining vestige of his own. Behr had passed Seymour and had reached the small town of Vallonia, where his ex-wife Linda, remarried and a stepmother, had lived for the last six years or so. He didn't need directions to get to her place. He knew the way. He'd be embarrassed to admit how many times he'd made the southbound drive, how many times he'd parked down the road from her house and watched her comings and goings. He'd managed enough restraint not to talk to her but seemed unable to stop looking. The visits had ended over a year ago though. A case had consumed him back then, and of course he'd met Susan. She filled a place in him he didn't think could be filled, and the need to drive south had vanished. Which was what made it all the more strange for him to be rolling down the smooth gravel drive past the mailbox that read 'Vogel', Linda's last name now, and parking right in front of the house. He seemed unable, or unwilling at least, to stop himself as he walked to the door and knocked.

After a moment, Linda's face, still beautiful to him, appeared in the door's glass pane. She still looked young – younger even than the last time they'd spoken several years ago. Her black hair was betrayed only by a very few grey strands. Upon seeing him, her eyes lit in an initial smile that quickly went out as she became guarded.

'Frankie,' she said, cracking the door, 'what're you doing here?'

'Hi, Lin,' he said. 'I'm not sure.'

They stood there for an awkward moment before she opened the door to him, and he stepped inside.

It was a nice home, not lavish but comfortable. There was evidence of early teenage children's artwork and sporting goods equipment and the like. The place had a familiar smell.

'Beef stew,' he remarked, mostly to himself, as Linda led him into the kitchen.

'Todd likes it,' she said, 'so do Gina and Jared.'

'Why not? It's the best.' It wasn't enough to put the smile back on her face.

'I just put up a pot of coffee. You want some?' she offered. Behr nodded. Some things didn't change. Linda drank coffee all afternoon long. She always had. It never stopped her from sleeping either. Until their bad time together, after Tim died. Then she swore off coffee altogether and endured the terrible headaches that going cold turkey brought on, but to no avail. Nothing she tried would allow her to sleep back then. They'd both lie awake all night, helpless in their grief. Maybe this resumption of her habit signalled a return to some kind of normal. He sat down at the kitchen table while she poured and delivered his cup.

'Are you in some kind of trouble, Frankie?' she asked. She was looking at his forearm, which the paramedics at Rubber House had wrapped and taped in a white bandage. He didn't answer for a moment. 'Because you're pale as a sheet. And you're here, so it must be for a reason.'

'I was, I suppose, for a minute there,' he allowed. 'I'm not any more.'

'That's good.' She stood uncomfortably across the kitchen from him.

'So you like it down here?' Behr asked. She nodded.

'It's nice. Quiet. People down here don't know what happened. If they do, they don't let on. I can be how I want.'

'And things with Todd?' Behr asked.

'It's good. He'll be home soon with the kids. You can meet them.' She paused and grew shy, and then: 'They call me "mom".'

He expected to feel like he'd been stabbed. But he didn't. A pleasant sensation washed over him with the words.

'So you're happy?' he asked.

'I've come to be,' she said.

'That's good,' Behr said, meaning it.

'And you?'

Behr didn't move and couldn't answer. The traitorous feelings he'd had before, that day after the lake, made their way back into his chest, but she cut them off.

'You've got to,' she said. *Got to what?* he wondered, but Linda went on. 'You've got to do it – whatever you want. Whatever you have to do. To get out of the tunnel . . . Back into life, Frank. There's a lot of ways to say it, I guess. Do you get it?'

Behr nodded and he recognized he had come there for absolution of some kind, and that her simple words had granted it. He sat there for another minute and knew he was looking on Linda for perhaps the last time. Finally, he got up to go. That was when he saw a stuffed monkey, a wooden fire truck and a few dinosaur figurines along her windowsill above the kitchen sink. He recognized them well – they were some of Tim's old favourites. There they were, just beneath the window she looked out of as she washed dishes. He realized she lived with it every day, even as she'd moved on, and that it was OK. He crossed the kitchen and picked up the truck and handled it. He saw there was a rescue hero action man in the driver seat. He looked to Linda.

'Sure,' she said, 'you go ahead.'

Behr drove north towards Indy, going slow, his eyes locked on the road, the little fire truck riding on the seat next to his leg.

FORTY-THREE

THE SHIT HAD truly hit the fan. The Schlegels had been blown up and burned the fuck down. Terry done, Dean done, Vicky locked down, and Kenny and Charlie apparently lit out for the territories. Knute Bohgen had just lost all the friends he currently had, along with the only thing in his life that passed for a semblance of family. He no longer had an income stream, or any real ideas on how to open a new one.

He had sat in his car down the street from Rubber House watching the police activity, and calling guys he knew who worked there. Rumours were flying thick and furious already. SWAT had taken the place down. Terry had wasted a handful of them before they got him. An ex-cop had shot him. They'd surrounded the place and after they lobbed in gas, Terry ate his gun.

Knute didn't know the truth, and he didn't much care to at this point. There was really only one thing on his mind, and that was getting a piece of payback for all of them.

The Tip-Over Tap Room was not currently open. Besides Terry, Knute was the only one with a set of keys, so it'd be a perfect place to meet with the Chicago guys, whom he'd called and told to hang back for a while until the cops had dispersed. After having a drink and seeing what was in the safe to pay them with, Knute would call the Chicago guys again, have them come in, and give them the assignment of punching this Frank Behr's ticket. Even if there was nothing in the safe, Knute felt pretty sure he could talk them into doing it on a payment plan. After all, their asses were riding on the outcome too.

The building was dark and locked, as it should have been. That was why it was such a goddamned surprise to Knute when he walked into the back office and saw they were already there.

'What the fuck's up, guys?' Knute said, reaching into his pocket and coming out with a slip of paper that had Behr's address on it. 'You're early.'

Tino nodded and kicked the office door shut behind Knute, who felt the air change in the room, just like out on the yard at ISP before someone got offed. It just changed. It got cold or dark or somehow unfamiliar and indistinct. Whatever it was, Knute didn't have much time to weigh it, because the quiet one, Petey, wrapped him up in a bear hug and lifted him straight off the floor. The guy was strong as fuck, and all of a sudden Knute felt weak as diner coffee . . .

When he'd recall it later, Petey wouldn't remember the man with the pink scar on his face fighting very hard, but then again, when it finally comes, there's not much use in fighting it. Before long it was over and they'd wrapped him in a blue plastic tarpaulin. They considered whether or not they should drop him in the same place they'd done the dumping the last time, but that spot hadn't seemed to hold up very well. Bobby B. figured he knew another one that was a lot closer and easier. Knute Bohgen never made it beyond the parking lot – specifically his own trunk. Petey remembered to pick up the slip of paper that Bohgen had dropped. Add-on jobs were not the way you stayed out of jail in their line of work. Eliminating the nexus was. Petey burned the paper before they made their way out, back to Chicago.

FORTY-FOUR

'**Y**OU WANT ANOTHER?' Neil Ratay asked, threatening to pour a fourth cup of coffee, black and strong. But Behr had had enough and waved Ratay off. Behr had gone straight home on the heels of the longest day he could remember and passed out into a dreamless sleep. Seven hours later he shot bolt upright. He'd sweated through his T-shirt and the sheets. He had a feeling that would be happening for the next few weeks, or months, or maybe even longer. When he noticed morning had slipped around the blinds and into the bedroom and there was no point in trying to go back to sleep, he rose and went to get Susan. And while Susan sat there listening, her jaw clenched tight, he'd told it all to Ratay – all except for Pomeroy, and the name of the big investigation firm. It was what he owed the man, plain and simple.

'So I can write it?' Ratay asked, jotting his final notes.

'Give me a day to think it through clearly,' Behr said, 'but yeah, you can write it.'

*   *   *

After that he took Susan home. They didn't talk along the way. Something he couldn't name wouldn't let him speak. All Behr could do was glance over at her every half-block or so and replay the events of the past week in his head. None of it made much sense to him, and the part that made the least was why he'd felt the same sensation when he learned Susan was pregnant as he had when he'd faced Terry Schlegel's gun: cold, chest-squeezing blackness. He could dress it up and tell himself he'd felt disloyal, that he'd been concerned that a new life would wipe away his memories of Tim, and even Linda, and those memories were all he had left of his son – they were all he'd had at all for a long while – but now he knew the truth. He was afraid, plain and simple. Because what she had given him with those words in his car that night was hope – hope, and a chance at joy, and a future. But it is a fearful thing to love what death can touch. And the prospect of losing it all again was more than he could face.

Too quickly they reached her house, and the thing that wouldn't let him speak kept on and she climbed out of the car. She looked at him for a long, disbelieving moment, then turned for her place.

FORTY-FIVE

THE STRAPPING YOUNG man got the first Whopper of the day when the breakfast menu switched over to lunch, backed it up with a chicken sandwich and, despite his pronouncement that he 'never eats this shit', wolfed them with a monster Pepsi. Then he walked down Scatterfield Road and entered the United States Marines recruiting station there.

Sergeant Fred Kilgen's eyes got big when the kid walked in. It had been a slow day, hell, a slow time altogether with the latest press the war was getting, but now he felt like a buyer at auction sizing up a prime Angus beef calf.

'I want to join,' the kid said. He was salty as hell, that was for sure, from the spiky hair right on down to the wise-ass T-shirt that read 'Jesus Didn't Tap'. They were gonna love him in basic.

'Sure,' Sergeant Kilgen said, getting out his sheet to start writing down the particulars and trying to look cool about it. 'Where do you live?'

'I stayed at the Motel Six last night. That's where I'll be until this is done.' The kid didn't mention the cell phone and car he'd dumped after his half-hour drive to Anderson.

'How fast you want this to happen?'

'I don't even want to go home.'

'Well, OK,' Kilgen said. This was the kind of signing that would help him 'make his mission', as they said at the productivity briefings. 'We'll contract you here. Then you'll head down to the MEPS in Indy for processing. It's a two-day thing – don't worry, we'll cover your room and board. You'll do your medicals, your ASVAB – that's your vocational exam. There'll be an Initial Strength Test, which, to tell by looking at you, will be a lay-up, and you'll be a shipper.'

'Head off to boot camp?'

'That's right. Next stop Parris Island,' Kilgen said.

The kid just bounced his head along to the information. He didn't have any of the usual questions: how long? How much money will I make? Do you pay for college? Do I get to fight? Will I have to fight?

'Now, you got your high school diploma or GED?' Sergeant Kilgen continued, bracing for the usual hurdles.

'I can get a copy,' the kid said. The sergeant didn't know it, but the kid figured he'd work one up on a computer at a Kinko's or use his brother's.

'Couple of standard questions. Ever do drugs?'

'No.'

'Ever been sick?'

'No.'

'Are you gonna change any of your answers for the doctor?'

'No.'

'Outstanding. Welcome aboard.' Sergeant Kilgen threw a laugh that sickened him a bit over the last part, and he had a strong stomach. 'So you sure you don't want thirty days? Go say goodbye to the folks?'

'I'll send 'em a fucking postcard from Afghanistan or wherever the hell else you put me.'

The recruiter nodded. 'Good idea. And you're gonna want to check that language, son.'

'Got it,' the kid nodded.

'Name?' the sergeant asked, his pen poised to write.

'Kenneth Schlegel' was the answer.

FORTY-SIX

BEHR STEPPED OUT of the station house on King Street where he'd just confirmed his statement, and he could feel the end of summer in the slight evening breeze. The two-day wait had been worth it. He'd gotten what he needed. He moved towards his car, adjusting his gun, which had been returned to him. When he reached the parking lot, he saw that someone awaited him there. It was Pomeroy, alone this time, and in full uniform. Gone were his captain's bars, in their place the oak clusters of a major.

'A farmer's combine turned up the rest of Bigby and Schmidt in a cornfield,' Pomeroy said.

Behr bowed his head at the inevitability. 'You knew that their murders and Santos and the Schlegel crew were connected,' Behr said.

Pomeroy shrugged.

'How?'

'Flavia Inez was a person of interest. We had her working in one of their houses. Then we lost her, until you turned her up. We had Santos as a player.'

'That wasn't in the file I got.'

'I said I'd give you the file, I didn't say I'd give you the file.'

'Dominic told you I was at Santos's Academy that morning. That I was personally connected,' Behr said, unnecessarily.

An imperceptible nod came from Pomeroy. 'I knew you'd push and keep on pushing, and that's what I . . . that's what the department needed.'

Behr absorbed the words in silence.

'This is for you,' Pomeroy said, and handed him an unsealed envelope. Behr glanced inside. It was a money order, in the amount of $9,990. 'That's from the Caro Group.' A higher amount would have triggered bank reporting to the IRS or other paperwork that opened everyone up to scrutiny, Behr supposed. Or perhaps that was how much they figured he was worth.

'Karl Potempa wants to offer you a job with them,' Pomeroy said.

The big firms all liked having a 'radioactive' guy around, Behr knew, someone who would go into the grey areas and beyond. Case management meetings were held without this guy, and no one wanted to hear a rundown on what he'd been doing. It was fake smiles around the water cooler and thanks for the results, but no invites to the bar later, and a fall guy if things went badly. The fact was, most big firms would go under without their radioactive guy, but like someone who'd been exposed in a nuclear plant accident, no one really wanted to get close.

'I don't like wearing suits,' Behr said, thinking of what he really wanted.

Pomeroy shrugged and produced a small black velvet box from his pocket. 'This is also for you,' he said, and handed it to Behr, who noticed right away that it was too small to hold a badge. He opened the box, and what was inside sparkled. It was a gold ring, with 'IMPD' written in diamonds atop the band. Behr looked at it, then up at Pomeroy.

'What's this?' Behr asked.

'What you did means a lot, Frank,' Pomeroy said.

Behr nodded, his eyes falling to the ring again.

'Go ahead, put it on,' Pomeroy urged.

Behr took the ring out of the box, and slipped it on.

'They don't generally make 'em that big. Had to be done up custom. Your size was still on file.'

Behr flexed his fingers, unused to the weight.

'You're a friend to the department is what that signifies,' Pomeroy said, meeting his eyes. 'You know what that means?'

Behr nodded. It meant access. Courtesy. All the things he hadn't had for the last bunch of years. He also knew what it didn't mean: that he was back on.

'We'd talked about a spot for me,' Behr said, each word costing him something deep inside him he knew he'd never get back.

'You know how we do it: let's kiss first, see how it goes,' Pomeroy said. A cheque, a ring and a handshake. Pomeroy had worked him like a pro. Behr had threatened, entered, hacked, pushed, bribed, hurt and even killed for him. And for what? A cheque, a ring and a handshake. He still didn't know how much he didn't know, and suspected he never would.

Behr looked at Pomeroy's outstretched hand. Then he shook it. He didn't see another choice.

Behr drove towards home making a mental list of what he'd need for his trip. He'd gotten his gun back. That was good. He had plenty of rounds for it still. He fingered the money order in his front pocket. Now he had cash. He'd bring his computer. He'd need his peephole viewer. Binoculars. His lock-pick set. His jumpstick for opening security chains. A shotgun and shells.

Clothes. He had no idea how long he'd be in Chicago. As long as it took, he supposed, to find the three – Bobby B., Tino and the quiet one.

He pulled up to his place and parked. He got out of the car and was walking towards the steps when he saw motion inside and stopped. Then he saw who it was. Susan was there, moving about in the living room. She spotted him and came outside and down the steps towards him.

'I'm getting my stuff, Frank,' she said, holding up her backpack. The finality of what she was doing, and what he had done, landed on him.

'Susan,' he said, and she stopped across a strip of grass from him.

'Yes?'

He fought to find more words. This time he wasn't willing to fail. Finally he spoke, his voice raw. 'I've gone a long time thinking there are mistakes you can make that afterwards, no matter how you live, you can't make them right.'

Her face changed, and she crossed to him. 'If the past guaranteed the future, we'd all be screwed,' she said. She saw the pain in him and must have seen the doubt in his eyes. 'It can be different, Frank. It will be. You'll see . . .'

'Yeah,' he said.

They stood in silence as the twilight hardened into darkness around them.

'Are you done?' she asked.

He wasn't sure what else he owed Aurelio, but he was sure what he owed Susan now, and maybe even himself. He didn't want to go to Chicago any more. He wasn't going. He wasn't going anywhere.

'I'm done,' he answered. She closed her eyes in relief. His hand waved between them. 'You want to do this?'

'I do,' she said.

They found themselves in each other's arms, shaking.

After some time had passed she went back upstairs, and he stayed outside for another moment drinking in the evening air. There it was. On mats in empty studios, in garbage bags dropped in fetid water-filled ditches, in stubbled cornfields, in empty garages, on raw mattresses in stripped houses, in bleak hospitals and out in the streets and beyond, was where the dead lay, waiting, to be found, to be tended by the living, to be solved, to be remembered, and finally to be put down to rest. He'd reached an end in himself, and a new start. It was time for him to lay them down too. He went up the steps towards his place. Susan had paused at the door, and she swung it open wide for him and smiled as he reached her. They stepped inside.

ACKNOWLEDGEMENTS

The author wishes to thank Chris Santos for the introduction to Brazilian Jiu-Jitsu, and John Danaher for the continuing education. John's generosity in sharing his estimable knowledge, both theoretical and practical, was invaluable in the writing of this book.